I've travelled the world twice over,
Met the famous: saints and sinners,
Poets and artists, kings and queens,
Old stars and hopeful beginners,
I've been where no-one's been before,
Learned secrets from writers and cooks
All with one library ticket
To the wonderful world of books.

KING OF THE OUTLAW HORDE

Continues the adventures of Arizona Ames, the title character of one of Zane Grey's novels. As a young man, Rich Ames lived as a range drifter. After a gunfight that left two men dead, Ames' skill with a sixgun made him one of the most feared and respected men in the West. In the stories in this volume, Ames faces bandits, marauding gunmen, and gamblers who stand on the wrong side of the law.

Zane Grey's Arizona Ames:

KING OF
THE OUTLAW
HORDE

ROMER ZANE GREY

Based on characters created by Zane Grey

ULVERSCROFT
Leicester

First Large Print Edition
published December 1982

British Library CIP Data

Grey, Romer Zane
    King of the outlaw horde.— Large print ed.
    (Ulverscroft large print series: western)
    I. Title
    813'.52 [F]   PS3513.R6545

    ISBN 0-7089-0897-7

575169

Published by
F. A. Thorpe (Publishing) Ltd.
Anstey, Leicestershire
Printed and Bound in Great Britain by
T. J. Press (Padstow) Ltd., Padstow, Cornwall

CONTENTS

King of the Outlaw Horde

1

IT was a long way to Arizona as the crow flies. And a horse couldn't fly, not even Cappy, Arizona Ames' big sorrel.

From the north, Ames heard the distant booming of heavy Sharps buffalo guns, standard equipment for the professional hunters slaughtering the bison, what was left of them.

Nobody knew how many buffalo there had been. Some said fifty million, but in a few seasons the vast herds had been reduced to pitiful remnants, while the insatiable killers pushed over the Staked Plain, seeking the last of the great beasts.

Ames had been headed for the camps to see if he might get information from the hunters to help him in his dangerous, difficult quest. But he'd been diverted and was now riding southeast. Late the previous afternoon he'd sighted a big party of Indians pushing down the old War Trail with a large gather of

3

horses, cows, and what looked like two or three women captives slung like sacks of grain over the backs of mustangs.

Spying from a high point with his powerful binoculars, he'd been able to make out enough to satisfy himself this might be the clue to what he was seeking. That morning he'd watched the savages returning. They'd delivered their loot and were rushing back to Indian Territory before the Army or Texas Rangers patrols might intercept them. They carried new rifles, belts of ammunition, trinkets and bolts of cloth; also small casks, no doubt filled with forbidden liquor traded with renegade Comancheros for what they'd stolen from the far-flung ranches of the Texas Panhandle.

Cappy was blowing so Ames pulled up, cocked a long leg to ease his muscles, and made a cigarette. The steady wind blew away the light smoke as the grit it carried stung his leathery bronzed cheeks.

Tall, gaunt from days of hard riding and trail fare, Ames' dark-gray eyes were slitted against the brilliant sunlight. Behind his sweated hull was a blanket roll; saddlebags held his razor, spare ammunition for the fine carbine in its boot, a few provisions, the odds and ends needed on a long journey.

He alerted. He'd seemed relaxed, but a man didn't keep his hair for long in this country if he let his mind wander. And Arizona Ames was on one of the most perilous missions he'd ever undertaken, an apparently impossible task.

The Indians had passed hours ago, their dust gone with the wind. What he now spied was a thin spiral, a small party headed southwest. They'd cut his course if he kept straight on.

He wondered if they'd noticed his sign in the warm air. He got down, ground out his quirly, and led Cappy back. The Staked Plain, the Llano Estacado, seemed flat as a table top, covered with short, curling grama grass, excellent fodder not only for bison but for cattle and horses. The surface was broken by numerous gulches which were unseen until a rider was almost upon them, many dry, some with springs at the bottom.

It had recently been discovered that just beneath the arid plain lay a reservoir of fresh water and underground rivers which could be tapped by windmills. The white men, always land-hungry, were taking over the Indians' hunting grounds.

Ames moved back a short distance and led Cappy down a deepening split with undercut red-clay banks which he'd seen as he'd passed by. A rider going over that in the dark would probably be crushed under his falling horse.

As he moved farther down, he knew there was water in the bottom, for he saw scrub bushes and then a stand of bluestem. A pair of wild canaries flew off, chittering in alarm. He dropped rein by a shallow pool; Cappy lowered his head and sucked up a drink. By the way he relished it, Ames figured it wasn't gyp water but would be palatable enough even for a man. The sorrel began cropping off mouthfuls of the tall bluestem.

Ames pulled his carbine from the boot, checked the action, and threw a cartridge into the firing chamber. He slung the belt of ammunition for the rifle over one shoulder, and moving with cougarish agility, started for the east end of the cut. Around his lean waist was a carved black-leather cartridge belt with a wide silver buckle. The long, oiled holster holding his sixshooter was adorned with a large silver "A." The revolver was a special Colt .44, a fine weapon.

Rich Ames, known far and wide as Arizona Ames, had a reputation as a square shooter from the Dakotas to the Mexican border.

Reaching the other extremity of the gulch, he put down his carbine and again brought his binoculars into play, lying on his belly up the slope so that only his head was exposed. He'd known it was a small party, Comanches or Kiowas, probably hoping to ambush a few whites.

For the Indians were possessed of murderous fury. They hated the accursed white men for destroying their main means of life, the buffalo herds.

"Kill off the buffalo," William Tecumseh Sherman, Chief of the Army, had advised. "This will force the savages onto the reservations."

The buffalo was sacred, the Indian's brother. He gave them meat, the hides for tepees. Sinews made good bowstrings, bones excellent scrapers. They used glands for medicinal purposes. They wasted nothing, only killing what they needed for life.

The Army and Texas Rangers, in many pitched battles, had defeated the Indians, captured and killed men, even women and children, burned their villages, and drove them onto reservations in the Indian Territory.

The white hunters had invaded the lands reserved for the savages' hunting grounds, though it was forbidden by law. Cheated, starved by thieving agents, the Indians would break out and strike at isolated ranches, shooting down the men, running off horses and cattle, firing the buildings. They would capture white women, alive if possible, and drive what they had taken down the War Trail, which swung southwest to the Pecos and on down to old Mexico.

Satanta's Kiowas, Quanah Parker's Quahada and Penetaka Comanches, said to be the finest irregular light cavalry ever known, still struggled against the hopeless odds, wreaking what vengeance they could.

The Indians no longer needed to drive all the way to Mexico. The Comancheros, the renegade breeds, would meet them with their carts at some hidden rendezvous and exchange firearms, ammunition, trinkets and rotgut liquor for the valuable stock. And a young white girl was most valuable; bawdy houses were filled with such unfortunate women.

Arizona Ames knew all this, and a good

deal more; it was why Governor David Lee Caldwell of Arizona Territory had sent Ames on this dangerous mission.

Studying the riders as they came abreast of his position, he saw they were whites, three of them. They were weary and so were their horses. They rode single file, intent on the cold trail left by the animals stolen by the Indians.

Ames was puzzled; he shoved back his hat and dried his brow with his bandana. If they were honest men, they were fools. Though the savages had sped back to Indian Territory, the three would soon bump into the Comancheros, who had taken over the gather.

Maybe they weren't honest, in which case it might pay to mosey along and see just where they were headed with such dogged determination. He returned to Cappy, and washed himself in the pool. He tasted the water, and it was not too alkaline so he drank his fill. He snapped the carbine into its boot; mounting, he rode from the gulch the way he'd come in.

He began rim-riding, keeping just below a low north-south spine so he'd be out of sight. Occasionally he moved up to make sure they were still in view. The character of the land was changing; he figured they had crossed the boundary between Texas and New Mexico. In the distance, high mountains reached to the sky, and the foothills were forested with pines, live oaks and heavy bush.

As he jogged on, he recalled the interview with Governor Caldwell, his good friend. Years before, Ames had avenged the seduction of his twin sister, Nesta, killing her betrayer and the crooked sheriff involved. He'd run for it, on the dodge, claimed by wanderlust. Finally he'd returned to his homeland, the Tonto Basin.

There he found Nesta married to Sam Playford, a fine young rancher. And an assassin's bullet, intended for Ames, had killed his lovely fiancee, Esther Halstead.

The stigma of outlawry had paled, and Ames' reputation as a fair, decent man had earned him a full pardon from Governor David Lee Caldwell. For a while, Arizona Ames had been an Arizona Ranger.

Once again, Caldwell had called on him. In the Governor's office in Phoenix, the chief executive of the great territory had told Ames of tall trouble besetting Arizona. Not only Arizona, but Texas and New Mexico.

Caldwell was a distinguished looking man with silver hair, a thick beard and sun-tanned face. His steady eyes studied the strong features of his top secret agent as he spoke.

"I've had numerous complaints from the governors of New Mexico and Texas. Wholesale thefts of stock, and worse, kidnaping of young women carried off and never again heard from by their families, and many killings. Texas has her well-organized Rangers, but New Mexico so far isn't as well organized, and particularly the northeast quadrant is wild, hardly mapped. About a month ago, while you were away, I sent Ranger Ken Wells over to make a preliminary investigation."

"It's a long run," drawled Arizona Ames.

"Yes, on horseback. But a railroad spur has just been laid from eastern New Mexico to join the Southern Pacific. Stock could be shipped over it. Settlers are flocking into both Arizona and New Mexico, eager to buy beeves and horses."

"Ken Wells is a top man. He's an old pard of mine. I'd ride the river with him any time."

Caldwell nodded. "That's why I want you to find him."

Ames jumped. "He's lost?"

"Captured, or more probably, killed. I had two telegrams from Wells. The first said he'd arrived and would wire me at least once a week. The second reported he'd hit something important. He'd spotted Burch Taisley."

"Taisley! Wells caught him and Taisley was condemned for life in Yuma Prison. But I did hear his outlaw pals had bribed some prison guards to help Burch escape."

"Right. Those guards are doing time now in Yuma. But Taisley's been free for nearly two years. He hates me; I refused him a pardon. A shady attorney tried to bribe me if I'd free Burch Taisley."

"He don't send me valentines either, Governor. I helped Ken Wells deliver Taisley to Yuma, chained to three other rapscallions. And a year later I killed his kid brother in a shootout after he'd mowed down two bank tellers and a woman during a holdup."

Caldwell nodded somberly. "Yes. You know Taisley is a sadist, worse than any Apache. His chief lieutenants, who got him out of Yuma, are Brazos Ole Svenson, a giant Swede, and Percy 'Lord' Roberts, a tiny

12

Cockney devil who's killed more men in cold blood than John W. Hardin."

"I've seen photos of Svenson and Roberts on Wanted circulars."

"It's over two weeks since I last heard from Wells. I'm sure something's happened to him."

So Arizona Ames had ridden to smash Burch Taisley, King of the Outlaws, and try to discover the fate of his pard, Ken Wells.

His alert mind jumped back to the immediate problem as a flurry of gunshots shattered the warm afternoon air.

2

WHEN he took a look-see, he saw the trio below had left their horses and scurried to a nearby pile of rocks. Ames got down, dropped Cappy's rein, and pulled the carbine from its scabbard. Stooped low, he trotted to a bluff from which he could command the scene.

He'd brought his binoculars and focused them. The rocks protected the trio but not their horses. Ames heard the screams of the animals as bullets drilled into them, saw them stagger and go down. More lead spanged into the stone, sending up showers of fragments, or shrieked close over the rocks.

One of the besieged stuck out his head and shoulders to let go with a long-barreled rifle; the felt hat he wore flew off into the air. Ames wondered if the bullet had smashed through the man's brain, but then he saw the bare-headed fellow hastily ejecting a cartridge and shoving another into the open breech. The rifle was an ancient model and single-shot! Then a shotgun blasted from the other side of the nest. A shotgun! Even loaded with buck, it was a short-range weapon for such a fight. Next, the third let go with a six-shooter!

Arizona Ames found it hard to believe. They were fools, all right. A single-shot rifle, a shotgun and a Colt, and they were riding the most dangerous trail in the West! They couldn't be professional outlaws, not with weapons and plug horses. They had to be pilgrims or maybe loco.

He turned his attention to their opponents. He could see five of them, lying in cover to the south; there were six saddled mustangs behind a stand of hackberry trees, held by a squat man in rough clothing. He studied them; they were firing repeating rifles of the newest make.

Dark-faced, bearded, grinning fellows. Not Indians, not cowboys or buffalo hunters. Breeds mostly, Mexican and maybe French blood in their veins. The answer came to him a moment later: they looked like Comancheros, wolves of the Southwest.

Numerically, it was two to one. Weapon-wise, it was the same as a squadron of veteran soldiers rounding up a few helpless civilians.

He could tell that the Comancheros, for that's what they looked like, didn't aim to take any prisoners. They meant to kill them all. One opened a hot fire on the rock pile, while the others, rifles in hand, scurried expertly off to the right. The other pair moved to the left, and while their comrade kept the victims down, the wings would quickly get in behind and finish them off. It was that simple.

Ames decided it was time to take a hand. He dropped one of the attackers on his side with a carbine slug through the heart. The man rolled head over heels and his pal pulled up short, staring at the dead one in sheer amazement. Ames downed him a breath later.

The one holding the horses began shouting and pointing up at the man who'd opened up. He had his hands full controlling the skitterish mustangs, who didn't like the echoing reports of guns. He drew a Colt and wild slugs shrieked over Ames but he paid no heed, turning his attention to the pair farther off, who had swung and were looking his way, trying to locate the source of the sudden foul-up.

One yelled and raised his carbine as he took aim at the man he saw on the rise, but

Arizona Ames hit him and the bullet plugged into the dry earth, kicking up a spurt of sand. The fourth panicked, turned, ran back for the horses.

A slim figure rose up from behind the rocks and fired the shotgun again.

The buck spread, pellets widening to an arc. Some spattered into the hackberries and stung several of the bunched horses, who began rearing and fighting, pulling free of the excited holder, though the man managed to hold tight to one of the reins, yanking the animal's head down. His friend evidently felt some of the wild pellets, because he yelped in pain and tried to reach the small of his back. He wasn't seriously wounded, though, and held to his rifle. The range was too long and the buckshot had lost much of its force.

The horse holder was swinging into his saddle as his pard rushed in and vaulted up behind him. Arizona Ames ran at a slant down the slope, after them. The cursing man in the rear swung and raised his carbine as he saw the tall figure hustling up.

It was a mistake. A fatal mistake. Ames heard the bullet whine past his head; it was a good shot or maybe a lucky one, from the back of a moving horse. So Ames knelt and

17

took careful aim and pulled the trigger.

The carbine flew from the man's relaxing grip; his legs relaxed, too, and he fell off. This worried the running mustang and he whirled around, almost throwing his rider, who brought his fist down hard between the horse's ears to force him into line. The excited horse stepped in a dog hole and crashed, head over heels, before the man on his back could kick his toes free from the stirrups.

Arizona Ames glanced back at the rocks. Three forlorn figures stood, watching, and he waved. They waved back, realizing it was this unknown marksman who had saved their lives. Ames trotted on, carbine at the ready.

But that was it. The weight of the mustang had caught the rider and broke his neck. The horse tried to get up but he had a broken leg. There was only one thing to do and Ames did it. He ended the animal's agony with a bullet to the brain.

Reloading his hot carbine, he swung back to the three people he'd assisted. They were walking slowly toward him, and as they saw him watching them, they waved again in friendly fashion.

The one in the lead was tall and spare. He

wore Levi's, faded and patched, like his rough shirt; both had been washed many times. He'd retrieved his battered felt hat, which was holed from back to front, and gray touched his temples. He hadn't shaved for several days, and the beard stubble was gray, too. Ames figured he was in his mid-forties. His boots were farmer boots, not cowboy style, and his drawn face was seamed, his eyes showing his anxiety and utter weariness. He had shouldered his old rifle, carrying it like a marching soldier; maybe he was a veteran of the Civil War, hc was of that generation.

Next came a younger replica, a youth who couldn't be much over twenty. He toted the double-barreled shotgun, muzzles down, under one arm. He was smiling, his white teeth and clear eyes showing he was a healthy lad. His beard was still soft and sparse.

The third was even younger and not as tall as the first pair, a hat pulled low over the violet eyes, face peach-smooth, in a shapeless man's shirt much too large, and hanging down over worn jeans.

Arizona Ames stared; the shape was all wrong, and he was slightly puzzled, but then the third one swept off the battered hat. A wealth of raven-black hair escaped, draping

19

in natural curls down the back of the shirt.

The third was a girl, a young one, maybe seventeen or eighteen at most. She flashed a brilliant smile, full red lips parting to show small, even white teeth.

"Mister," she said, "you sure saved our bacon. We were dead!" Impulsively she ran to him, reached up and threw both arms around his neck, kissing him.

The Colt sixshooter, a familiar old Frontier Model, was thrust into the sash which held up the oversized pants.

Ames was even more astonished than he'd been. A pretty girl, out here!

"You folks are way out of line in these parts," he drawled. "Hoemen, ain't you?"

"I reckon," nodded the elder somberly. "Mainly though we run more and more stock. I'm George Ince, and this is my son Bob and my little girl, Belinda."

Ames cradled his carbine under an arm and made a cigarette with one hand. He offered the makings to the father who said, "Obliged. I'll stuff my brier if you don't mind. Run out of plug yesterday."

Bob and Belinda didn't smoke, and the girl's eyes smiled as she watched the tall man's stoic face, bleached hair showing under his Stetson, chinstrap taut under his granite jaw. "Rich Ames. Some call me Arizona, folks."

"You a lawman?" asked George.

"Well, I drift a lot. I can take care of myself."

"We seen that, Mr. Ames," agreed Ince fervently. "We'd be goners if you hadn't popped out of nowhere like you did."

"You still haven't told me what you're doing in Comanche country armed with pop-guns, Ince." There was a hint of severity in Arizona Ames' voice.

"It's like this. My brother Jim and me own a spread back east below the Cap Rock. Run cows and had broke a good number of wild mustangs to saddle. The boy here is a top rider and Belinda'll take a crack at it if you don't tie her down. Rides and shoots good as most men." A bit of pride crept into the father's voice.

"So why did you leave home?"

"It was hard scratchin' for years but it looked like we'd make a go of it. Jim and I are widowers but Belinda does the cookin' and plants a garden. Jim had one son, Taze. He was twenty."

"You talk like they were dead."

21

"They are. Shot out of their saddles at dawn four days ago by rovin' Indians. They run off all our stock, and would've burnt us out and killed us, too, but we were inside our cabin and after we'd winged a couple, the rest of 'em rode away. It was only a small war party, maybe six or eight, I guess they was mainly after our beeves and mustangs. They fired our barn but after they left we doused the blaze. We had a few work horses in the stalls, and that's what we were ridin'."

Ames thought it over. The savages had struck several ranches and made up the big gather he'd seen from a distance, the separate bands meeting at a prearranged rendezvous as was their habit, then delivered the critters to the Comancheros. "And you thought you could recover your stolen stock by trailin' 'em? Didn't you notice how the sign showed your animals joined a big band, driven by a horde of Indians?"

"We noticed. But we got to get our stock back. We was hid off the trail and saw forty, fifty braves ridin' home in a hurry. And we kept goin'."

Ince puffed at his old brier pipe, and looked down. Then he said, "We knew we might die. But we might as well be dead. We're ruint. Had to fetch Belinda along; we couldn't leave her back there alone. Now we ain't even got our work horses left." George shook his head.

Ames ran his long fingers down his bronzed cheek, dark eyes brooding as he thought it over. He realized how desperate Ince was, and as for the young 'uns, well, they were frontier-bred and reckless. "Fetch your gear. Here, I'll help you unsaddle the dead horses."

Ames toted Belinda's saddle and some of the slim bags and packs: George and Bob shouldered their own hulls, while the girl carried her father's old rifle and two blanket rolls. Single file, they trailed Ames back to Cappy, who was cropping at short bunch grass on the hill.

The girl started gathering dry sticks to make a fire but Ames stopped her. "No smoke. The Comancheros must have a depot, not far off, where the Indians delivered their gather. That's where the cusses who hit you come from. Eat cold. I'll be back."

"You figger our stock's right down the line?" asked Ince.

"Maybe. I aim to find out. Lie low till you see me again."

He picked up Cappy's rein and led the big sorrel down the steep slope to the beaten trail. Mounting, he rode south; he only glanced at the dead ones, he'd see about them when he came back. Alert for any sign of trouble, he kept going for a half mile, and then he sighted the canvas-topped cart. It stood near a rough corral formed of tree limbs cut from the surrounding timber. He held his carbine at the ready, across the pommel, as he scouted the clearing.

It was deserted and the corral gates stood wide open, the pen empty. Three saddled mustangs who'd run off from the dead holder grazed close by. They raised their heads but didn't run. Ames made sure of everything before dismounting and checking the wagon. There were axes, other tools, rolled blankets and a few other items in it, but the renegades had traded their goods to the Indians for the stolen stock.

A blackened area, still smouldering, marked where they'd had their fire; he kicked out a couple of partially burned boards, the tops of boxes which had held rifles and ammunition. A necklace of cheap glass beads sparkled in the light; it had fallen unnoticed during the swappings.

24

He rode in a wide circle and came on the cut-up trail, pointing southwest, along which the mustangs and cattle had been driven by eight or ten riders, maybe more of the Comancheros. Plainly they were headed for a bigger depot, perhaps the main one he was seeking. The half dozen who'd struck the Inces may have stayed behind to clean up the camp and fetch the wagon. He figured the big gather had started off that morning.

Back at the empty pen, he uncoiled his lariat; in a jiffy he'd roped the three loose horses and lining them out, started back.

He paused to pick up the carbines, ammo belts, and pistols from the stiffening dead ones at the scene of the fight, tying them on the spare mustangs.

He found the Inces resting; they'd eaten hardtack and jerky, and some cold coffee they'd had in a canteen. George was grave but the two young ones acted as though they were on a picnic, joking and laughing.

"Now, Ince," said Arizona Ames, "here's good mounts and weapons for you. I want you to start back home and I want your word you'll head straight there, Savvy?" His voice was stern.

"Thanks, sir, many thanks." George Ince

spoke, a weary note creeping into his tone. "But we still ain't got back our stock. Like I told you, we're done in for good without that, bankrupt, ruint."

"Tell me just where your place lies and I'll see you get back your animals and more soon's I can. You got my promise on that. You rest up and go on home, like I said. And keep a sharp eye peeled for rovin' Indians."

"All right," George said finally. "Prob'ly it's best."

"I know it is. I'm going to snatch a bite and then I'll be off on the trail. You'll only hamper me, understand?"

"Yessir. And—well, we're obliged."

Ince offered his toil-hardened hand and Arizona Ames shook with him and Bob, who also thanked him. Belinda smiled up at him and kissed him again; she'd taken a shine to the big fellow, that was plain. Ames ate cold, washed down the salt meat and biscuit with what was left of the coffee, and with a wave, moved down to the trail.

He knew he might well be riding straight into the jaws of death but he meant to find Burch Taisley. This might be a clue.

3

HE glanced back as he reached the camp with the empty wagon. In the intense blue sky hovered black shapes, others swooping down on the dead bodies and horses. He heard coyotes, knew Nature's cleanup gang was at work.

He picked up speed, Cappy's long legs pacing off the miles. The sign was easy to follow, with all the fresh hoof marks of cattle and horses. He pulled his hat brim low against the sun, dropping low ahead of his course, his narrowed eyes flickering right and left, always watching for danger.

Night fell. Cappy was blowing, and he pulled the sorrel to a walk. They came to a rill crossing the trail; horse and man drank. He refilled his canteen with fresh water, and loosened Cappy's girth, then munched a biscuit and a piece of jerky, squatted on his heels.

After awhile he led Cappy among the

nearby trees and unsaddled, drove in his stakepin, and let the animal graze. Rolling in his blanket, he stretched on the pine needles and was quickly asleep, weary from the hard drive.

When he awoke, the moon was up. He fixed a cigarette and smoked and had a drink. Cappy was munching on leaves from a low branch.

Ames had hoped to reach the thieves' main depot before dark. Even if he sighted it now, he'd have to wait until the next night before creeping in close; it would be too well guarded to chance that in daylight.

His gunbelt with the holstered revolver and the carbine lay on his tarpaulin, close by him as he'd slept, head on saddle. He left his Stetson, hitched up his trousers and swung up into the big live oak nearby, keeping a tight grip so he wouldn't slip and fall.

Higher up, he was able to see over the lower growth, and make out a sweep of starry sky, paled by the moonlight.

Suddenly he saw what he'd been hoping for, a reddish-yellow glow which must be from a fire. That meant a camp. He climbed up farther and sighted smaller yellowish twinkles, lanterns or lamps. Maybe this was it! If he was lucky, it might be Taisley's stronghold.

He descended, put on the sweat pad and saddled Cappy. He shot the carbine into its boot and buckled on his gunbelt. Leading the sorrel back to the trail, he began jogging slowly on, pulling up now and again to check.

Finally he came to it and drew off. The clearing was a large one, and a river meandered through its center. He left Cappy tethered in the trees and stole closer. Squatting down at the edge of the extensive installation, he studied the layout.

There were several small wood fires going, and he could distinguish the outlines of many corrals. A few steers bawled, and occasionally a horse would whinny. Against the faint light, he saw riders patrolling the great camp. And to the south were low buildings, clustered together. One had a number of lighted windows, and seemed the largest of all.

He kept sighting more and more sentries, no doubt guarding not only the huge gather of animals, but on the alert for intruders.

He nodded to himself, Burch Taisley took no unnecessary chances.

They'd surely watch the track he was near

in case of possible pursuit, as the stolen animals had been driven that way. Flat on his belly, he checked the terrain. He thought the land rose higher west of the camp; if he could work around that way before dawn . . .

He picked up Cappy and led him off, roughly north, crossing the trail, working slowly through the broken woods and brush.

It was hard going and he had to be careful. He spent two hours at this before he figured he was far enough off to chance a swing to the west so he could get up to the heights that way.

The light was improving, for dawn was near, increasing the chance he'd be seen. He kept threading west for a time; the stars began blinking out as the day took over. He led Cappy back and staked the sorrel where the horse could graze on a patch of grass. He unsaddled, hung the hull on a low tree limb. He slung his carbine and the ammunition belt for it over a big shoulder, along with the strap of the binoculars.

He flitted south, from tree to tree, from bush clump to bush clump, pausing now and then to listen, hunting a point from which he would be able to study the encampment when day broke. Already, red and purple streamers streaked the eastern horizon.

He wanted to get a full picture of the layout before making a move. Alone, it must be after dark, if he went in at all.

Finally he found a safe spot on a ledge west of the big clearing, creeping under a thicket, where he laid his carbine and its belt by him, along with the heavy sixshooter and cartridge belt. He loosened his chinstrap and added his Stetson to the collection. Smearing dirt on his face and hands to kill sheen from the flesh, he took care to shade the lenses of his binoculars as he focused on the scene.

There were numerous large corrals filled with cattle and horses. A couple of armed riders were keeping an eye on them. As the sun came up, bathing the world in yellow light, he sighted loading chutes along the south margin and the glint of railroad tracks. Down the tracks were several cattle cars. The thieves had laid a private spur to connect, no doubt, with that new line mentioned by Governor David Lee Caldwell!

The stolen stock could thus be shipped to points in New Mexico, Arizona, even on to California. This had to be Taisley's work.

Grudging admiration for Burch Taisley's

evil genius touched Arizona Ames as he studied the elaborate layout. There was nothing picayune about this operation; it was a big scale. Well into New Mexico, Taisley was outside the jurisdiction of the troublesome Texas Rangers. And this far off, wild area was not yet policed at all, for New Mexico was still hardly organized.

Breakfast fires were being lighted at several outdoor hearths. A number of Mexicans, peons mostly, emerged from one clump of the brush shelters. They began baking sourdough biscuits in Dutch ovens, making pots of coffee, frying steaks and tortillas, heating clay vessels of frijoles.

A corral over toward the in-trail held a number of ready horses, saddles hung over on the top rails. There were structures formed of surrounding forest timber.

But the main building was a large, one-story affair with several wings. The front, with a shaded veranda on which stood several chairs, faced toward Ames, and he examined this. There were four stone chimneys, and smoke issued from two in the rear. Breakfast was being prepared in there, too.

It took patience, and Ames knew he'd have to stay where he was through the day, till night might offer him a long chance of stealing in. He wanted to be prepared to make a detailed report, so that a large force might be able to seize the stronghold without undue loss to themselves.

If Ranger Ken Wells had located this hangout, he would have reported it to Governor Caldwell, unless—well, a thousand to one Wells had been captured and would already be dead.

One of the Mexican cooks struck a big frying pan with a heavy iron rod. The clanging resounded in the morning air, and before long, more figures came from shacks closer to the hacienda. They were yawning, rolling the first cigarette of the day, strapping on hats and gunbelts. These men had a different aspect from the peons. They were Anglos, mainly, a few tough-looking breeds scattered among them. Some fancied high-peaked sombreros, others flat-topped Nebraska hats.

These were fighters, who lived by the gun. Ames counted over forty, and there were also the night sentries still around the place.

The gunnies filled tin plates with steaks, frijoles and biscuits, pouring mugs of steaming coffee from big pots, obsequiously

33

waited on by the peons. They squatted as they ate their meal, and when they'd finished, made fresh quirlies, some touching off cheroots. Several went to the ready corral, saddled broncs, and relieved the guards, who came in, handing their animals over to Mexican wranglers, who took off the saddles, rubbed the critters down, turned them into the pen. A wooden conduit led from a high point up the little stream, feeding by gravity into a long watering trough at one side of the enclosure, so the horses could drink at will. The wranglers forked in fresh hay—apparently Mexicans did all the menial work around the camp.

The night sentinels stoked up, smoked, then went into the shacks to sleep.

The sun rose higher, losing its ruby tint, becoming a bright golden orb.

The front door of the rambling hacienda, obviously headquarters, was opened and men came out, stepping off the low veranda into the sunlight. Ames didn't need his field glasses to recognize one of them, who was picking his teeth with a hunting knife.

He was huge, with hulking shoulders and mighty arms. A sweated Stetson hung down his broad back by its loose strap; the sun glinted on the cartridges in his belt, Colt .45 in place.

The thick hair on his great head was straw-colored, contrasting with his sun-bronzed, ugly face.

Brazos Ole Svenson, tough and strong as a buffalo bull and with even less conscience.

Behind Svenson, a scrawny little man stepped daintily forth. He was so slight he looked like a boy. But he was no boy. A cartridge belt was strapped at his narrow waist, an oiled, open holster holding a walnut-stocked Colt .45 revolver. The holster was secured to his thin leg by a rawhide cord. He was fresh-shaven. Before he donned his Nebraska hat, Ames noticed the thin hair was carefully parted in the middle and plastered with pomade to his round head. The ends curled up in a cupid effect.

This would be Percy "Lord" Roberts, the Cockney killer, said to be the fastest gun west of the Missouri. Idly, as gunfighters will, Arizona Ames wondered if he could beat Roberts to it in a pinch. It was always a question. Until the fatal instant; nobody could say for sure.

Ole Svenson bent his head to touch off a cheroot; the blue smoke slowly wreathed around his mighty shoulders. A couple more armed toughs joined the first pair and they all walked over to the in-trail and stood there, staring east. Some of Taisley's riders must have driven the latest gather of stolen animals over from the Comanchero rendezvous a day or two before, rather than more Comancheros.

The Swede and Lord Roberts talked together for a time, the Cockney gesturing with his thin hands. They seemed undecided, but finally all swung back to the hacienda. Svenson went inside. The other three, including Roberts, sat down on the porch.

Before long, the Swede came out again with another man.

Now Ames eagerly focused his binoculars, studying this one. He was tall, with a sallow complexion, his brown hair touched with a carrot hue. He wore a cartridge belt, a silver-filigreed handle on his revolver. Ames recognized the hawklike, cruel face of Burch Taisley, known as King of the Outlaws. Nobody, at least nobody living, had argued with Taisley over the crown. The King was lightning-fast with a gun; he was a sadistic killer who enjoyed torturing his victims before finishing them off. No Comanche or

Kiowa had ever taken such pleasure in watching another man's agony as did Burch Taisley, with his vulture's beak over a small, rat-trap mouth.

Arizona Ranger Ken Wells was a fast gun himself, but he'd admitted it was partly luck that he'd managed to crease Taisley and capture him.

Few prisoners ever escaped the horrors of Yuma, the Arizona Territorial prison, yet Taisley had, with the help of loyal confederates. Svenson, Roberts and others had brought it off, with large bribes. They'd done it because they knew nobody else had Taisley's imaginative evil genius, that he could plan to rake in illicit fortunes, and it was rumored that the King had fortunes stashed away.

Svenson, Taisley and Roberts went to the trail. They talked for a short time, then Burch made a decision. Svenson nodded, and went to carry out the orders. Taisley and the Cockney went back to the main house.

A couple of pretty Mexican girls came from the hacienda. They wore flimsy silk and their dark hair was done up with high, jeweled combs. As Taisley stepped up on the veranda, their white teeth gleamed in smiles as

37

they took his arms, fondling him, but he impatiently shoved them off and went inside. Roberts followed, not glancing at the girls; Ames had heard the Cockney hated females.

A clot of gunnies, armed with Colts and carbines, had gathered around Svenson. They all went to the ready corral, roped mounts, saddled up, and moved out. The Swede had a powerful bay capable of bearing his extra weight. Ole mounted with surprising agility for such a big fellow, and led off eastward, the party soon disappearing around a bend.

Ames could guess what this was all about. The Comancheros should have arrived at the depot well before, and Taisley had sent Svenson to learn why they hadn't. When Ole got there, he'd find the abandoned cart; then he'd discover the dead ones, what the buzzards and wolves had left of them, anyhow.

This didn't worry Ames, for by now the Inces should be well on their way home, many miles off, beyond pursuit.

The renegades who traded with the Indians in west Texas would be paid for what they delivered to Taisley's drovers. The King would see to that; he had a keen eye for business. A tally of the beeves and horses had begun; Mexican wranglers, supervised by a few armed Anglo toughs, were jotting down figures on pads. Fires were going, running irons heating. With a running iron, brands could easily be altered. A "C" was made an "O" and an "L" a Box. "I's" could be crossed to form a "T" or several other letters or symbols, bars and new marks added. Horses carried an owner's brand, as a rule smaller than a cattle brand, and this would be blotted out and a new one burned in when the horse was sold. Counterfeit bills-of-sale would be given to buyers by the rustlers. Horses often changed hands.

With narrow confining chutes, it was not necessary to throw and hogtie each critter; one was held the few moments required to doctor marks and brands.

The operation was going on at the pens along the north margin of the great clearing. Bawls of cows, snorts and whinnies of horses could be heard, while Ames detected the distinctive odor, a familiar one to him, of burnt hair and hide.

It was hot but the bushes overhead shaded him. He dozed lightly, aware he must be rested, alert when action was required.

At noon, there was a break. The Mexican

39

cooks served food and drink, the weary wranglers lounging in the shade. They ate and smoked. Ames chewed a biscuit, slicing thin strips from a piece of jerky, washing it down with swallows of water from his canteen.

It was siesta time. Men pulled sombreros and Stetsons over their eyes and napped. Ames dozed along with them.

Suddenly a new sound aroused him. It came from the south, where there were more corrals filled with cows and mustangs. He heard the puffing and clang of a small locomotive approaching on the track, to the bumper at the end of the spur.

More peons went down, watched by some of the armed outlaws. They began poking the animals up ramps into the cattle cars. It took three hours to complete the operation, and Burch Taisley came from his hacienda and watched for a while, as the cars were crammed with uneasy critters.

The engine was a wood-burner. Ready to move, black smoke poured from the bell stack, and steam hissed from the cylinders. The wheels spun for a time, then took hold, slowly drawing away the string of loaded cars. It could be heard in the distance after the train had vanished into the woods, headed southwest toward the main line.

A couple of beeves for the commissary were being butchered, skinned, and quarters carried off for the cooks, peons doing the work.

Late in the afternoon, Burch Taisley was seated in a rocking chair with Percy Roberts nearby when shouts sounded from the trail.

The King of the Outlaws got up and strolled over, trailed by Lord Roberts, who seemed to be his special bodyguard.

They waited, watching Ole Svenson come up. Behind came the gunnies he'd led off that morning, and in the rear rattled the Comanchero supply wagon, driven by one of the toughs, the mustangs Ames had given to the Inces lined out on lead-ropes behind the vehicle.

It was seldom that Arizona Ames' cool mind was stunned with horror, but it was now, as he recognized the three captives herded along in the procession. They were roped together, lariats knotted around their waists. Their wrists were tightly secured by rawhide cords to short poles passing behind the neck, forcing the head down. They either

41

trotted to maintain the pace, or they'd be dragged.

First was George Ince, then his son Bob, and last Belinda. They still had their hats strapped on, low over their foreheads, and were coated with reddish dust. Ames decided that the killers hadn't yet discovered they'd snared a young female. The oversized man's shirt and her slender figure must have fooled them, and they'd been in a hurry to get back to the stronghold with the prisoners.

Brazos Ole Svenson swung from his saddle, handing his rein to a Mexican, who led the big bay off to rub him down before turning him into the pen. Other peons dumped several bags of grain into feeding bins, forked in more hay; there were tall stacks nearby, handy to the corrals.

The sun had enlarged, becoming red in the sky behind Ames.

The driver swung the cart around. In back were the mangled corpses of the Comancheros, stacked like cordwood. By now, they would be smelly. Mexican laborers found shovels and drove the wagon off to the far side, began digging a mass grave for the remains.

Ames guessed why Svenson had fetched

back the bodies; they'd been on Texas soil, and the tough, hard-fighting Texas Rangers kept an eye on the distant region with their patrols. The Army, too, sometimes policed the Llano, watching for Comanches and Kiowas who'd broken off the reservations. The recent raid, during which the Inces had been attacked and robbed, would have been reported by other victims.

Beads of sweat rolled down Ames' bronzed cheeks, dropping in the leafy bed on which he lay. Yes, the Inces were fools, worse fools than he'd believed, even. He couldn't blame the two young ones, who had stayed with their father. But George Ince, instead of turning back and heading home, as Arizona Ames had ordered, must have trailed on, still determined to recover his stock or die—and he would, as would Bob. Belinda's fate would be even worse.

4

BURCH TAISLEY, King of the Outlaws, stared at the three prisoners. He'd had them brought into the large main room of his hacienda. Shadows were lengthening and the light was dim. Taisley said, "Light the lamps, Ole."

Svenson struck a match and touched off wicks of three lamps on stands around the room. He replaced the chimneys, adjusted the flames as they came up, and put on the milk-glass globes.

The parlor was furnished with easy chairs, tables, plenty of lamps, a desk with papers stacked on it, a small safe in a corner. In another corner, out from the wall, was what looked like a bear cage. The contraption had heavy wire sides and roof and a padlocked gate.

In the trap a man slouched with his back to the wire, a man with a long, strong body. The cage was too low for him to stand erect. He had on a torn gray shirt, wisps of straw sticking to it; and to his denim pants. His feet were bare and he had no belt. His drawn face was disfigured by welts and scabbed bruises, while one eye was so swollen, he couldn't fully open it. Unshaven, his dark hair was a tangle.

Save for a slop bucket and the unfortunate captive, the cage was empty. Dully, he watched as Taisley sat down, and said, "Cut 'em loose, Roberts."

Lord Roberts, the scrawny little Cockney, produced a razor-sharp knife and slashed the bonds from the trio's wrists; the poles fell on the thick mat. The pretty Mexican girls stared at the scene, and Taisley called, "Conchita, you and Maria go to your quarters!" The women reluctantly obeyed, passing through a door leading to the rear.

Ole Svenson sank into a chair with a grunt and lit a cheroot.

Roberts suddenly cursed. There was disgust in his piping voice as he cried, "Gawdamighty, this 'un's a female!" He drew back from Belinda as though she was a coiled rattlesnake. Her long locks had fallen free as Roberts had swept off her hat, snapping its strap.

45

Taisley jumped up and went to examine her; he looked carefully at her from all angles as he might judge a prize horse.

"You're right, Percy. A pretty one, too!" He took hold of her shirt front and tried to rip it aside, and Belinda slapped him in the face.

Angered for a moment, Taisley stepped back, but then a faint smile touched his rat-trap mouth. "Spunky, too. I like that. When you get to know me better, dear, we'll be good friends."

"She's my daughter," said George Ince, choking back his anger. "This is my Bob, sir. I'm George Ince, own a little spread back from the Cap Rock. Injuns killed my brother and his son, and run off our stock. We were followin' to try and get 'em back."

"So you drygulched six of our amigos," growled Svenson. "Took their guns and mounts. Lucky we went huntin' for 'em, Boss. The fools was headed this way when we spotted their dust and snared 'em."

The smile wiped off Taisley's sallow face. "Ole, you mean this yokel told you he and his two brats drilled six well-armed fightin' men, and took their horses and weapons?"

"I guess he did. Anyhow, he let me think so."

The King swung on George Ince. "You're a liar, mister. Somebody gave you a hand. Who was it?" As Ince didn't reply quickly enough, Taisley hit him a sharp smack in the face that nearly knocked him off his feet.

Belinda cried, "Stop that. Don't you hurt my father!"

Lord Roberts grunted in disgust, a sulky expression on his wizened red face. He lit a spirit lamp under a small samovar, heating water for a cup of tea. Burch Taisley returned to his chair.

"Sit down, all of you," he ordered, "till I figger this out."

He put his chin in his hand as he glared at the three, who perched uneasily on chairs, facing him.

The water in the samovar began to boil, whistling as steam came from the spout. Percy Roberts daintily sprinkled tea from a can into a china cup, and poured in the hot water. Then he sat down and began to sip the brew, little finger extended from the cup handle.

George Ince finally had thought up a good story. He said, "I did sort of lie, mister. We had help. A passel of buffalo hunters come along and they shot down your friends."

Taisley kept staring at the rancher's face. "So, then the hunters handed over the mustangs and weapons to you, gave you their blessing, and let you ride on."

"Yessir, that's how it was."

If Taisley didn't swallow this, he pretended he had. "Ole, tell Fernandez to rustle up some grub for our guests. They must be hungry."

"We sure are, Mr. Taisley. We'd be obleeged for a bite. We're mighty thirsty, too, from that walk we took to get here."

Taisley rose, went to a side stand and fetched over a tray with a carafe and glasses on it. He poured a drink for Belinda, and took it to the girl.

"Ladies first," he said gallantly. She hesitated but her mouth was dry as flannel, and she took the glass and drained it. Burch passed the tray to George. "Help yourself."

The father and his son drank greedily.

Svenson had risen to carry out the King's order; he shucked his vest, saying, "Hot in here." On the breast pocket of the giant Swede's sweat-stained gray shirt was pinned an Arizona Ranger's badge. As Ole started toward the kitchens, Taisley called, "Have Fernandez fetch in the usual slops for Ranger

48

Wells." Svenson waved a ham hand and went through to the rear of the hacienda.

Ranger Ken Wells, slumped in the bear cage, stared at Taisley, his tormentor, eye bloodshot, bruised face drawn. He'd been there four days, held by his arch enemy, the man he'd sent to Yuma.

He'd shot down four outlaws before he had been overwhelmed by Brazos Ole Svenson and his horde of killers. Sometimes he wished they'd finished him off during the hot fight; it seemed better than what he was enduring, endless hours in the cage, taunted by Taisley. After he'd sent his second telegram to Governor Caldwell, saying he'd sighted Taisley, he'd begun carefully scouting around the big depot, getting the full picture with the idea of returning with enough of a force so he could crush the bandit horde. But a man couldn't go forever without sleep, and while he was napping, a couple of sentries had spotted him, called Svenson, and Wells had been captured.

Anyone but Taisley would have executed him immediately. Only the King would enjoy slowly torturing a man to death. For Wells knew he was doomed. There was no possibility of escape, no chance of rescue.

Taisley took immense pleasure in goading Wells, jeering at him, dragging out his victim's agony for a long time, as savages did, before a merciful death could release the sufferer.

Svenson came back, poured himself a liberal glass of redeye, sat down and lit another cigar. The Swede's pale-blue eyes were like twin marbles in his pouchy face. Lord Roberts ate some biscuits with his second cup of tea.

Before long, a Mexican in a white apron came through, bearing a large tray laden with foods, chile, fried steaks, tortillas and a bowl of frijoles, which he set down on the central table.

"Pull up your chairs and enjoy yourselves," the King said to the Inces.

They couldn't help but enjoy the first sumptuous meal they'd had since they'd left home. Young Bob ate wolfishly, and his father stowed it away, too. Belinda was more dainty, and she seemed worried; she kept stealing glances at Taisley.

Burch picked up a tin plate with leavings of food on it and went to Wells' cage. He produced a key ring and opened the padlock on the little gate, shoving the plate in with his foot, then refastening the entry. "There you are, Ranger Wells. It's better'n the slops we were fed in Yuma. Not enough, mind, but that was the rule at the prison, too. We lived like animals in tiny, miserable cubicles hardly big enough for a man to stretch out when he tried to sleep, if he could sleep. How do you like it? Maybe you realize what you did to me, and I ain't forgot Governor David Lee Caldwell, either. Soon as I get around to it, we'll capture him and I'll even up the score."

Wells crawled over and took the plate; his hand shook, but he began eating with the wooden spoon given him. A man had to cling to life, no matter how desperate his situation might be, and for another thing, he'd soon lose what strength he had if he didn't have food.

George Ince had cleaned off his heaping plate, and mopped up the last of the gravy with a tortilla. He glanced around. "You say that hombre in the bear cage is an Arizona Ranger, Mr. Taisley?"

"He is, the one who captured me and had me condemned to Yuma Territorial Prison, the worst hellhole on this earth. Fortunately I had loyal friends who managed to set me free. But I never forget an enemy, never." His mouth pursed tightly, his sallow face worked with seething inner fury.

Night had fallen over the wilderness. Lights blinked in the shacks and from lanterns on poles around the perimeter of the camp. Sentries rode circle, on the watch for possible intruders.

"You must be worn out, Ince," said Taisley. "You and your son go and sleep. Ole, put them in a bedroom, post a guard at the door, in case they don't enjoy our hospitality enough to spend the night." The King prided himself on his quick wit and sarcastic tongue.

George and Bob stood up. "Thanks for that fine meal, sir," said the father. "We're mighty grateful to you. See, when we lost our stock to the Comanches, it ruined us. We'd worked hard for years to build up our spread, all of us. The Indians killed my brother and his son. So the three of us set out. We just had to recover our critters."

Brazos Ole Svenson finished his drink in a gulp, snubbed out his cigar in a tray, and heaved from his chair like a buffalo bull rising from a wallow. His massive shoulders drooped. "This way, gents," he said, starting for the door into the rear of the house.

Ince nodded. "Thanks again, Mr. Taisley. C'mon, Belinda."

She started to follow her father and brother, but Taisley seized her arm. "I want to talk with you a few minutes, dear."

Ince looked alarmed. "See here, that's my daughter—"

Svenson gave him such a hard shove that Ince fell to his hands and knees. Bob hurried to help his father get up.

"Don't you dare hurt them!" cried Belinda, darting past Taisley.

The King seized her arm and drew her back.

"Don't worry your pretty little head about it, dear," he said. "If they do as they're told, we'll take fine care of 'em. Ole, you go easy, savvy? I don't want Mr. Ince and the boy harmed. Give 'em anything they need."

Svenson scowled and grunted, hulking over George and Bob. Taisley said, "Ole, you can have Conchita. Maria, too. I'm sick of 'em."

"Why, gracias, Boss," said the big Swede. "I always had a yen for Conchita. I'll move her to my quarters. As for Maria, Vern Hansen, one of my best men, is pinin' away for Maria."

Taisley shrugged. "They're yours, Ole. I

53

don't give a hoot what you do with 'em. Now take care of Ince and his son, and remember, handle 'em gentle."

Svenson herded George Ince, still dazed from shock and weariness, off to the rear of the spacious building. Bob held his father's arm to steady him. Taisley shut the door after them and threw a heavy bolt.

Belinda sat by the center table, her young face drawn with alarm.

Percy Roberts had watched the scene without stirring from his chair. Now he calmly poured another mug of tea for himself.

"Those fellers're disgustin'," he remarked. "H'all they thing h'about is femyles!"

"Douse that lamp by you, Perce," ordered Taisley. "Drop the front jalousies and take your tea out and wait on the veranda."

" 'Arf a mo'," replied the Cockney testily, but noting the scowl on the King's sallow face, he rose and lightened his gunbelt. He blew out the light on his stand, and went along, dropping the blinds. The side windows were narrow embrasures, but the half dozen giving out on the porch were somewhat larger. The Cockney darted venomous glances at Belinda's back as she sat stiffly, facing the rear of the hacienda.

"What'd you say?" demanded Taisely sharply, as Roberts muttered to himself.

"H'l sye ye're no better'n the rest of 'em," he snapped. Taisley grinned. "Hustle to it, Perce."

Roberts shut all the jalousies, picked up his mug of tea, and went out the front way, slamming the door behind him.

Burch Taisley glided over and bolted it shut. He picked up a light chair and set it close to Belinda's, looking hungrily at her young face.

"Don't be afraid of me, dear," he said gently, but seemed to relish her obvious alarm. "We'll get along famously. Here, I'll pour you a glass of the finest wine ever produced by Spain."

"I—I don't drink, Mr. Taisley," she said.

"How charming! Innocence such as yours is seldom encountered in these crude regions. Virtue is so unusual I admire you very much."

He poured a glass of liquor for himself and drained it, then filled it again, took another swallow, and set the glass on the table.

Belinda was trembling. Taisley hitched his chair closer and put an arm around her shoulders. "I'll protect you from harm,

Belinda. They call me King of the Outlaws. Well, I will make you my queen. You shall have everything your heart desires—jewels, silken gowns, fine horses. Your father and brother will have the best of everything, too. I can see how devoted you are to them."

"Please, please let us go," she begged, brokenly.

"You won't want to leave when you realize how much I intend to do for you."

Her face was drawn, pale under the tan. "I'm wore out, Mr. Taisley. I need to sleep."

"Of course! Forgive me for not realizing it, Belinda. Here, lie down over on the couch. Close your eyes and sleep." He helped her up, then took her in his arms and carried her to a soft, wide divan along the inner wall. He spread a blanket over her, smiled down at her, and returned to the table. He swung his chair so he could watch Belinda as she lay there, drank off the wine he'd poured and again filled the glass. He chose a fine Cuban cigar from a cedar box, and lighted it, smoking and drinking, a faint smile on his rat-trap mouth.

Slouched in his seat, he watched Belinda. She was utterly exhausted. With the blood of youth in her, she was quickly asleep, lying on her back, her red lips parted as she began breathing easily.

Burch Taisley seemed to gloat over his new prize. Sadistic as he was, some quirk in his brutal nature took pleasure in this cat-and-mouse game.

"You're a swine, Taisley," Ken Wells suddenly said from his cage.

Taisley jumped, rudely startled from his reverie. He got up, pulled a large Spanish shawl from a hook, and went over to Wells. He secured the shawl at the top of the wire bear cage, draping it so that the captive could not see him and the couch, though the other sides were still uncovered.

"You can go to sleep now, Ranger. I'd really forgotten about you. No reason why I should give you the pleasure of watching."

"I'll kill you with my bare hands if I ever get out of here!"

"You won't. Tomorrow I aim to be shut of you. You won't die easy. I'll put a bullet through one shoulder, then the other, next shatter your kneecaps. After you've screamed a while, I'll gutshoot you. It'll take a long, long time to die. And you won't be planted. I'll have the boys dump you in the bush for the buzzards and coyotes. Now dry up, or you'll wake the little lady."

Taisley spoke through gritted teeth, keeping his voice down. Belinda hadn't stirred; she slept deeply.

The King of the Outlaws went back to his seat. He poured drink after drink, occasionally turning the glass in his long fingers, holding it up to the light. He liked the play of colors in the fine Spanish wine, murmuring to himself.

He relished the wine and the anticipation of the sport he'd soon enjoy with the pretty young captive.

5

ARIZONA AMES bellied as close as he dared to the rim of the big clearing. It was very late, and a chunk of yellow moon was near its zenith. The lanterns blinked in the night wind, attached to their high posts. Most of the lamps and candles in the shacks had gone out an hour ago. The ready corral was the closest of the pens to his position, and the horses waited quietly, some standing quiet, a few moving slowly around. Farther west were the enclosures holding the latest batch of stolen stock; some of the cows were lying down, others standing with lowered heads. The mustangs were more restless, and a whinny or snort would sound. Bad-tempered critters would bite or kick at others who crowded them. Big haystacks loomed black against the moon sky.

Night sounds came from the woods, hoots of owls, distant yipping of coyotes baying from hilltops at the moon.

He was at the north of the bandit eyrie. The hacienda was dark for the night, save for a faint yellow glow behind the drawn front jalousies and glinting through two narrow embrasures at the end that Ames was facing. This was probably the hacienda's main parlor, its doors giving out on the long veranda, as the building faced the west.

The mounted sentry, slowly covering his beat, rode past again. He wore a steeple sombrero shading his face; he had on easy clothes. He was riding a light gray, and the leather creaked faintly, accoutrements jingling. The man rode with his chin down, and carried a carbine at a slant across the pommel. He would go to the end of the in-trail from Texas, where he would raise his arm and signal a horseman patrolling the east margin, turn and come back. At the west end, he would wave his rifle to the sentinel on that side. They hadn't, so far anyhow, drawn close enough to exchange words. Ames figured there would be a fourth one to the south, but the buildings cut him off from where Ames lay spying.

Ames regretted having to do what he must do. If he hadn't seen Brazos Ole Svenson fetching in the Inces, he could have snaked round after dark and ridden back to Texas for enough men to capture Burch Taisley's powerful outlaw horde. But this would have taken time. He would have had to collect enough buffalo hunters, if they were willing to assist, or had he been lucky, might have been able to contact an Army patrol, even connected with a troop of Texas Rangers. By now, word of the latest Indian raids would have reached the military and Rangers.

He knew what he was attempting was fool-hardy. Locating the Inces in the big hacienda, taking them out and furnishing them with mounts, seemed impossible. But Ames also knew he'd never sleep easy again if he didn't make a stab at it, though he'd probably die in the operation.

As soon as dark had fallen, he'd worked his way back to Cappy and seen to his big sorrel. He'd moved the horse in closer, where he'd have a chance of reaching him when he needed him. He'd tethered Cappy in a small grove where the sorrel might graze and wait.

He had smeared his face with fresh dirt, left his hat and cartridge belt, even his carbine. He'd bound his hair with his bandana, and took only his hunting knife, sheathed at his back, and his heavy revolver, fully loaded. He had a few spare shells for the handgun carefully distributed in his pockets so they wouldn't clink together. He wore his moccasins, riding boots stowed with his other gear under a live oak near Cappy.

The big Colt was thrust into his pants belt behind his lower ribs so it wouldn't interfere with crawling. It was uncomfortable but he had to have it with him.

He'd already been lying there at the edge of the clearing for over an hour. If he was to have the slightest chance, he must be sure of the sentries' routine; one shot or warning shout in the night would bring out the whole ravening pack of killers and spoil the play. Up to the moment, he hadn't had any luck.

The first, probably the last wild gamble he'd get came fast, and Arizona Ames had to seize it or lose out.

The sentry came along, horse at a walk, its head lowered with the easy pace. He was hardly past Ames' position when he pulled up, half turning his mustang to the faint light from the clearing, and thrusting his carbine into the boot with an audible clunk. Cocking up a leg to ease his muscles, he drew out a tobacco sack and papers and began carefully building a cigarette. The horse stood resting.

Something in Arizona Ames' brain clicked, "This is it!" Crouching, he made a panther-ish lunge, leaping in a single bound up behind the rider. The startled mustang snorted and might have reared but the sentry grabbed his rein with both hands to hold him down.

This left his throat wide open and before he could do more than gasp, a band of steel circled his neck from the rear. The powerful muscles in Ames' arm tightened, shutting off the man's wind.

The struggle was brief; Ames held with his long legs around the mustang's barrel ribs; he pressured with his left, swinging the animal toward the edge of the woods.

It was over in seconds; the outlaw went limp and Ames held him up, keeping hold of the horse's rein with his left hand, he pulled the unconscious sentry off the saddle. A breath later he had dragged him out of sight; he looped the rein to his shoulder, and knelt. He tightly gagged the bandit, tying him quickly but efficiently, hands behind his back and ankles crossed, with the man's own lariat.

He grabbed the extra pistol and thrust it into his belt, unbuckled the chinstrap and put on the sombrero, pulling it low to shadow his own face. Rolling the still unconscious fellow into the bush, he pulled the horse out and mounted.

He had the carbine in the boot, and drew it, holding it across the pommel; its ammunition belt hung from the horn. Riding slowly on, chin down, he moved west to signal the other sentinel who was coming up that way.

Within some yards of the other horseman, he raised his carbine in one hand and waved; the other waved back, returning the salute, signaling all well. The steeple hat, gray mustang with the slouched rider against the dark wall of trees, looked normal to the west sentry, who pulled on his rein and started his slow run back.

Ames rode east now, glancing in at the sprawling hacienda, its front windows still showing a light. How to get inside? If he went over, the other guards would quickly miss the north line rider and come hunting him. He'd have no time to accomplish anything much.

Arriving at the margin of the beat, the east sentry was waiting, the signal was exchanged, and both swung back. A second time he waved to the west man. Then he noted the large haystack a few yards past the northernmost corral, which was filled with mustangs.

It might be what he needed. If he drew off the sentries, he'd make more precious minutes for himself.

When the west guard was well on his way, Ames quickened the gray's pace. Reaching the haystack, he struck a wooden match and tossed it at the base of the dry hay. He waited a moment to be sure it took hold. As the flames began licking up and spreading, he swung and angled over to the hacienda.

The hay was completely cured and there was a night wind which whipped it up even faster than Ames had expected. Flames began leaping high in the air, smoke circling in clouds. The animals in the pen began whinnying in panic at the fire, crowding against the rails into the corner farthest from the terrifying blaze.

The reaction was even faster and more violent than Ames had anticipated.

"Fire, fire!" somebody bellowed, and several shots blasted the alarm as the west sentinel pointed his gun into the air and pelted toward the northwest corner of the clearing. A confusion of shouts rose as men emerged from their sleeping shacks. "Bucket lines, bucket lines!" leaders ordered, and Ames, pressed against the wall in the shadows, saw other line sentries and everybody else galloping toward the blazing haystack.

Sitting his saddle, he looked through the narrow window by him into the front room of the main house. A lamp on the center table gave enough light so he could make out details inside. First he saw Burch Taisley hurrying over to the veranda door; the King pulled the bolt open and stepped outside. Then, on down the large chamber, he saw Belinda Ince. She was sitting bolt upright on a couch, staring at the open doorway.

And then he noticed the wire bear cage. A cloth covered one side but the other three were open, and a man inside got up and turned, so that Arizona Ames could see his face and figure quite distinctly.

Ames' breath sucked in sharply. His friend, Ranger Ken Wells, was in that cage, a prisoner of Burch Taisley's!

Now Ames knew he must get in there. He'd been convinced Wells had been shot down by the outlaws, but for some strange reason, Taisley was holding him captive, maybe as a hostage, maybe for his own sadistic pleasure.

Ken Wells couldn't stand erect in the cage,

but he gripped the heavy wire with both hands as he tried to see what was going on out there. Men were yelling as confusion gripped the bandit hangout.

Ames swung just in time, hearing a door to the rear of the place bang open. The huge figure of Brazos Ole Svenson catapulted outside, other men crowding behind him. Svenson saw the rider with the steeple sombrero on the gray mustang, and Ames shouted "Fire! Fire!"

Svenson lumbered on by, calling, "C'mon, get shovels and buckets, whole passel of you! Wind's this way, don't let that fire spread!"

As the knot of dark figures pelted past him, Arizona Ames coolly rode to the door into the rear of the hacienda. Nobody had bothered to close it. He got down, ground-hitched the gray, and stepped inside, carrying the carbine he'd taken from the sentry he'd knocked out. He had his own Colt and the spare revolver which had belonged to the fellow he'd laid out and left trussed and gagged in the woods.

Somebody had lighted a lantern in a bedroom which gave off the hall leading toward the front of the house. Ames glanced in and saw a pretty young Spanish woman sitting up

67

in bed, silk nightgown over her voluptuous body.

He almost bumped into a man, standing with grounded carbine against the wall, outside a closed door. He was a tough looking rascal with a red face and shaggy brown hair. He had no hat on. Ames' face was shadowed by his sombrero, and the man seemed to accept him as one of the crew, for he said, "What the hell goes on out there?"

"Mean fire, got to keep her from spreadin', wind's this way. Better go help. Svenson wants every hand he can get."

"Shucks, he told me to stick here and guard them two stupid hoemen we snaffled. What you doin'? Why ain't you out there?"

"Svenson sent me to fetch a hose from the front, then I'm goin' back. They're riggin' up a pump—"

"Two 'hoemen' captives—" Ames immediately guessed George and Bob Ince must be held in the side room.

He started past the gunny, who was trying to see out the open door though all he could make out was a reddish glow from the fire.

With one swift movement, Arizona Ames swung the carbine barrel, connecting square with the house guard's temple, knocking him sprawling. The man's eyes widened, then glazed as he quivered and lay in a heap at Ames' feet. Arizona Ames stepped over him and rapped sharply with the carbine butt on the closed door.

"Ince, you in there?"

George called, "We're in here, me'n Bob. Who's that?"

"Ames. Stand back, I'm coming through."

There was a padlock outside. Ames pried the hasp hard with the rifle barrel and the screws pulled from the wood. He flung the door open.

"Hustle, follow me," he ordered, seeing the two dark forms of the Inces standing nearby in the small room.

He padded up the long corridor toward the front, where he'd seen Ken Wells, Belinda and Burch Taisley. George and his son trotted in his wake. He reached the closed, wide door giving into the parlor. He carefully lifted the latch and shoved, but the door was locked from the other side.

"Take this," he said, voice low, passing the loaded carbine to George. He gave young Bob the spare Colt.

"Don't shoot unless you have to," he warned. "We're going in there."

"Taisley's in that room and he's got my Belinda!"

"I savvy. Keep quiet and back me up."

They could still hear the excited uproar from across the clearing, men calling out, the frightened neighs of horses, and cattle bawling. But it wouldn't be long before the haystack burned itself out, and the bucket brigades doused the embers and last of the blaze.

He put a powerful shoulder against the door, above where the inside bolt would be, and shoved with all his power. The door was thick and heavy and resisted the pressure; he thought he heard the bolt screws starting to pull from the wood.

He drew back a couple of feet and hit it with all his weight. The bolt let go so suddenly, screws flying from their seats, that Ames catapulted through the opening as the door banged back.

He was several feet inside the big room, sliding to a halt as he skidded on a mat, before he could check himself. Belinda screamed, startled at the sudden commotion.

Burch Taisley, who had gone out on the veranda but had seen it was only a haystack burning, had just come back inside. He was

70

bolting the door onto the porch, but the sharp noises behind him caused him to turn quickly.

There was a wall rack holding rifles, shotguns and small arms only a few steps down to the King's right.

But it might just as well have been a mile away, for all the good it did Taisley at the moment. The same went for his own fancy six-shooter, lying in its holster on the center table by the bottle of wine.

The sallow face, the cruel eyes, rat-trap mouth trying to work but unable to say anything because Taisley was so shocked and horrified, gave Arizona Ames a feeling of the deepest satisfaction.

"Howdy, Taisley," he drawled.

Burch found his voice, and in a falsetto, pitched with panic, screeched, "Roberts—Svenson!"

He couldn't believe it. Arizona Ames, his old enemy, had him under the gun!

6

AMES knew he must not lose a precious moment. He crossed over, seized Taisley by the shoulder, and propelled him to an armchair in the center of the room. "You die first of all, Taisley, if they bust in here or fire at us, savvy?"

Taisley's eyes were round with the fear of death. "Don't kill me, Ames!"

"Pronto, Ince, grab that lariat off the hook and help me tie this cuss to his chair."

Belinda had run to her father and brother. "Belinda, you keep back and stay down low, hustle. We got no time to fritter away."

"Do as he says, Belinda," ordered George Ince, hurrying to fetch the rope.

"Now tie him good, tighten the knots." Arizona Ames was watching Taisley with one eye and the front windows and door with the other. The jalousies were down, the bolted portal thick wood.

He checked the ties Ince had made.

Taisley's wrists were fastened to the chair arms, his ankles to the lower rungs.

Ames set the lamp, turned low, on the floor, giving enough light to maneuver by, but dimming the big room. He hurried to the cage and ripped down the Spanish shawl which Burch Taisley had fastened over one side.

"Ken!"

Wells was squatted down, holding the wire with both hands. "Arizona Ames! I thought it was your voice but I couldn't believe it!"

"You better, pard. Pull yourself together. We got an army to hold off. Where's the key to this padlock?"

"Tailsey's got it on a ring in his pocket."

In a jiffy Ames found the keys, undid the padlock, and helped Ken Wells crawl from the pen. "You hurt bad?"

"No. Only feel like I've been drawed through a keyhole!"

His bruised, unshaven face was stained, his cheeks hollow. He staggered the first few steps and Ames grabbed his arm, but then his friend straightened and said, "I'm okay, Rich."

"Arm yourself. Plenty guns in that rack across the room."

Wells started over; he grabbed a pitcher of water from a stand and drank deeply from it. Then he took down a double-barreled shotgun, loaded it, chose a fine carbine, and hung two cartridge belts, with .45 Colts in the holsters, over his shoulder.

"Get on back here, Ken," commanded Ames. "Squat down behind Taisley. If they bust in on us, kill him first off. Blow his head off his shoulders with that shotgun."

"That'll be a pleasure, a pleasure," grated Ranger Wells, a grim smile flitting across his haggard face.

"Don't—don't kill me, gents," begged Taisley again. Ames' bloodthirsty order to Wells had shaken him, as Ames had intended.

"That all depends on you, Burch," replied Arizona Ames.

The door into the interior was a problem. Ames had torn the bolts from the lock. He made sure it was closed as tightly as possible, then, with Bob Ince's help, dragged over a heavy sideboard and blocked the entry.

"Everybody's gone to the fire, lucky for us," said Ames. "But they got it most out and they'll come swarmin' back on us. We ain't got long to make ready."

He gave more orders. George and Bob Ince

74

assisted as Ames formed a small semi-circle of upended tables, stands and chairs, a little fort within the large parlor. He took care to back this against the wall, away from the door to the interior; high-powered rifles could send bullets through the panels, and the sideboard might not stop them as they tore through the wood.

He had Ranger Ken Wells sit with his back to the wall, just behind Taisley, tied to his chair and facing the front of the house. "Remember, Ken, your job is to blow Burch to pieces when the moment comes, though his own men'll riddle him if they ain't mighty careful." Arizona Ames watched Taisley's sallow face, as Burch licked his dry lips. He meant to impress his prize prisoner.

Now he set the Inces at narrow gaps between the jumble of furniture they'd assembled as a crude barricade. "I want you all to lie down flat, amigos. You got carbines and ammo, and revolvers. Don't fire till I give the order, savvy?"

Belinda took her place in the line; she could handle a rifle as well as most men.

Ames had a loaded carbine, two sixguns, a shotgun and a pile of ammunition for the weapons by him as he set himself behind the overturned table. He was puffing, and it took a few moments for his breathing to quiet down. Now he made a cigarette, and Ken Wells said, "I ain't had a smoke for days, Rich." Ames tossed him the makings.

He could hear the voices of the firefighters in the clearing, but the haystack had burned itself out, and the glow had died off. Embers and sparks had been doused.

Pretty soon heavy steps sounded on the front veranda.

"Hey Boss," sang out Ole Svenson. "It was only a haystack. All out now. You okay?"

Ames looked back at Taisley. "Answer him, tell him you're fine, Burch," he whispered hoarsely.

"I'm—I'm all right, Ole," he called, but his voice quavered.

"We're turnin' in again," Svenson said from the porch. "Perce is right outside here if you need anything."

They heard more steps on the veranda, and the querulous voice of Lord Roberts. "H'I sye, what a todo over a little burnin' grawss!"

They heard Ole Svenson give a coarse laugh, and utter a ribald jest.

The bandits were returning to their sleeping quarters and the big hangout was quieting

76

down again. Arizona Ames crunched out his smoke, waiting. George Ince asked in a low voice, "How do you expect ever to get out of this trap? When day comes they can smoke us out, or maybe get at us from the roof by tearin' off the shakes."

"Don't let it worry you," Ames replied. "Keep down low, stay shut, and be ready. The baille has just begun."

But his alert mind had already been hunting a solution to the main problem, escape from the outlaw stronghold with the Inces and his pal, Ranger Wells. His ace in the hold was Burch Taisley. Somehow, he hoped to use his star prisoner to effect a getaway, though he hadn't figured how as yet.

True, he might trade Taisley for horses and a start back to Texas. But it would still be a long way to the nearest buffalo hunters' camp, and Svenson was no fool. The murderous horde had plenty of fast animals and spare relief mounts.

With the Inces in tow, Arizona Ames really didn't believe they could make it to safety.

He could only hold tight and watch for some slight chance.

Ken Wells said nothing, but as an

experienced lawman, he could calculate the odds as well as Arizona Ames could.

It wasn't long before Ames' prediction that the ball was just starting came true. Men were coming through the hallway leading from the back of the place to the parlor. Someone rapped sharply with a gun butt on the door, jammed shut by the sideboard.

Ole Svenson called, a worried note in his deep voice, "Looka here, Taisley, something's sour. The Inces have escaped. The guard I set by their room was laid out cold. I brought him to, and he claims some hombre he thought was Guiterrez buffaloed him. Guiterrez was on the north margin as sentry, but we can't find him. He's disappeared."

Arizona Ames had laid down his carbine and stepped close to Burch Taisley. He wore his Colt .44 in the holster at his hip; the weapon was seldom far from his hand. An old trapper named Cappy Tanner had given it to him in Tonto Basin, and he'd used it many times to save his life in desperate duels. Ames had named his big sorrel in honor of the trapper who'd presented him with the revolver.

"Tell him it's all right, Burch," Ames

78

whispered in Taisley's ear. "Send out search parties for the Inces in the mornin'."

Taisley gulped, then obeyed. "Don't bother me again, Svenson. I'm busy. You can hunt for 'em when dawn breaks. Go back to bed."

"Open the door and lemme speak to you, Boss," argued the Swede. "I don't like the smell of things around here. What's wrong?"

"Nothing's wrong, you jackass!" Taisley's voice shrilled with the fear that dominated him, dominated every fiber of his being, with Ken Wells right behind him with that shotgun. At close range, such a weapon would blow his head off his shoulders.

"Look out, Ames—"

Ken Wells' sudden warning caused Arizona Ames to whirl; he'd been watching that door to the rear of the house as he stood by Taisley.

At the south end of the long parlor he saw Lord Roberts just as the tiny Cockney rose; the man was so small, he'd been able to squeeze through one of the narrow embrasures.

Percy Roberts came up to shooting stance, teeth bared.

It was an even draw, Arizona Ames with his blinding speed against the fastest gunhand west of the Missouri.

79

7

THE heavy revolvers roared, belching flame and lead as though in a single explosion; any difference between the two shots could not have been measured, save perhaps in a thousandth of a second.

Percy Lord Roberts flipped back, a clean hole between his fierce bloodshot eyes.

The Cockney's slug shrieked past Arizona Ames' ear, missing by inches, burying itself in the opposite wall with a dull thud. The deafening bang of the guns reverberated through the room.

Ames, still in his gunfighter's stance, suddenly realized another weapon had spoken even as the ace marksman had squared off. He glanced left, and saw Belinda with her carbine still pointed toward Roberts, a curl of burnt powder smoke slowly rising from the muzzle. The girl had fired without waiting for Lord Roberts to pull trigger. She'd evidently seen Roberts squeeze through the embrasure and without hesitation had thrown a quick one at the Cockney.

Ames trotted over, kicked away the gunman's pistol. He checked, making sure Percy Roberts was dead; Arizona Ames had hit him square between the eyes. Belinda's hasty bullet had only slashed his left shoulder but the shock had been enough to deflect his aim.

Ames pouched his .44 Colt and returned to the improvised fort.

"Now I'll never know," he said, in a low voice.

Ken Wells knew what he meant. "And if he'd beaten *you* to it, Rich, you wouldn't savvy, either!"

Svenson had heard their whispering, and he sang out. "Who's that in there with you, Chief?" The Swede was no fool, but a shrewd, competent leader second only to Burch Taisley.

"Go on back to bed," called Taisley, voice thick.

Instead, a covey of bullets ripped through the door panels, some stopped by the bureau blocking the entry, others singing near the little group, off to one side.

"Cut that, you fool!" screeched Taisley in the lull. "They got me under the gun! They'll blow my brains out if you try to bust in. Arizona Ames and Wells have me hogtied to a chair. While you dumb jacks were cavortin' over at that little haystack fire, Ames snuk in, and he freed the Inces and Ranger Wells! Ames just killed Perce Roberts; even that little lame-brain run over to join the fun."

There was a silence. Finally Svenson called, "Look, Ames, I don't know how you done it. How about a deal? You savvy you ain't got a snowball's chance in hell of escapin'. I'll smoke you out."

"Do that. You'll find Burch dead, even if we're still kickin'."

"Ole," shouted Taisley, "tell 'em we'll furnish 'em with horses and give 'em as long a start as they need. Fact, we won't even try to catch up if they free me."

"All right, I'll do that, Ames, sure enough. Just let Burch loose and the passel of you can ride off." Svenson sounded too glib.

"I might, only Taisley goes along with us till we can get to a safe place. Say a big buffalo hunters' camp on the Llano."

"So when you make it, you arrest Burch and run him back to Yuma Prison!"

"You got my word I'll free him."

"How about Wells? What's he say?"

"Anything Arizona Ames says speaks for me," called Wells.

"Do like he says, Svenson," ordered Taisley anxiously.

"I'll think it over."

Ames listened, Colt in hand; he heard footsteps as the enemy went back into the interior of the big hacienda.

He knew Ole Svenson had the advantage over him, for while Ames would keep his promise, the Swede wouldn't be troubled by such scruples. Svenson was probably figuring how to fool the captives, make them believe he was carrying out the bargain. Maybe he'd post sharp-shooters, hidden at high points along the route back to Texas, who would pick off Ames, Wells and the Ince men without warning. Svenson knew very well that even if Arizona Ames and Ranger Wells were willing to give Taisley a chance of escape, that wouldn't guarantee what the tough buffalo hunters might do. There were large rewards posted for Burch Taisley's capture, dead or alive, and blood-money scavengers were as ruthless as the King of the Outlaws.

Arizona Ames was about as weary as he'd ever been; he'd had only catnaps, he couldn't remember when he'd last relaxed. His grim face, still stained with dirt, was drawn, his eyes would scarcely stay open. With a grunt, he sank to the floor, back to the wall, long legs extended before him.

"Rich," a soft voice said at his side. It was Belinda: she'd come up near to him and sat down. She laid down her carbine, and took hold of his arm, looking earnestly at him.

"You're wonderful," she whispered. "I never met a man like you before. You saved our lives and you saved me from—from that beast!" He felt her shiver as she glanced at the trussed Taisley.

Now she began to stroke his cheek with her gentle hand. It was very soothing; Ames shut his eyes, lulled by the pleasant caresses and nearness of the pretty girl. She was soft and warm as she pressed against him.

Ken Wells said, "Take a little shuteye, Rich. I ain't tired, all I've done in that cage was sleep! I'll keep guard."

"Maybe—" Arizona Ames began . . .

When he jumped awake, he found he was

in Belinda's arms, his tousled head cradled on her bosom.

It took a second before he brought himself back to the situation, with sudden death liable to strike them all at any instant.

The brief sleep had helped. He straightened up.

A yellowish-red glow sent streamers of light through the embrasures and the slats of the jalousies.

Ken Wells, seeing he was awake, said, "They've lit big fires all around the clearin', Rich."

Ames nodded, rubbing the sleep from his eyes. "Makin' sure we don't sneak out while it's dark. Blow out that lamp, Bob. We don't need it any more; we can see well enough without it."

Bob Ince blew out the lamp, which was turned low. Then Ames heard faint noises; for a moment, he couldn't place them exactly, but they seemed to come from above, toward the end of the big room. He watched, Colt .44 ready. Finally he saw a small hole; a shake had been quietly removed from the roof. The opening was easy to make out because of the outside bonfires.

A head was outlined in the gap as a gunny

peeked in, trying to see just where the beseiged were, so he might pick them off. Ames threw a quick slug from his revolver; there was a sharp yelp of pain, a rolling sound, and another cry as the man fell off the roof and landed on the ground.

The twin barrels of a shotgun were thrust through the hole, and a blast of spreading buck came through, spattering too close for Ames' liking, and he let go three more, while George and Bob Ince fired their carbines at the shotgunner.

This time they heard the body rolling off the roof, but there were no outcries. Probably the flurry of slugs had killed or seriously wounded the outlaw.

They waited, watching the little opening, but nobody else seemed willing to take a stab at it again. "They won't try that any more," drawled Ranger Wells, with a short laugh. He borrowed Ames' tobacco and papers and fixed a quirly, Arizona Ames joining him.

"I don't reckon we'll ever get our stock back, do you?" asked George Ince.

Ames chuckled. "You sure got a one-track mind, Ince! If it hadn't been for worryin' over you and Belinda, I wouldn't be trapped in here. On the other hand, if I hadn't peeked in, I'd never have known Ranger Wells was caged. I'd have ridden off, fetched back enough fighters to smash Taisley's gang, and—"

"By that time I'd have been dead, Rich," broke in Wells. "Taisley promised to kill me tomorrow."

"You saved us," murmured Belinda, again pressing close to the big fellow. "No matter what happens now, I'm glad. I'll die right by you, Rich. I never met a man like you before." Her large eyes betrayed her admiration.

"That tomorrow you spoke of is here already, Ken," said Ames.

A faint grayness had come over the wild land. Dawn was breaking, dimming some of the bonfire light. "Svenson savvies he'll have more chance of pickin' us off in the daytime," said Arizona Ames.

He made sure his Colt .44 was reloaded and checked over his other weapons.

Taisley was whimpering. His head was sunk on his chest, and he complained, "You got me tied so tight, all the circulation's cut off!"

"Don't let a little thing like that worry you, Burch," Wells told him. " 'Fore long, you won't be able to feel at all. I got a hunch Svenson won't wait for Christmas to come."

Arizona Ames had the same idea. Brazos Ole Svenson was a fighter, a man of direct action; the Swede had no trace of fear in his makeup.

"Take your places, friends," Ames ordered. "Make sure your guns are loaded and ready, and whatever you do, keep low behind your barricades."

Wells remained with his shotgun behind Taisley; Belinda and her father and brother spread flat at the gaps, facing the front of the house, backs to the wall. Ames had his .44 Colt, a spare pistol, a shotgun and carbine by him as he waited.

The attack opened with sudden blasting fury. Guns bellowed through the embrasures on both flanks; shotgun blasts smashed the windows and ripped the jalousies to shreds. The lead seemed to rain all around, rapping into the walls, shrieking close overhead, tearing at the crude protective barrier they'd erected. George Ince gave a sharp cry, and Ames glanced over, saw the father's cheek was bleeding, but Ince wasn't badly wounded; he opened fire with his rifle, aiming at the front windows, at dodging figures on the veranda.

Nothing could be heard now above the roaring explosions. Ames decided Svenson had mustered every available man for the strike, meant to overpower the handful of defenders. He heard a few loud curses, from men hit by the lead from inside. Bob and Belinda, Arizona Ames, Ken Wells, the shotgun reserved for the last instant when he'd kill Taisley across his lap, wielded his revolver, shooting close past the terror-stricken prisoner whose shouts were lost in the din.

The bolt holding the front door was shot out. The door banged open, and Ole Svenson rushed in with the impetus of a charging buffalo bull, revolvers blaring from both hands. Close behind him crowded a dozen or more tough gunnies, fanning out for the kill.

Arizona Ames took cool aim at the heavy, half-stooped Swede. He fired once, twice, three times, all his bullets striking dead center, but Svenson charged on straight for the low barricade. Ken Wells let go at him, too, and Bob Ince swung his carbine on the huge man.

Ames dropped his revolver and snatched

up the double-barreled shotgun, pulled both triggers as fast as he could. The wads of buck literally tore Svenson's body to pieces; he finally went down, almost at the barricade.

Wells, Bob, George and Belinda were making hits on the gunnies, halfway across the big room. Several went down; others cried out, dropped their weapons, grabbing at punctured arms and thighs, turning back. The survivors hesitated, then beat a hasty retreat, diving out the open doorway, scrabbling off to safety.

The echoes died off, and acrid powder smoke drifted through the room. The handful of defenders, dazed by the fury of the strike, could hear only the ringing of their ears for a time as they pulled themselves together.

Burch Taisley gasped, "You fools! I—I'm hurt."

Ames inched over, and Ken Wells said hoarsely, "He's hardly touched, Rich. Bullet parted his hair, that's all." Blood was running down one side of Taisley's face from a shallow scalp crease.

"Reload and be ready," cautioned Ames. "They ain't finished with us yet."

He could see the massive Svenson, lying with his huge arms stretched out, still holding his Colts in a death grip. Several others had died nearer the door, while down the line lay the Cockney killer, Percy Lord Roberts.

Ames suddenly realized his upper left arm stung; a bullet had cut the flesh behind the muscle; then he found blood trickling down his right cheek. Both wounds were superficial. George Ince had been slightly wounded, and young Bob complained, "My leg hurts, Pop." The concerned father quickly cut the boy's trousers leg, and then heaved a sigh of relief. "It ain't bad, son. I'll wash it and pour some of that whiskey in, then bandage it."

Belinda was unhurt, Ken Wells had been behind Burch Taisley, and the attackers had tried to keep from hitting their chief, though a wild slug had burned his scalp.

The girl hurried to Arizona Ames, fetching a bottle of water. "You're wounded, Rich. You feel bad?"

"Just scratches, honey. Tear a piece off that silk shawl and clean me up, then pour some likker in."

Tenderly, she dabbed the damp cloth on his cheek and arms, concern for him in her large eyes. She brought a bottle from the stand across the room and poured the alcoholic liquor into the wounds, then carefully bound his arm. The cheek stopped most of its bleeding after a few moments.

"Take care of your father, Belinda," Ames said. "Keep a sharp watch, though; they ain't through with us yet."

The lull had helped but it was brief. They all scrabbled back to defensive positions as they made ready for a fresh attack. Heavy firing had erupted, blasting of rifles and pistols, hoarse yells, and the beat of galloping hoofs.

They could hear men at the rear of the hacienda, and shouts echoed through the corridors.

Guns ready for action, they waited tensely for the new strike.

Suddenly Arizona Ames realized they were no longer the center of attraction.

8

AMES, .44 Colt in hand, rose and hustled over to a front window, pushing aside the mangled jalousy, peering out.

"What goes on?" called Ken Wells.

"The Texas Rangers are here! They got the place surrounded, and—" Confused shouts rose, and he saw Taisley's desperadoes throwing down their weapons, raising their hands high in surrender.

"There's Cactus Ed Fraley, Ken! The rascal's hit just in the nick. Must've heard the firin' and rushed the place."

Big fellows in white hats, silver star on silver circle pinned to flapping vests or shirt pockets, heavily armed with twin Colts and repeating rifles, were expertly herding the prisoners against a corral fence, handcuffing them to the rails.

Arizona Ames went to the door, smashed in by Ole Svenson during his final charge. He sang out, "Fraley, don't shoot! It's Arizona Ames and Ranger Ken Wells!"

Cactus Ed was as tall as Brazos Ole Svenson, but he was lean sinew and muscles. His halfboots, decorated with the red Lone Star, were run over; he was dressed like his men, in white Stetson dirtied from much use, whipcord pants and a blue shirt, a tobacco sack tag hanging from one pocket.

The noise had abated, and Fraley heard Ames' loud call, swung and strolled over, pouching his sixguns, letting his repeating Henry rifle point at the ground as he moved. There was a wide grin on his lips, and one leathery cheek bulged out with a tobacco cud.

He stomped up on the porch and thrust out a big hand to shake. "Arizona Ames! What in tarnation you doin' here?—No, why should I ask? You could pop up most anywhere." He slapped his old compadre on the back.

"Come inside, meet some amigos of mine. Arizona Ranger Ken Wells, you savvy him. That's George Ince, his son Bob, and his girl Belinda. Ince is a Texas rancher, he come trailin' his stolen stock."

"Who's the gent you got tied to that chair?" asked Cactus Ed.

"That? It's Burch Taisley."

"Taisley, can't believe it!" He crossed over and took a closer look at the miserable prisoner. "By gee, it is! Texas wants that cuss. He belongs in Huntsville."

"That's where we're going to have an argument, Ed. He goes back to Yuma Prison. It's better'n Huntsville."

Fraley stopped grinning. "No Texan will admit anything outside the Lone Star is better'n anything Texas has, Ames! Well, you caught him, so just let's say Yuma is *worse* than Huntsville!" Cactus Ed smiled again and shifted his cud.

Ken Wells got up to shake hands. "Howdy, Lieutenant."

"Cap'n now," corrected Fraley, with a wink. "In charge of the whole danged Trans-Pecos! We had a bunch of complaints from ranchers up this way about Indians shootin' 'em up and runnin' off their stock. We wiped out a gang of Comancheros on their way up here, then marched on north. Run on a beaten trail, and our scouts claimed wagons and plenty riders had come along it. So we tracked along."

"You're out of your jurisdiction, Ed. This is New Mexico."

Fraley's grin grew wider. "I claim hot pursuit, that's legal."

"Lucky for us," nodded Ames. "They'd have finished us off."

"I didn't savvy what we'd find here, thought it might be another Comanchero depot. We camped last evening. Our sentries seen a fire in the sky, and more soon after, so I ordered a night march. After awhile we heard heavy gunfire and stole in, left our horses back in the woods, and hustled up. It was easy; all those rascals were concentrated around the front of the hacienda, so we drew a circle and closed. Even snaked a few Rangers into the back door, and we grabbed some who tried to take cover inside."

Belinda clung to Arizona Ames' hand as they said good-bye. "Please, Rich, come back to our ranch with us. I sure wish you would." She reached up and kissed his lips, holding the big fellow.

"Belinda, nothing I'd like better, but I got to take Taisley back to Arizona and report to Governor Caldwell. Next time I'm over this way, I'll stop and see you."

She sighed deeply. "Remember, you promised, Rich. I—I guess I'll never meet another man like you."

"Sure you will, honey. You're a beautiful girl."

Captain Ed Fraley had made his dispositions. He was sending a detail under a Ranger sergeant to drive the stolen cows and horses back to Texas and restore them to their owners. The Inces would assist, and in addition to their own stock, Fraley said they should have a number of mavericks and a herd of the outlaw mustangs in return for their help.

Fraley and his other Rangers would escort the shackled bandits, marching them to the nearest rail connection east; they would end up in Huntsville. The captain had decided to leave most of the furnishings and outlaw equipment for the peons. The Mexican leaders had convinced him that Taisley had treated them no better than slaves; they'd been abused and paid very little for their labor. Ames knew they'd taken no part in the fighting. Conchita and Maria were young daughters of two of the Mexicans; Taisley had taken them for himself.

They would leave the Rangers to clean up. Cactus Fraley would destroy the arsenal of guns and ammunition along with running irons and whatever else might be used

97

illegally. He gave a few hunting rifles to the Mexicans. The peons buried the dead.

Fraley was still busy at this when Arizona Ames and Ken Wells said so long. Wells had retrieved his Arizona Ranger badge from the dead Ole Svenson, and pinned it proudly to his shirt.

Armed to the teeth and well-provisioned, Ames and his friend set out with their captive, Burch Taisley, King of the Outlaws. Ames rode his big sorrel, Cappy, while Ken Wells had a fine bay gelding. Taisley was on a gentled, strong black, ankles roped under the horse's belly, wrists manacled to the saddlehorn, and Wells looped the lead-rope of the black to his horn as they started off.

They followed the crude spur track Taisley had laid to his stronghold. When they reached the main line, they'd wait at a water tower for the first train southwest, which would connect with the Southern Pacific.

"First telegraph station we come to, we'll wire Governor Caldwell we got Taisley and you're okay, Ken," said Arizona Ames. "He'll be mighty glad."

"And he'll be glad to hear we're escortin' Taisley back to Yuma for the second and last time."

He scowled back at the prisoner. But all the ginger had gone out of the King of the Outlaws. With Svenson, Roberts and his chief lieutenants dead or bound for Huntsville, Taisley knew he would never again escape from Yuma Territorial Prison.

"I wish," he muttered brokenly, "you'd shot me back there!"

"Yuma's worse," drawled Arizona Ames. "And you'll have a lot longer to think it all over, Taisley!"

He pushed Cappy on, headed back for the Tonto Basin and his beloved Arizona land.

Marauders of Gallows Valley

1

IT was near dusk when Arizona Ames topped the small rise and looked out over the verdant and pine-sloped terrain of Northern Nevada. He leaned forward in his saddle, patting Cappy's wind-blown mane gently; in the distance he could see the snow-peaked outlines of the Santa Rosa Mountains.

He was at last nearing the end of his long ride—a journey that had begun two weeks earlier in Salt Lake City. He had gone by train from that Utah settlement to Reno—with Cappy in one of the stock cars—and then continued by horseback in a straight line to Winnemucca. He had followed the general course of a tributary of the Humboldt River from there; and now, after three days, he had come in sight of the Santa Rosas.

Gallows Valley, his ultimate destination, lay in their near shadow.

Tall and weather-tanned, wearing a sheepskin jacket and the brim of his wide sombrero pulled low over his ears—for the air was chill here and smelled of snow and Ponderosa pine—Ames was a stoic man with inscrutable gray eyes. He wore faded blue denims, an old woolen shirt and well-traveled boots, and the sparse simple clothing seemed to accent the raw power in his slender yet muscular frame.

There was a carved black leather cartridge belt with a hammered silver buckle at his waist, and in the single holster ornamented with a large silver "A" rested an aged but meticulously well-cared-for Colt .44—a weapon which Ames had been forced to use many a time since it had been given him by an old trapper named Cappy Tanner in Tonto Basin, Arizona. It had saved his life on more than one occasion.

"Reckon another day's ride will bring us to Gallows Valley," Ames murmured to the great, sleek sorrel, who had been named after that same old trapper. "We'll bed down for the night in one of the valleys below, and head for Wade Lamont's holdings come sunup."

With a gentle prod of his bootheels, Ames took Cappy forward along the meandering trail. They started down the gradual slope, heading into the nearest of several lush green mountain valleys which were connected like arrow-straight markers pointing the way to the Santa Rosa Mountains.

There was, Ames knew, a wide and fairly well-used wagon road which passed through the string of valleys to the fertile Paradise Valley, where settlers from the East and Midwest were building new lives. Gallows Valley, to the southwest of Paradise, would soon be just such a mecca as well, for the federal government had recently sold parcels of land in the arca.

Wade Lamont, whom Ames had come to see to negotiate the purchase for his brother-in-law Sam Playford of several thousand head of prime beef stock, had "owned" all of Gallows Valley before the government's decision to sell over half of it to the land-hungry settlers. Lamont, unlike most land barons threatened with losing a good portion of their holdings, had resigned himself to the loss of some of his open range and to a reduction in his stock operations.

But being a shrewd if fair-minded old man, he had seen the chance to make large sums of money by shipping the settlers' farm produce to California and elsewhere, for he controlled all transportation facilities in the Gallows Valley area.

From all Ames had heard about Lamont— he had never laid eyes on the man—he imagined that shipping fees would be cut to accommodate the new landowners, and that Lamont would make his money on volume rather than outrageous prices. Too, Ames had heard that Lamont was planning to set up credit stores for the settlers, all of which would be run properly and honorably.

If all this were true, the Arizonan couldn't begrudge Wade Lamont whatever profit he would make from the coming of the settlers into Gallows Valley.

As he and Cappy dipped lower into the vale, Ames could at last make out the wagon road, winding along its floor toward the separating hills between this valley and the next. Great pine forests dotted the facing slope which made up the high boundaries of the glen, as they did on the side down which Ames was working his way. Birds spoke and sang softly in the growth to the trail's sides, and the cold wind hummed through the trees. It was the only sound, and a comforting one in Ames' ears as the cowboy eased Cappy down the twisting trail.

The first volley of gunshots, none too distant, startled Ames, and he snapped back on Cappy's reins to bring the sorrel to a complete standstill. A frown creased the tanned-leather surface of his forehead, and he craned his neck forward, listening intently.

There were more gunshots—single and in rapid-fire bursts.

Ames was able to pinpoint the general direction of the reports. They seemed to be coming from the wagon road, at a point which was not visible to him because of a thick growth of pine to his right, toward the winding tributary of the Humboldt River.

The Arizonan debated for a brief moment: should he ride there to see what the cause of the gunfire was, or not? The resolution was an obvious one, for Ames had seen much injustice done in his many hard years of wandering across most of the west. He had seen and been a part of the havoc wreaked by bandits both Mexican and *Norte-americano*, by raiding Indians of a dozen different tribes, by liquored-up cowhands with a month's pay swelling their jeans.

He had been in many a tight spot where he had wished for a helping hand—too many for one man—and if the opportunity presented itself to aid a fellow in trouble, then he was more willing than most.

Besides, he told himself as he spurred Cappy quickly forward, if it looked to be a fair fight of some sort, or a bunch of ranch-hands having target practice, he didn't have to venture any nearer than was necessary to make sure of that.

The sure-footed sorrel carried him at a much more rapid pace down the winding trail than might have been expected. Just before the pines thinned out enough for Ames to look upon the wagon road where the commotion was taking place, he slipped off the cowhide thong across the butt of his .44. In a swift, sure almost indistinguishable blur, the weapon was in his hand with the hammer pulled back and his finger touching the trigger.

At last, Ames reached a point where he had a clear view of the wagon road—some two hundred yards east and another hundred down to the valley floor—and as he did so a fresh volley of shots reached his ears. He took in the scene before him in a single, sweeping glance.

A large, white-canvased Conestoga wagon, hitched to a pair of skittering mares, sat in the middle of the trail. Its right front wheel was off, lying on the ground below the strapped-on water barrel, and that side of the wagon's forward frame rested on the axle. Inside the Conestoga, lying prone with a rifle cradled in her slim arms, and visible beneath the rolled canvas side, was a young girl with raven-black hair that fanned out in the cold, early evening breeze. Up on the wagon's seat, a man was trying to control the frightened horses with one hand and squeeze off shots from an old Colt Frontier revolver with the other.

And circling the wagon Indian-fashion, firing at the gallop, were four men in cowboy garb and wearing kerchief masks.

"That sure don't look like a fair fight to me," Ames muttered under his breath, his face setting into grim lines. "Let's see what we can do 'bout that, Cappy!"

Leaning low across the sorrel's burnished neck, gun arm extended straight out at a diagonal to the animal's head, Ames left the trail to traverse a grassy slope and finally intercept the wagon road a hundred and fifty yards from the Conestoga. Cappy seemed to respond to the urgency of the situation, his long legs reaching in great strides, hooves pounding over the sod of the rutted roadbed.

The gap between Ames and the wagon closed to one hundred yards, to seventy-five.

When the Arizonan was within fifty yards of the beseiged Conestoga, one of the raiders fired two shots as he came around the front of the wagon. The man aboard seemed to stiffen, releasing the reins and the Colt Frontier at the same time, and then he toppled sprawling into the roadway. He lay still.

The girl inside the Conestoga screamed a name which Ames could not make out and unleashed a barrage of shots from her repeating rifle. One of the circling bandits flew from his horse and was dragged several feet with his boot hooked in the saddle stirrup before being jerked free.

At the same instant the girl cried out and begun firing, Ames squeezed off three quick shots from his leveled .44. Almost simultaneously with the one bandit being shot from his horse by the girl, the marauder who had felled the wagon man threw up his arms and rolled backward off his mount with two of the Arizonan's bullets in his chest.

The other two bandits reined up, turning their horses, uncertain about what to do now that two of their comrades had been felled.

Ames, still pressed low over Cappy's surging neck, sent another slug their way as he closed in on them, missing high.

One of the attackers—a tall man, taller than Ames, with a livid red scar across one temple and wearing a raw-edge railroad hat with a silver band—wheeled his horse about and dug his spurs sharply into the animal's flanks. In a moment, both rider and mount were a single retreating blur fleeing into the surrounding hills.

The one remaining bandit made the mistake of standing to fight.

He snapped three wild shots in Ames' direction, jerking hard on the reins held in his left hand to steady his skittish horse. None of the lead came close to the Arizonan. Ames leveled the .44 again, less than fifty yards from the raider, and emptied the weapon of its final two slugs, knowing that he had to make at least one of them count or face certain death at the hands of a cold-blooded killer.

He made both of them count.

The bandit threw up his hands and cried out in surprise and pain as two blackened holes, less than three inches apart, appeared just over his heart. He seemed to stare down at the blood which had started to flower out of the wounds, sitting immobile in his saddle, and then he toppled sideways to fall noiselessly into the soft grasses beside the roadway.

Ames brought Cappy up, releasing the breath which he had taken and held prior to squeezing off his final rounds. With swift agility, he swung down off the sorrel before the animal had come to a complete standstill, slipping the .44 back into its holster and taking into his hand the sharply honed hunting knife which he wore in a buckskin sheath decorated with Navajo beads on the left side of his belt.

It was quiet, almost tranquil again now that the shooting had ceased, and Ames could hear the softly lamenting wind as he ran to the bandit he had just shot. The raider lay on his stomach, arms flung out. Ames held the hunting knife at the ready as he turned the man with his boot, but he had nothing more to fear from this attacker. He was dead.

He next checked the first man he had felled, the one who had shot the Conestoga's driver, and found him dead as well. The third bandit, the one who had stopped the bullet from the girl's rifle, lay unconscious but still breathing on the thick grass. His left leg was twisted oddly, and Ames decided it had been broken as the attacker was dragged with his boot caught in the stirrup.

Ames examined the wound high on the marauder's right shoulder. It seemed to be superficial, although it would undoubtedly leave the man in considerable pain. Serve him right, Ames thought wanly as he rose to his feet again.

He re-sheathed the hunting knife, turning toward the Conestoga wagon. As he did so, he saw the raven-haired girl who had been firing from inside kneeling beside the still form of the wagon's driver.

He took a long breath, released it, and then walked slowly toward them.

2

AMES stood next to the grief-stricken woman, his hat held firmly in his hands as a token of his sorrow. The woman—hardly more than a girl, he could see—had her back to him as she knelt beside her fallen companion, gazing tenderly at the man with downcast eyes, and smoothing the rough front of his woolen shirt with one gentle hand.

"He's dead," she whispered in a trembling voice.

Ames did not reply. He was unsure whether she had made the statement to him or was merely voicing the grief in her heart. "He's dead . . . dead . . ." she repeated.

The man was young, no more than twenty-five, Ames guessed. He had black curly hair of the same coal-like luster as the girl's and prominent cheek and jawbones which gave him a strong, masculine look. His clothes were threadbare, patched, and wash-faded,

114

but he did not strike the Arizonan as a saddle tramp.

He impressed Ames as having been a good man when alive, a man he would have been glad to shake hands with. Rage over such senseless murder welled in Arizona Ames and he tightened his lips to hold back the hot and merciless words he had for the killers.

The girl turned her head around and looked up at Ames, focusing her brimming eyes on him with a silent plea for help and understanding. "They never gave us a chance. They shot my brother down in cold blood."

Ames shook his head and scuffed the toe of one boot in the gravelly dirt. He never was one for words at the best of times, and when confronted by the situation of death being mourned, he always felt at a loss for the proper things to say.

He had seen many a fallen man—and some he felt had deserved to die more than others—but he had never lost the humanity to feel saddened. He had never grown callous or disrespectful of suffering, and as he met the watery, doe-eyed gaze of the girl, he was hit by the full impact of the tragedy.

He could see the family resemblance

between the girl and her brother. The bone structure which had given the man his handsomeness had been softened for her, but that gave her a unique expressiveness and an alive kind of beauty. She was tanned deeply, with her black hair cameoing her face and cascading over her shoulders, and her eyes were wide and almond-shaped, smoky gray. Perhaps she would cry, Ames thought, but he doubted it. She struck him as the kind of woman who would not find her release in tears.

Her clothes were simple and much like her brother's. She wore men's jeans which accented her slim, boyish hips, a woolen shirt of fancy, colorful knit, and a sheep-pelt-lined leather jacket.

"Thank you, Mister," she said. "If you hadn't come along when you did, I'd be alongside my brother by now."

Her voice broke as she glanced at the still figure.

"Sorry I wasn't sooner," Ames replied. "Maybe if I had . . ." He let his sentence trail off, the meaning clear.

"Perhaps," the girl said softly.

She turned back to look at her brother again. As she did, a gust of wind tore down the westerly slopes and whipped through a large stand of pine and scrub growth, echoing across the valley in a weird banshee wail. The girl shivered and wrapped her coat more tightly to her slender frame.

"The cry of the dead," she said in an odd voice.

Ames said nothing.

"The Chinese believe that when a man dies, the wind comes to collect his soul. My father wrote that to Mom when he was a section leader with the Chinese when the railroad was being put through the Sierras. He died a year later, up in those mountains somewhere. When his boss shipped his things back home, he didn't say whether the wind blew for Dad or not. I bet it did." She stifled a sob. "Now, now it's blowing for Tom."

"Tom," Ames said. "That's your brother?"

"Yes. Tom Holmes." She rose, unsteady from her grief and shock. "I'm Jan Holmes." She stared intently at Ames, as if the first look she had had of him was cursory and she had missed some detail. "Who are you?" she asked. "You're not part of the train."

"No, I'm alone, Ma'am. The name is Ames."

"Ames," she repeated.

"You mentioned a train. Reckoned you must be part of one. Where's the rest of the wagons?"

"They went ahead."

Ames frowned, then declared, "That doesn't sound right! I can't believe that you and your brother would be left alone with a broken wagon."

"You don't understand. You see, we've come a long way to get to Gallows Valley, and it is so close that—well, it was decided to have everybody go on and set up camp there, and then come back to help us."

She took a deep breath and then said in a wavering, unsure voice, "Who could have known that after all this time and in this peaceful little valley there would be any trouble? Besides, Tom wanted it that way. He thought he could fix the wheel himself and catch up."

Ames turned and took a couple of steps to the wheel, where he squatted for a moment, studying its box. Then he checked the bare axle shaft, fingering the smooth metal. He bit his upper lip and worried his left ear.

"Not often a wheel comes off nowadays," he said. "Not since Sarven's patent hub. I can't figure how it loosened."

"Neither could Tom. But it did—rolled right out from under us about two hours ago. Tom said that a part was missing, but before he could find a replacement, those men rode up.

Ames stood and scanned the valley floor and surrounding slopes, peering into the gathering shadows of twilight as best he could. He caught no outline of wagons or riders, nor the tell-tale plume of dust, not anything except the gently waving vegetation and the sentinel like trees and the unwinding thread of the rutted road as it snaked through the valley and into the next.

"Couple of hours," he murmured to himself. He returned to stand beside the girl. "They can't be so far ahead so's not to have heard the gunfire. Kinda slow getting back," he added pointedly.

"Nothing much they can do now, anyway, Mr. Ames."

"Folks call me Arizona, ma'am."

"All right . . . Arizona. If you'll call me Jan."

Jan went to the listing wagon and climbed

119

up on the board seat. She reached through the canvas flap front cover and after a moment of searching, produced a thick, old horse blanket.

"It's the best I have," she said, stepping down. She covered her brother carefully, taking a last look at his slackened features before settling the end of the blanket over his face.

"He will be buried properly," she said tersely, "and that's more than I'll do for the three we killed."

"Two," Ames corrected. "The hombre you winged is alive."

He thought of the wounded man lying nearby and wondered what he might have to say for himself. This had all the earmarks of a simple raid on a lone wagon by a bunch of desperadoes, but the intuition sharpened by years of living with trouble told Ames that there was more to it, though he did not know what.

He could smell it, taste it, almost feel it, and he had the strong suspicion that the man in the grass could shed some strong light upon the matter.

"Beggin' your pardon . . . Jan," he said, "but I'm going to fetch that jasper now." He placed his sombrero on his head, fitting it carefully over his thick hair, and then pivoted and started to walk away. "I'll be right back."

"I'm coming, Ames," Jan said.

She grabbed her rifle and together they waded through the grass. Jan looked back once at the wagon and the covered form of her dead brother, but she did not say anything, only tightening her slim fingers into clenched fists.

Ames was impressed by Jan Holmes, by the grit and determination which kept her together at this time of crisis. She kept pace with his long-legged stride, matching him step for step, and the Arizonan couldn't help but likening her to rawhide which rough usage only seems to toughen.

Ames examined the still unconscious killer more carefully this second time. He slipped the red kerchief from his face and studied the man's features dispassionately.

"Know him?" he asked Jan.

She shook her head.

"How about any of the others?"

"How could I? They all wore masks."

"I mean by their dress or horses or the way they acted."

"No." Jan Holmes fingered the rifle as she

looked at the man. "Why us, Arizona? We don't know anybody out here. The whole wagon train is from Kansas, and none of us have been in Nevada before. We're just simple farm folks, coming to Gallows Valley to settle, and there's not enough money between us to make it worth anybody's while. Why us?"

"I don't know," Ames said grimly.

He thought of the government's recent land sale, and concluded that Jan and Tom Holmes were one of the many families who had taken advantage of the offer. He wondered how anybody could benefit from robbing and killing these poor people, and then he began to think of the cattle baron, Wade Lamont. No, it was impossible that a man like that would be involved, and yet . . .

The answer lay supine on the ground. The man had thinning brown hair and long sideburns. He breathed noisily through his open mouth, which showed his dirty teeth. He had a fat, round face and a flat wide nose with lumps of broken cartilage. He was pale, but Ames figured that his face was normally flushed, for he had the fine spider-web arteries on cheeks and nose, and the thick stomach of a heavy drinker.

122

Ames checked for identification, but there was no wallet on the man, just some change, an old silver pocket watch, and a pouch of cigarette makings. His empty holster was on the left side, indicating he was left-handed.

Ames took a deep breath. "Hired," he said. "Just another saloon dog bought by the pound. I wouldn't doubt that we'll find the other two are the same kind."

"Leave him here for the buzzards," Jan said harshly. "Two down isn't price enough for my brother."

"The law will swing him soon enough, Jan," Ames said. "But in the meantime, he just might be able to answer some of those questions of yours. As soon as he comes to he'll start giving us the reason he and the others were hell-bent on wiping you out."

Ames slitted his eyes as he gazed down on the comatose killer. "I'll see to that," he promised.

Suddenly Jan Holmes looked up and pointed to the northern edge of the valley. "Somebody's coming!" she said excitedly.

Ames saw the small dust cloud and the black outline of two horses and riders galloping fast across the earth. They were heading directly for the wagon.

Jan dropped to one knee and brought the rifle to her shoulder. "If those are more of them, I'll—"

"Hold on," Ames commanded. "If they were, they'd come out of the hills, using the trees as cover. No, I bet those are from your wagon train."

They waited in silence until the two horsemen got within recognizing distance, and then Jan said, "Yes, you're right, that's Matt Harlen and Jake Ellison!" She raised the rifle and shot once in the air, attracting their attention.

The two men swung their mounts off the road and through the grass to where Ames and the girl stood. One of them barked out, "What happened, Jan?"

Janet Homes outlined the tragic events and while she did, Ames studied the man who had spoken. He seemed to be in his fifties. His hair was silver and his white moustache well clipped; his eyes were blue and candid. He sat astride a large roan, his calloused, big-jointed hands folded awkwardly over the horn of his saddle.

There was a moment of stunned silence when Jan finished, and then the younger man swung toward the other and snapped, "I told you, Matt! I told you to stay, but you wouldn't! And now look what's happened!"

"You hush up, Jake Ellison," Jan flared. "You have no right to speak to Mr. Harlen that way!"

"No? Well, I think I do. It just goes to show what me and Tom been saying all along is true. Matt Harlen is not the right man to lead the train!"

"Mr. Harlen's a fine man, and a far better leader than you, you ill-mannered little boy!"

"Boy!" Ellison sputtered. "I'm older than you—"

"And another thing," Jan continued. "It was Tom who insisted upon staying to fix the wheel alone. You and Tom have been after Mr. Harlen almost from the day we started, and he gave into Tom this time to try and stop some of the friction you two have been causing. He had no way of knowing that there were bandits nearby!"

"And I still say he had no business allowing you and Tom to drop out!"

"You're never satisfied unless you boss everything, are you? Well, I see that we made it from Kansas to Gallows Valley in one piece!"

"Almost," Ellison said sardonically. "Tom is dead."

There was an unearthly groan, and everybody's attention suddenly shifted to the wounded man on the ground. He was still unconscious, his eyes tightly shut, but he writhed in pain, his hands fluttering weakly at his sides.

"Is he one of them?" Harlen asked.

"Yes," Ames answered. "There are two more nearer the wagon. They're dead."

"This one looks as though he'll live long enough to hang," Ellison said, fury heavy in his voice.

"We'll pick up Tom first," Harlen said. "Hold the burial tomorrow, if that's all right with you Jan. Reckon he'd like to rest in the valley."

Ellison stared intently at Ames. "Who are you and how come you're biting off a hunk of this trouble?"

"M'name is Ames," the Arizonan said. "I was riding nearby when I saw these varmints, and I thought I should pitch in and help."

The man reached down and shook Ames' hand. "I'm Jake Ellison." He paused. "Sorry you didn't save Tom's life."

Ames couldn't decide whether to be angry

at the man or not, for the implication—if it was one—was veiled well.

Ames said tersely, "So am I," and dropped the other man's hand quickly.

Ellison was big, as tall as Ames and almost as broad-shouldered. His eyes were a shiny brown, like buttons, and his hair was fiery red—no doubt, Ames thought, indicating the obviously intemperate nature which seethed just beneath his surface. He was dressed in the same plain but warm clothing as the others, and he carried a well-used old Harrington and Richardson in a worn leather holster.

"Look out!" Matt Harlen cried suddenly. Before Ames or the girl could react, Harlen's pistol boomed in their ears.

3

AMES reacted instantly with the instincts born of long and ruthless years. With the shot still ringing in his ears, he took two quick steps to his right, drawing his pistol as he moved, and pivoted in a crouch, fanning the area.

Ellison's horse, a blood bay, reared and snorted, obviously gunshy. Ellison tried to rein him in and to keep the flashing forelegs from Jan Holmes, who had, in that brief moment, been struck immobile by the unexpected yell and blast.

Ames glanced at Harlen next and saw the man straight in his saddle, holding a smoking pistol in a hardened grip. It was a Colt, but not the Peacemaker; rather the smaller .41 caliber Double Action. The muzzle pointed like an arrow shaft at the wounded man on the ground.

"No trouble," Harlen said. "Now."

Ames pivoted and looked at the outlaw.

There was a clean hole drilled in the middle of his chest.

"He was pulling for a derringer," Harlen said as he moved his hand. "If I hadn't, he'd have plugged you in the back, Ames."

The outlaw was dead when Ames knelt beside him. His hand was across his stomach as Harlen had noted, but when Ames checked under his shirt and around his wide belt for a small gun, he found none. He came to his feet, saying, "No derringer, or any kind of gun for that matter, on him."

"What?" Harlen said uncomprehendingly, his forehead furrowed. "I don't understand! He looked as though he was reaching for some kind of weapon."

Ellison said sharply, "I didn't see the man move. Did anybody else?"

"I didn't," Jan said, "My back was turned to him."

"You, Ames?"

The Arizonan shook his head.

"No loss, anyways," Ellison said. "Dirty sidewinder."

Ames' lips tightened. "A man's got a right to a legal hanging, and besides, this maverick would have talked. This whole thing has a bad smell to it, because these men were

129

apparently waiting to get Jan and Tom."

He looked up at the now contrite Matt Harlen. "You got any ideas?"

"No, none." Harlen rubbed a finger over his moustache. "I guess I was a little hasty, but I figured I was saving your life, Ames."

"Rather have you wrong this way than the other," Ames replied. "But it's done. We'd best bury them and get the wagon back with the others."

Ames turned and picked the rifle from Jan's fingers. "I'll carry it back to the wagon and bring some shovels."

"Wait a minute, stranger!" Ellison called out. "We're mighty obliged, I reckon, but we can handle our affairs from here."

"Call me Ames," the Arizonan said evenly. "Miss Holmes here said you all were headed for Gallows Valley. So am I. I wouldn't be put out none by lending a hand."

"Ride along," Harlen said. "And Ellison, I've had just about enough out of you. If it weren't for your sick Pa, I'd have sent you packing a month ago. We can use all the men like Ames that we can find, and if he wants to help, we'll treat him kindly, you ungrateful whelp."

The wagon master's icy tongue-lashing

made Ellison livid for a moment, and his eyes flashed, but he didn't reply. He settled himself in his saddle and remained in a sulky mood all through the burials and wagon repair. Searching for the missing part of the hub proved futile, as did locating a spare, and Ames was forced to fashion a makeshift one out of wood and rope and cotter pins.

"It should last until tonight," he said as he wiped his hands on a rag. "If one of the other wagons doesn't have a spare, you can probably get one in Gallows, or from Wade Lamont."

Jan Holmes climbed onto the seat and then Ellison said, "I better ride with Jan, just in case the wheel comes off again." Before Jan could protest, he had tied his bay to the back of the wagon and climbed up beside her, taking the reins from her hands. There was an easy familiarity in his attitude, as though he considered Jan his property. Ames, turning in his saddle to look back, could tell little from the girl's set, frozen face.

The traveling was slow, as the front wheel still wobbled a bit, and for quite a while neither Ames nor Harlen said anything. The valley where they had been opened out into another, wider valley. This was rugged country, with thick stands of forest which covered miles, and brush and boulders and wind. The wind was something special in the Sierras, blowing cool and fresh, unlike the extreme blasts of the plains.

Ames caught glimpses of stray cattle now and then, which he did not find unusual. With as large a herd as Lamont's they would be scattered widely in the hills. Ames was glad that it was not him but Lamont's cowboys who would be doing the brutal job of combing them out of the brush and canyons once they were sold.

Harlen turned to stare at Ames, his gaze running from the sombrero down his long body, pausing momentarily at the bone-handled gun and the engraved holster set against Ames' thigh.

Then he asked, "What's your business in Gallows Valley, Ames?"

"I'm here to buy cattle from Wade Lamont. He's cutting his herd some, what with you settlers moving in, and mighty fine stock it is, I hear."

"Knew you weren't one of us, all right. You look more like a tumbleweed, to me, son."

"Not any more," Ames said thoughtfully.

132

Harlen smiled. "I'm too nosey, I guess." He waved toward the crest of an approaching hill. "On the other side of the rise is the reason for my poor manners. One wagon train. Seventy-five wagons and almost two hundred people, counting the kids. We left Kansas early this spring, soon as word of this land opening up came."

He pointed to the surrounding hills with one knob-jointed finger. "This is our destination, Ames, virgin territory begging to be homesteaded."

"It can be a tough land," Ames said flatly.

"No worse than the dust and heat and snows of Kansas. We'll work, and we've been saving and doin' without to raise the money to get that chance. And we're going to make it, too."

They reached the hill crest, and Ames looked down into yet another valley, perhaps five hundred yards below, and at the double line of wagons stretched out along the road.

"As soon as we heard the shots, we halted," the wagon master explained. "I was hoping to get a little closer to Gallows Valley itself before nightfall, but I guess this is as far as we'll go tonight." He twisted in his saddle and looked behind him. "Guess the kids are

133

all right. I still see 'em coming, and they're both there, squabbling like a mess of chickens." He turned back to Ames. "Stay for dinner, won't you?"

"Mighty kind to offer."

"In fact," Harlen continued, "unless you've got another place to roll your blanket, I'd be obliged to have you stay until we arrive at the Valley."

"Well, now—"

"I don't mind telling you that I'm worried, Ames. This affair with the wagon is unsettling, especially not knowing why Jan and Tom were attacked. And believe me, I'm as sorry as you over what happened back there, and I could curse myself blue for being so quick on the trigger."

Harlen urged his horse into a canter, and the Arizonan drew abreast. "I've got a nasty feeling, Ames, that this isn't over. I could use a gun like yours."

"Maybe you're right," Ames told the wagon master.

"Jan Holmes is unprotected now, and if there are killers after her . . ." Harlen shook his head. "No, I can't help thinking that there's more to it. More like us moving in to the Valley, taking over Wade Lamont's land."

Ames was taken aback for a moment. "It's hard to believe that. Everything I've heard of Lamont is that he's a good man, and not against settlers. He's got plans for credit stores and shipping, and he should do better than he is now."

"A man can put an odd value on his property, Ames," Harlen said quietly.

The two rode down the line of wagons, Harlen waving to the many shouts of greeting from the settlers.

"Close 'em!" he yelled. "Close ranks! We're down for the night!"

The wagons closed the gaps between them, and then there was the noisy bustle of dinner preparation as the cool evening settled around the train. The campfires were a hundred winking stars in the black valley. Ames was invited to have supper with Harlen, and enjoyed the repast of boiled beans and coffee, the smell of the crackling pine fire, and the long-winded tales of the wagon master.

Ames checked the Holmes wagon afterwards, and helped Jan take her dead brother from the wagon. She gave Ames a fresh cup of coffee, which was blacker than the night, thicker than gumbo, and hotter than sin. It was good cowboy coffee. After a bit, Ames took his bed-roll from Cappy's flanks and spread out near the girl's wagon. If there was an attempt on her life tonight, he wanted to be close enough to head it off.

Ames slept lightly, coming instantly awake the way an Indian brave does at the slightest odd noise. He was going to make sure that they—whoever they might be—were going to have to kill him first.

The next morning he was awakened by the crying of children and the sharp sounds of their mothers preparing breakfast. Daylight came slowly, and Ames nursed his coffee with chilly fingers, shoulders hunched. Then he moved restlessly around the camp, talking to the other settlers, and after a time located a spare hub. With the help of a couple of the men, Jan's wagon was soon good as new.

For most of the day Ames and the wagon train continued through the valleys which made a chain through the hills. The birds sang and a slight breeze rustled the trees and sunlight speckled the trail with leaf shadows. There was little talking among the settlers, each of them caught up in the excitement. this was the last day of traveling for them—the long, grueling journey was drawing to a close. . . .

There was the jangle of chains and the creak of leather as a rider shifted weight and the rattle of spurs and the creak of tired wagon, but little else. From time to time Ames saw the sign of cattle tracks, or those of deer and elk, and as he had the day before, he occasionally caught glimpses of Lamont's sprawling herd.

Most of the stock were longhorns, which were excellent beef animals, even if excitable at times, because of their ability to go for days without water. Like other breeds, the longhorns' quality depended upon the amount it had to eat and drink, but unlike the lighter strains from New Mexico, or the whitefaced or shorthorns from the East, it would walk good beef off but would still be alive when it reached water.

Lamont had a reputation for mixing longhorn blood with the other varieties very successfully, breeding cattle with excellent combinations of stamina and marketability. It was just such a mixture that Arizona Ames was after. He was looking forward to meeting Wade Lamont, for a man who would breed varieties for other reasons than necessity interested him, indicating a deep and abiding love for cattle and the industry. For in these mountain valleys there was water and food enough for the weakest of breeds, and the Eastern stock would do well without longhorn help. Nowhere was the grass eaten away, and Ames concluded that there was enough for more cattle than were already there.

In Arizona's hotter, dryer climate, the mixed blood would be better than stock of either breed alone. Sam Playford, Ames' brother-in-law, would be mighty pleased to see them, he thought. Mighty pleased.

Harlen, who was riding point, drew up suddenly. A few of the riders, including Ames, circled around him.

"There," he said with pride. "There is Gallows Valley."

Before them was an opening in the trees which lined the road, and several miles away could be seen a wide, rolling lush, green valley, full of meadows and patches of trees and split by a meandering stream of clear, sparkling mountain water. It was big and grand, stretching as far as the eye could see, and Ames saw in his mind the houses of the

138

settlers in place of the few head of cattle which dotted the landscape.

"Home . . ." one of the other men whispered, and then with a whoop, he tore his hat off, waved it high in the air and galloped to the train, bellowing the good news.

The wagon master chuckled, then said, "I see a cluster of trees near a natural pool not too far away. Just the place, I'm thinking, to set up camp." He stood in his stirrups, raised his hand, and gave a hoarse shout: "Move out!"

Ames rode beside Harlen as the train followed them to its final destination. "The Valley," Ames asked, "where does it get its name?"

"I understand that farther up, the creek bed forms a double loop, sort of like a hangman's noose. I don't know for sure, of course, not having been hereabouts before." The older man shifted uncomfortably in his saddle. "There might be other reasons," he added darkly.

"Looks peaceful enough," Ames said.

"Just the same, I'm putting the wagons in a circle tonight, and posting guards. I've come too far to have things go wrong at the last minute."

The wagon train reached the spot Harlen had chosen two hours later. Again the quiet of the day was broken by the sounds of the settlers preparing dinner, scolding children, and stretching their legs and jaws. Ames walked Cappy back to where the Holmes wagon was grouped and dismounted, glad to see that Jan had regained some of her composure.

He helped the girl take her brother's body from the wagon once more, though this time it was canvas-wrapped through the efforts of the train's doctor, Ebenezer Benton, the previous night. He and Jan carried Tom to a site near the stream, one not far from the camp nor too near the fire, and one which Jan thought, Tom would have liked.

"I'll stay for the funeral tomorrow," Ames said as they returned to her wagon.

"You don't have to, Arizona," Jan said, placing a hand on his arm. "This isn't your fight."

"Well, now, I guess I've done no more than any other man would." He was about to add more when there was the sharp sound of Ellison's voice.

"Jan!"

"Oh!" Jan turned, startled, and saw the young man coming toward her. "What is it, Jake?"

Ellison swung suddenly and faced Ames, eyes lit with anger. "Leave," he said harshly. "I want to talk to Jan alone, without you around. Besides, I don't like you always hanging around her anyway."

"Sounds like you're looking out for her," Ames said softly.

"Sure as hell am. Somebody has to, now that Tom is dead. Me and Jan is getting married afore long."

"The devil we are!" Jan cried out. "I wouldn't marry you, Jake Ellison, if you were the last man—"

"It was what Tom wanted," Ellison broke in.

"A woman's got the right to make up her own mind," Ames said. "Even in a train like this."

"I told you to git!" Ellison shouted. He shot out an impulsive fist at Ames in a looping swing.

Ames stepped inside, and wishing to end the altercation quickly, regretfully hammered the hot-tempered man with a short jab to the

141

jaw. Ellison sat down in the dust, one knee drawn up underneath him, a confused and stunned look on his face.

Ames stood back, hands easy at his sides, waiting for Ellison's next move. The man slowly got to his feet, shaking his head and rubbing his jaw with his hand. The fire light reflected the deep anger and resentment which gripped him. Without another word, he wheeled around and stalked away.

"I guess I should thank you again," Jan said softly. "I'm sorry that you had to see that."

"I'm sorry I had to put him down, Jan. He has a lot of spunk and . . . I think he cares for you quite a lot."

"That—oh, he's impossible sometimes!" she sputtered.

Ames' grin was a quick, sharp break across his tanned face. "Let's let it pass, Jan," he said. "Now, didn't I hear you say something about biscuits for dinner?"

The Arizonan spent an agreeable time with Jan as he ate, but try as he might, he couldn't erase the lines of worry which etched her face. Jake Ellison bothered them no more that night, and after a couple of cups of coffee and a cigarette, Ames bid the girl goodnight.

4

AFTER a breakfast of boiled coffee, flapjacks and slab bacon, Arizona Ames rode directly to Wade Lamont's Bar L ranch to discuss the hoped-for cattle purchase which would replenish Sam Playford's depleted stock. Before leaving the wagon train encampment, he agreed to meet Matt Harlen and the still sulking Jake Ellison in the little valley town of Gallows, situated to the north.

The two trainsmen were riding there for supplies after the noon meal, and would be needing assistance in getting the staples they purchased back to the train.

Ames rode south, following the wagon road toward Paradise Valley. The grasslands through which he passed were rich and green and fertile, good grazing land for cattle and even better farming land for settlers like Jan Holmes and the others. He saw none of the fine beeves which Wade Lamont raised, and judged that most were pastured in a less-traveled area to decrease the danger of rustling.

It was rumored in Salt Lake City that the Bar L had in the neighborhood of ten thousand head of prime white-faced Herefords and longhorns in the rolling terrain of Gallows Valley.

Ames let Cappy have his head, and the sorrel took him at an easy canter along the road. He was thinking about Sam Playford, the husband of his twin sister, Nesta, and Sam's growing ranch in Tonto Basin, Arizona. It was fast becoming one of the finest spreads in the area, thanks to Playford's hard work and good business sense. Much *too* big, Ames' brother-in-law had said in a letter which had reached the Arizonan in Albuquerque some three months before; too big for just one man and his wife to handle.

Sam Playford wanted to take in a partner, someone he could trust, someone who was experienced in cattle and ranching, who had courage and conviction and just plain horse sense.

That man was Arizona Ames.

The tall, leathery cowboy had considered his brother-in-law's offer carefully. He had long thought about settling down, establishing roots, putting an end to his aimless wandering of the past fifteen or more years. It seemed as if trouble was Ames' constant saddle partner, for he had an accursed knack for getting into some scrape or other no matter where he drifted.

It had all begun in Tonto Basin, where young Rich Ames had avenged the despoilment of Nesta by killing the man responsible, as well as the town's crooked sheriff. He had been a hunted man then, a man who for fourteen years rode alone, building a reputation which now preceded him everywhere he went, a reputation as a strong-willed, fair-minded man who never shied from danger and was always ready to lend a helping hand to those beset by problems and hardships.

Tragedy, too, stalked Ames' path. Shortly before his impending marriage to the beautiful Esther Halstead—the Arizonan had saved her father's ranch in Troublesome, had been made part owner of the spread by the grateful rancher, and had fallen in love with Esther—an assassin's bullet meant for Ames had felled his betrothed in the streets of the town of Yampa.

Esther had died in his arms, and Ames had

never allowed himself any strong ties with a woman—though many would have wished it, until he had returned to Tonto Basin last year in response to a plea for help from Sam Playford and Nesta.

Briefly sworn in as an Arizona Ranger, he had put an end to the reign of terror being wrought by a crooked saloon owner named Slade Gorton—and during that period of time had fallen once more in love, with the beautiful Anna Belle Tate. But his nomadic existence, the restlessness which he couldn't seem to control, had forced him to leave Tonto Basin again in spite of his feelings for Anna Belle, in spite of the pleas of Sam and Nesta. Once more, he went in search of new adventures—alone.

Before drifting down to New Mexico, Ames had had a close call in the Dakota plains, near Phileaux River; there, he was framed for the murder of a young cowboy by a con man named Jersey Jack Kelson, who operated a traveling Dollar Wagon as a cover for crooked gambling. He had, after no little trouble and a bullet wound in the shoulder, succeeded in capturing Kelson in a ghost mining town. He had left the Dakotas with his skin and reputation intact, but only barely.

The more the Arizonan had considered Sam Playford's offer, the more he had decided to try once again to put down roots. It did a man no good to drift constantly, forever turning up trouble, for sooner or later he would wind up dead in some little cow town, or in some draw, or on some windy slope. No matter how tough, how skilled with a gun a man was, there came the time when his luck would run out.

Ames had been pressing his for too long now, and unless he wanted to die alone, with the buzzards and coyotes to pick his bones clean, he would have to find a permanent place for himself.

He had accepted his brother-in-law's offer.

He found, upon returning to Tonto Basin, that Anna Belle Tate had married a young rancher in the area and was expecting a child in the fall. He had been saddened, for he had still loved Anna Belle, and had put himself hard into his new-found job—discovering finally that he enjoyed being with Sam and Nesta again, enjoyed the idea of having a home and being surrounded by people he loved and respected. He had at last found some measure of happiness, and he wondered why he had not come back to Tonto Basin sooner.

Ames and Playford had taken the train and stage to Salt Lake City three weeks ago to negotiate with a man named Bachelor for the cattle Sam needed. But Bachelor's price had been much too high for Sam's liking, and they had not come to terms.

Ames had heard of Wade Lamont there, and he and Playford had sent the cattle baron a wire outlining their needs and requesting a firm quotation on two thousand head of white-faced Herefords. Lamont had replied two days later and his price—very low, because the coming of the settlers forced him to cut back his stock—had given Sam Playford occasion to grin joyously.

It was agreed that the Arizonan would go to Gallows Valley with a letter of credit from the Cattleman's Bank in Salt Lake City and full authorization to sign a contract with Wade Lamont if there was no last-minute increase in price. He would wire Playford in Salt Lake that the deal had been made, and Sam would then go by train to Reno, where he would arrange for rail shipment of the cattle to Arizona. Lamont would have the beeves driven to Reno, and final payment would be made there. Ames, if it could be arranged, would accompany the trail drive from Gallows Valley.

Ames had little difficulty locating the Bar L Ranch. He came upon a well constructed and well-tended private road which branched diagonally off the wagon road and wound down into a wide, naturally hollowed-out section of the valley. There, nestled at the foot of high, pine-covered boundary slopes, lay a series of brilliantly white-washed buildings and an intricate network of barbed wire and split-rail fences, all of which were painted the same gleaming white.

At the entrance to the private road was a white wooden gate, but it was not barred or locked. A huge sign, painted white with professionally-drawn blue letters, was fastened to the gate's middle; it read: *The Bar L Ranch—Gallows Valley, Nevada*. Below it was another sign, crudely printed on heavy cardboard, which invited: *Hands Wanted, See Roy Stringer—Foreman*.

Ames took Cappy up to the gate, swung it open without dismounting, and then closed it again once he and the sorrel were through. They started down the road, and as they approached the buildings which comprised Lamont's ranch proper, Ames marveled at the care and precision with which the buildings had been constructed. Lamont was obviously a man who took a great deal of pride in his possessions—and no doubt in himself and his accomplishments.

When Ames came into the ranch yard, he could see that there was a great deal of activity surrounding a white-railed horse corral at the rear of a long building which the Arizonan knew to be a stable. Cowboys in heavy jackets, trail denims and well-scuffed boots were shouting and laughing encouragement to one of their number, a rail-thin, craggy-jawed man who was about to mount a gleaming black stallion. There were two ropes looped about the animal's muscled neck, held by four of the cowboys, and a heavy russet leather halter with a single length of rope for reins.

Ames walked over, wedged his way between a couple of the men at the fence, and watched as the craggy-jawed cowboy climbed onto the stallion's bare back, caught up the halter rope, and shouted. "Let 'er go, boys!"

With a whoop, the four men released the ropes holding the untamed bronco, and the sleek animal gave a sharp, angry snort. Then it began to buck and kick wildly, tossing its head, twisting and arching its back, deadly hind hooves flashing angrily as it tried to rid itself of the cowboy astride its back.

The craggy-jawed man hung on grimly, but the raw stamina of the horse won out finally; the stallion gave a tremendous buck, and then lurched sideways, dropping its head as its forelegs locked into an abrupt halt. The cowboy went sailing over the bronco's neck, somersaulted in mid-air, and landed on the seat of his pants in the dust.

Quickly, he scrambled to his feet and scuttled to the fence, climbing through to safety just as the bronco charged toward him. The circling men hooted derisive comments to the craggy-jawed fellow, laughing up-roariously and urging him to try again. Ames, too, found himself grinning at the antics.

And then a voice at his elbow said equably, "Something I kin do for you, stranger?"

Ames turned, and stood facing a heavy-set man with restless blue eyes and a dark, beard-shadowed face. The man was unsmiling, but there was no malice in his expression as he regarded the Arizonan. His hands were knuckled at his waist, just above the cartridge

151

belt which contained, in a brown leather holster, a new Colt Single Action Bisley revolver.

"Maybe," Ames said laconically.

"Name's Roy Stringer," the man told him. "I'm foreman of the Bar L. You lookin' for work?"

"No," Ames said. "I'm here to see Wade Lamont. Chanced to notice the fun over here, and thought I'd give a look-see."

"You got business with Mr. Lamont?"

"That's right."

"What's yer name?"

"Ames."

"Arizona Ames?"

"Reckon I'll admit to that," Ames said dryly. "Would Mr. Lamont be hereabouts?"

Stringer broke into a tobacco-stained smile. He put out his hand, and Ames, after a brief second, shook it. "Sure would!" Stringer said. "He's been expectin' you, Ames. Come on, I'll take you up to the house."

Ames nodded, following the Bar L foreman away from the corral. They returned to where the Arizonan had left Cappy, and took a cinder path which wound toward a sprawling white ranch house with a huge red brick chimney and a small neat garden fronting it, set back from the other ranch buildings. A huge and gnarled oak tree cast shade over the veranda-ed front porch, and the smell of the flowers growing in the garden was strongly aromatic on the cool morning air.

Stringer led Ames up onto the porch. The door was open, and he knocked on the fly-screen's wooden frame. "Mr. Lamont?" he called out.

"What is it, Roy?" a gruff baritone answered from within.

"Got a fella to see you."

"Who be it?"

"Arizona Ames."

"Well, now!"

There was the sound of quick footsteps inside, coming nearer, and then the flyscreen was jerked open and a big, burly, white-haired man in his late fifties stepped onto the porch. He had a good-humored, weather-eroded face, and his black eyes were shrewd.

Ames had the feeling that they wouldn't miss much of anything they touched upon. He wore an old pair of Levis and a plaid Pendleton shirt.

He looked Ames up and down, grinning. "So you be the famous Arizona Ames, eh?"

The Arizonan felt uncomfortable; he did

not take to compliments particularly well. "Don't know about the famous part," he muttered embarrassedly, "but I'm Ames, right enough."

Lamont chuckled appreciatively, extending his hand. The two men shook firmly, and Ames decided he liked this big, open bear of a man—though there was in that immediate warmness a certain reservation; after all, he still knew very little about Wade Lamont other than what was rumored. And rumors, Ames knew, were not that often accurate.

"Thanks for bringin' this hombre up, Roy," Lamont said to Stringer. The foreman nodded to him, then to Ames, and ambled down off the porch and back along the cinder path. Lamont said to Ames, clapping him on the shoulder in a friendly way, "Well, come on inside. Reckon you could use some coffee?"

"Reckon I could," Ames told him.

"Come on, then. I had Wes Oldham, my lawyer over to Paradise, draw up the bill of sale for the cattle Sam Playford wanted, and you can read it over to make sure it's to your satisfaction afore you make your X."

"The price in your wire   still firm, then?"

"Sure! When Wade Lamont names a figure, he stands by it."

The rancher led Ames inside the house and into a mahogany-paneled den. It was expensively furnished with carved mahogany chairs and couch, a Morris recliner opposite a library rocker—both finished in mahogany—and several glassed bookshelves. Hanging library lamps were strategically located about the dark room.

Lamont bade Ames sit down at a flat-top mahogany office desk with paneled sides and a leather top. When the Arizonan had done so, the cattle baron placed the bill of sale before him, having taken it from one of the desk drawers. While he went to fetch coffee for both of them, Ames looked over the bill of sale and found Lamont had been true to his word. It was perfectly in order, for the exact quoted price and amount of cattle Sam Playford had requested.

When Lamont returned with two pewter mugs filled with strong hot black coffee, Ames readily signed the bill of sale agreement and presented the rancher with the letter of credit from the Salt Lake City Cattleman's Bank. The two men then spent the next two hours discussing the time and route by which the beeves would be shipped to Reno, and a schedule satisfactory to both of them was at last worked out.

Ames made a note of the information for the wire he would send his brother-in-law from Paradise some time within the next day or so, and then leaned back to make small talk with the expansive rancher over more coffee.

Ames found himself liking Wade Lamont more and more. There did not seem to be any need for his reservations about the man now, or any reason to doubt the validity of Lamont's reputation for fairness. And it did not seem possible that Lamont could have been behind the attack on the Holmes' wagon the previous afternoon; what reason could the rancher have for wanting to harm Tom Holmes? Still, Ames managed to drop mention of the wagon train's recent arrival in Gallows Valley.

Lamont frowned over the rim of his pewter mug when Ames had finished speaking. "Sure, I knew them nesters had arrived hereabouts; soon's they was within twenty miles of Gallows Valley, I was aware of it. There isn't much in these here parts I *don't* know about, Ames."

"Did you know I came in with the train last night?" Ames asked mildly.

Lamont frowned again, and then grinned infectiously. "Hell! Caught me now, didn't you? Reckon a few things manage to slip past my nose at that. How'd you happen to latch on with 'em?"

Ames told him about the shooting incident resulting in the death of Tom Holmes, automatically and modestly playing down his own role in the episode.

Lamont said, "Say, that's a damned shame! Is there anything I can do to help?"

Ames described the dead bandits as best he could, as well as the one who had gotten away. "Recognize any of them, Mr. Lamont. Sound like local men, maybe?"

"Can't say I do," Lamont said. "Maybe outlaws; maybe rustlers on the prod. We get a passel of 'em hereabouts."

"Maybe," Ames said. There was nothing more to be said at that time, he decided. "Well, I want to thank you, Mr. Lamont. For both me and Sam Playford."

"My pleasure, Ames. Listen here, you tell these nesters—hell, reckon I'd best call 'em settlers, hadn't I?—you tell 'em that if there's anything I can do for 'em to let me know

157

pronto. I can't fight progress, and I can't fight the government, so I might as well make my peace with the folks'll be sharin' Gallows Valley with me right off."

He winked at Ames. " 'Sides, I expect to be doin' considerable business with 'em in the future."

Ames said that he would pass on Lamont's message, and the two men shook hands warmly. The rancher bade the Arizonan goodbye at the door inviting him to stop by at any time before the beeves were ready for the drive to Reno. Ames went along the cinder path, exchanged nods with Roy Stringer, who was issuing orders to a group of hands nearby, and mounted Cappy.

He took the sorrel back along the private road to the main wagon road, and headed for the valley town of Gallows to meet Matt Harlen and Jake Ellison.

5

GALLOWS was a company town, there by the grace of Wade Lamont. The rancher kept tight rein on his hands, Arizona Ames thought as he rode into the town, and it was just as well he did. The number of cowboys required to run a spread of such size would be considerable, and they would be a tough, hard-bitten crew, always looking for trouble. Given their head, they would drink and brawl and gamble all night and day until the pay in their pants was gone.

Consequently, Lamont had let the town of Paradise have all the headaches, stopping the expansion of Gallows from more than four small clapboard buildings. Paradise, on the other hand, had become wide-open, with saloons aplenty lining the streets, and hostesses swarming in the saloons. It attracted the miners and settlers and riders from all over, including the crew of the Bar L, but as far as Lamont was concerned,

159

temptation twenty-five miles away was a lot easier to control than one that was under his nose.

The four buildings were split with two on either side of the road, little more than a wide spot where a rider could stop on the way to Paradise. It was a few miles north of the Bar L ranch turn-off, not too far from where the wagon train planned to settle—a natural oasis which would by necessity grow as Lamont relinquished his control over the land. The growth, influenced by the women of the train, would not pattern itself after Paradise—of that Ames was certain.

The lean Arizonan reined in by the general store, dismounted and tethered Cappy to the tie bar. He noted one of the train wagons and the roan nearby and concluded that Jake Ellison and Matt Harlen were already here. He patted the sorrel fondly on its nose and glanced around.

Next to the general store was a two-story, whitewashed building, boxshaped and with no particular mark about it to indicate what it was intended for. Its windows were dark and the one door set in the middle of its front looked firmly locked. It had all the appearance of being deserted. It would be the combination church and town meeting hall, Ames figured, and would probably become the schoolhouse in the coming year.

Across the street was a combination blacksmith's shop and livery stable. The big double doors were open, and Ames could hear the clanging sounds of the smith at work inside as he pounded upon the anvil. Outside was an empty wagon and a cloud of flies swarming in the sunlight by the doors, but that was all. Even the small saloon beside the stable looked quiet, although there were half a dozen horses hitched outside the bat-wing doors. It was low and flat-roofed, with a tall false front gaudily painted and two fancy stained glass windows on either side of the doors.

The gilt-edged sign on the false front proclaimed this to be the *Great Western* in faded red letters, and the property of one Yakimaw Sam in green ones. A harsh, ribald laugh rolled out from the doors, breaking the stillness of the day, but it was quickly swallowed up with more silence, and Ames turned back to the store.

He climbed the worn, weather-beaten steps and opened the rusty screen door, letting it slam behind him like a waspish dog at his heels. Inside was dim and dusty, with dirt and sawdust on the plank floor and a film covering the windowpanes. From the exposed beams hung an assortment of metal and wooden tools and utensils, along with wagon parts, and what wasn't hanging was piled on long tables or heaped in barrels and crates. There were clothing, shoes, and medicines; saddles, blankets, and books; rifles, pistols, shells and knives. It was a hodge-podge of goods, centered around a large cast-iron potbelly, and the thousand and one smells of the country store assailed Ames' nostrils pleasantly.

"Ames!" a voice cried, and from the dark corner of the store walked Harlen. "We're back here, getting robbed, I swear."

Ames chuckled and went with the wagon master to the rear, where Ellison stood with the store keeper. Ellison glowered at Ames, but did not say anything, and the other man hardly glanced at him. The storekeeper was bald and one-legged, the flap of his unused pants leg pinned to his thigh, and he rested on the handle of his crutch with a nonchalance of a born Yankee trader. He slowly chewed a plug, occasionally adding a stream of brown juice to the already littered floor.

"Howdy," he said laconically.

"Ames, tell Mr. Sweetwater here we aren't rich," Harlen said.

"Don't matter one way or the other," Sweetwater said. He spat. "Take it or leave it."

"You know as well as we do that quantity price is always lower than single price," Ellison snapped angrily.

"Not here it ain't." He spat again. "It all gets sold sometime, and at my say. Whether it all goes at once or a little at a time is no matter to me. I ain't going nowhere."

"Why you—" Ellison growled.

"Might even charge extry for the barrels," Sweetwater added.

The bargaining went on with increased fury on the part of Harlen and Ellison, and calm stubbornness by the storekeeper. Finally Harlen gave in, vowing that this would be the last time he'd do business here; Sweetwater looked silently sure that he would be back.

Ellison read off the prepared list and the storekeeper hobbled around, taking down or pointing to or digging out from under other stuff the goods and food which was wanted.

"We're going to have trouble getting everything back to camp," Harlen said to Ames. "We ended up needing more than we thought."

"I saw another wagon over by the livery stable. If it belonged to the hostler he might let us use it."

"If he's anything like Sweetwater there," Harlen said, thumbing toward the storekeeper, "he'll only sell it to us at double the cost. But it's worth a try, I guess. Coming?"

"No," Ames said with a shake of his head. "Think I'll amble over to the saloon."

"It's a little early in the day for my drinking," the wagon master said dryly.

"Same here," Ames agreed. "I'm going there for a different reason."

He took his sombrero off and wiped his brow with the back of his hand, then fitted the hat back on. "I've been thinking about those men who waylaid the Holmes wagon. By the looks of them, especially the wounded one you shot, they would roost in just such a place as the Great Western. Now, one of them escaped, and if I could dab a loop on him—"

"You don't think that jasper is over there!" Harlen exclaimed in an astonished voice.

"He might be, especially if Wade Lamont

is mixed up in this, as you seem to think. Then again, he might not, but the bartender might remember something about him or the others."

"Now hold on, I never accused Wade Lamont of anything. It just seems to me mighty peculiar that all this trouble started the minute we neared Bar L property, that's all."

They had been walking toward the front of the store as they talked, and as Harlen crossed the threshold, he said, "You were at Lamont's today. What do you think?"

"That he's as he says. I took to him, and have no reason to doubt his word."

The two men walked into the street. "How did your business go?" Harlen asked.

"We came to terms. I'll be out in a minute and help load."

Harlen nodded and started for the livery stable. Ames adjusted his sombrero again, hefted his gunbelt, and began to walk slowly toward the Great Western saloon. He went up the three wooden steps and broke through the black batwing doors.

There was the whiff of stale beer and bad whiskey and the low murmur of voices as he entered. Four men were sitting at one of the

plain wooden tables which were to Ames'
left, and two lone men were bellied up to the
bar minding their own business.

Ames stepped in between the two men and
ordered a rye, and the fat, sleepy bartender
rubbed his hands on his dirty apron, reached
behind him for a shot glass and bottle, and
placed the setup in front of the Arizonan
without a word. Ames stood with his drink
between his fingers while he surveyed the
place for the man he had seen riding from the
Holmes' wagon.

The men at the table were dirty and un-
kempt, but did not have the hard, cold look of
killers about them. One was leaning forward,
gesturing and talking in a low voice. The
others listened intently until he was finished;
then they all laughed and the one who had
told the joke grinned broadly and poured
another round from the bottle beside him.

Ames turned and studied the man nearest
him, on his right, for he was by far the tallest
man in the saloon. But he was clean-shaven
and sloe-eyed and not at all like the missing
killer, in spite of his height.

Ames turned his attention to the last man,
aware that the chance of finding the
desperado in this bar were slim, but also

knowing that he had to try every possible chance, no matter how unlikely. Besides, there was the additional possibility that the bartender would remember four gunslingers passing through. Their kind, Ames knew, had a particular odor to them, some hidden scent which warned of their presence and raised the hair on the back of good folks' heads.

It was hard to tell about that last man. He was at the far end of the bar, leaning on the wood with a half-empty bottle and glass in front of his crossed hands. His head was down, with only the brown crown of his hat showing to Ames.

Ames gestured to the bartender, and when he came over, the Arizonan said, "The man at the end. He seems thirsty. Pour him a drink."

The bartender opened his mouth to question or possibly protest, but Ames gazed at him levelly, and the bartender did as he was bid. The sound of the bottle upon the glass as he poured seemed to stir the cowboy from his lethargy, and as Ames had hoped, the man looked up to see what was going on. He smiled wanly at the bartender and his fingers groped for the glass.

In that brief instant, Ames saw the hat and face. The hat was a railroader's, with a silver band. And the man had a scar across his temple. And the smell of a gunslinger was strong.

Ames felt a tremor of excitement run through him, and a certain degree of pleasure. His hunch had paid off! On the outside he remained passive and cool, with no sign that he had recognized the killer, and his hand remained steady as he picked up his drink, walked to the end of the bar, and hunched beside the man.

He waited until the man had downed his shot, and then when the agate-colored eyes of the other rested on him, Ames said, "You alone?"

The man straightened up. "Who the hell are you?"

"Call me Ames. Seems to me I've seen you around before, but I can't quite recollect the handle."

"Name's Guthrie. Lloyd Guthrie."

"Sure," Ames said as if pleased. "Sure, that's right. Guthrie. You used to ride with three others, didn't you?"

Guthrie's eyes narrowed into suspicious slits. "A time or two." He poured himself another slug and looked at the amber liquid before downing it. "What's it to you?"

"I could use a job," Ames said. "I heard tell you and them were pretty handy with an iron."

The man shook his head. "Nothing doing."

"What about the others?" Ames pressed.

"Forget 'em." Guthrie clenched his teeth, his jaw firm with savage anger. "Dead," he spat, "shot dead."

"South of here, wasn't it, Guthrie? While attacking a lone wagon and killing Tom Holmes? Isn't that how they got lead poisoning?" Ames voice matched Guthrie's in bitterness.

Guthrie staggered back a step, his eyes widening with shock. "How—" he started to say and then he choked out, "you! I remember you! You're the hombre who came out of nowhere and—"

"That's right, Guthrie!" Ames snapped back. "And I plan to hear you start talking on who paid you!"

Ames had his .44 half unholstered, but Guthrie reacted with the swift instincts of a hungry coyote. The killer grabbed the bottle of whiskey and smashed it against the edge of

169

the bar, splintering the glass and spraying the liquor. He took a vicious swipe at Ames with the jagged bottle neck, and Ames stepped back, throwing his draw off.

Some of the whiskey had splashed into the Arizonan's eyes, and he was blinded momentarily by the stinging, burning alcohol. His eyes blurred with tears and began to puff up, making his enemy a hazy outline. He lashed out and caught the man somewhere in the chest, but then a fist took him in the shoulder spinning him back into the bar.

At the instant of his impact, Ames heard the loud report of a handgun. He flinched slightly, tightening his muscles against the onslaught of lead which he was sure was headed for his gut. But then he made out Guthrie clutching at his own chest, his gun dangling from his finger, a wide, unbelieving look in his eyes. The man fell against the bar, groaning, and pitched forward. The gun clattered to the floor and then he rolled over and slumped into a still, quiet heap.

"This time there *was* no mistake," came the voice of Matt Harlen, and surprised, Ames whirled around to see the wagon master standing in the doorway, a smoking revolver held ready in his hand.

The bartender was peering over the bar at Guthrie. "Guess you had to do it," he said. "I saw him slapping leather."

"Sure I had to," Harlen said as he holstered the Colt and crossed to Arizona Ames. "I got worried about you and thought I'd see what was what. It was a—"

"I know," Ames said. "A lucky thing."

One of the four cowboys who had been sitting at the table, but who now crowded with the others around the body, looked up at Ames and asked, "Who was he, mister?"

"Yeah," Harlen said. "Who was he, Ames? All I saw was him reaching for his gun. I didn't take time to ask."

"The other man who killed Tom Holmes," Ames replied, and then explained to the bartender and cowboys the events of the preceding days and what had happened with Guthrie at the bar. There was some more talk, with everyone throwing in opinions and advice, and the bartender stood a round of drinks.

Finally Harlen clapped Ames on the back and said, "C'mon. No more can be done here, and I imagine Jake is getting tired of loading. We got that other wagon, and he can't do all the work himself."

A sense of failure clouded Ames as he walked out of the Great Western with Harlen. He had been close, so cussedly close, to some answers, and for a second time Harlen's Colt had silenced a man who might have talked. He was aware of how close to death he had trod just now, and that he owed the wagon master a tremendous debt . . . but somehow that failed to salve the frustration he felt.

6

THE burying of Tom Holmes was a somber affair. A member of the train who had been a preacher back in Kansas read several passages from the Bible and led the assembled settlers in the singing of *Rock of Ages*. The remains of Holmes, wrapped in canvas, were lowered into a deep grave on a grassy hillock sweet with the smell of blue lupine.

Jan Holmes—who had been standing between Arizona Ames and Jake Ellison during the service, dry-eyed but with trembling lips and jaw—turned away when four of the men began to fill in the grave. She walked quickly, with her head held high, back toward the circle of wagons.

Both Ames and Ellison followed her, and when they had reached Jan's wagon, the younger man said, "I'd like to talk to you a spell, Jan." His voice seemed to have softened somewhat from its usual belligerence.

"Not just now, Jake," she replied tremulously.

"It's mighty important, Jan," Ellison said. "For both you and me, now that Tom is gone."

"I said not just now!" Jan flared suddenly, and Ames saw that big tears were glistening on her cheeks. For all her calm exterior, she was filled with inner torment. "Oh, please, Jake, leave me alone!"

Ames took a long stride forward, stepping between Ellison and Jan Holmes. He managed a wan smile. "Reckon Miss Holmes made herself clear enough, Jake. You can have your say when she's feeling a mite better."

Ellison glared at him, dislike apparent in his shiny brown eyes. But then he seemed to remember the brief altercation he had had with the Arizonan the night before. He moistened his lips, said, "All right, then," in a gruff voice. And to Jan, "I'll come by later today, if it'll be suitin' you."

Without waiting for an answer, Ellison turned and strode off in the direction of his wagon.

174

"Don't think he cottons much to me," Ames observed ironically. He took makings from his shirt pocket and began to fashion a cigarette with one expert hand.

"Jake doesn't like anybody, I sometimes think," Jan said. There were no more tears in her eyes now. She took a long, sighing breath. "He's the most headstrong, obstinate man I've ever met; that is outside of Tom."

She turned, and looked toward the Santa Rosa Mountains; they were obscured somewhat by a bank of white fluffy clouds that looked as if they had been painted on the blue background of the sky. After a long moment she said, "Arizona?"

"Yes'm?"

"I think I'd like to go for a ride, to see just what there is in Gallows Valley. Would you mind keeping me company?"

Ames knew that she felt the need to get away from the train for a while to forget her sorrow, to concentrate her thoughts on something other than her murdered brother. He said, "It'd be my pleasure, Jan."

"I'll change into riding clothes," she said, indicating the simple, dun-colored dress and borrowed black veil she had worn to the service. "I'll just be a minute."

Ames nodded, and went to sit on an adjacent wagon tongue to finish his smoke. Jan emerged shortly, wearing a similar outfit to the one she had worn yesterday and the day before, and she and the Arizonan went to where the horses were kept at the far end of the wagon circle.

Ames saddled and mounted Cappy, and helped Jan onto a chestnut gelding which belonged to Jake Ellison's father. She insisted on riding bareback, and he offered no argument. She was strong-willed all right—and, he soon discovered, an accomplished horseman.

They rode toward the Santa Rosas, along the near boundary slopes of Gallows Valley. Jan showed no inclination to talk, and Ames, being a taciturn man, anyway, held his peace; if she wanted conversation, she would let him know it.

The conifers growing on the slopes cast long shadows over Ames and the girl as they passed below; twilight was fast approaching, and the horizon was purple and gold to the west. Ames wondered how long Jan would want to ride before returning to the train. He didn't know Gallows Valley well enough to be adept at traveling it by night, even though he felt sure he would have no difficulty in getting them back to—

He saw Jan's gelding stumble and fall to its forelegs before he heard the echoing report of the rifle.

He swung Cappy around, reaching out for the girl. But in that instant she cried out once, sharply, toppling forward off the flank-shot gelding's back and rolling over and over down the grassy slope in time to the echoing reverberation of the second shot.

Ames saw her come to rest and lie still beside several fallen and rotting scrub pine logs fifty feet away—but he was already out of the saddle and running by then, running and stumbling down the slope toward her. His hand was wrapped tightly around the Winchester .70 he had jerked from the boot on Cappy's flank before leaping down.

The third and fourth shots missed high over the Arizonan's head. The ambusher had made the mistake most men made when firing steeply downhill—aiming too high. Ames threw himself forward when he was ten feet from the girl, tumbling through the grass to land beside her prone form just as a fifth rifle bullet whined harmlessly above them. He caught Jan under the arms and dragged

177

her behind the larger of the pinelogs, holding the Winchester tightly under his arm.

When he and Jan Holmes were safely hidden, he inspected the scarlet ribon of blood which flowed along the shoulder of her woolen shirt. He breathed a soft, relieved sigh when he saw that the slug had only furrowed the skin, leaving a nasty gash but otherwise doing no damage. She was unconscious from shock and from the rolling fall she had taken downhill, but aside from a bruise here and there she would be all right. Her bosom rose and fell rhythmically.

Arizona Ames put his head up cautiously over the termite-ridden log and peered uphill. He could not see Cappy, but he knew that the sorrel would not be far off. Jan's gelding was lying on its side on the path they had been following, kicking now and then in its pain. He clenched his teeth bitterly, thinking that the fine animal would have to be put out of its misery and damned soon. But there was the predicament he and Jan Holmes were in to be given first consideration.

There had been no more shots for several minutes now, and Ames wondered if the ambusher had already hightailed it out of the area, or if he was still waiting on the chance that he would have another clear shot. There was no way of telling unless he, Ames, moved out into the open—and he wasn't about to do that. At least, not just yet.

Although he couldn't be sure, the Arizonan thought the shots might have come from a line of ponderosa pines some hundred and fifty yards above where they had been riding. He thought he had seen a flash from there just before Jan had been shot. It was a perfect spot for a bushwacker to lie in wait; hastiness or nervousness, Ames figured, were the only possible reasons why both he and Jan Holmes were not at that moment lying dead on the path.

The Arizonan reached out and pulled the Winchester to him. He levered a bullet into the chamber, the sound seeming magnified on the now-still dusk air, and poked the barrel over the log's rim, resting it there. He sighted along it, squinted, waiting for their attacker—if he was still there—to make another move.

Ames waited with the patience bred of instinct and experience, his finger curled on the Winchester's trigger, his muscles honed at readiness but not tensly corded. He listened to the soft moaning of the mountain wind, felt it cool on his leather-brown face, and he wondered who their attacker was.

Why was someone hell-bent on wiping out the Holmes family? What had they done to warrant an assassin's bullet? Ames frowned, because there were no immediate answers to his silent questions. He was by this time firmly convinced that whatever was behind these attacks, *whoever* was behind them, was directly connected with the arrival of the wagon train to settle in Gallows Valley. But the only logical explanation was that Wade Lamont was trying to frighten and intimidate the settlers off the land he had claimed for his ranch.

And yet, there were holes in that theory, too. Lamont had struck Ames as just the type of man he was rumored to be—fair-minded, shrewd, resigned to the coming of the nesters—and somehow the Arizonan could not picture the rancher to such cowardly tactics as hitting and running from blind ambush. If Lamont wanted to get rid of the settlers, Ames was sure he would have mounted a major offensive against them to drive them out. He had plenty of men to do so, to start a bloody range war that only

Lamont's seasoned veterans could hope to win.

And, Ames reflected, even if Lamont was content to play cat-and-mouse games, why had he specifically chosen the Holmeses as his target?

There was a soft whimpering sound beside him, and the Arizonan looked down to see Jan Holmes stirring, coming awake. She raised her head, her eyes wide with sudden fright, and then she winced as the movement sent pain shooting through her wounded shoulder.

"I've . . . been shot," she said in a wondering tone, staring at the blood on her shirt.

Ames reached down and put a gentle, quieting hand on her forearm. "Easy, now," he told her. "You'll be just fine. It isn't any more'n a flesh wound."

"I remember a sharp pain in my shoulder, then falling, rolling," Jan said haltingly. "What happened?"

Ames told her, briefly, and the girl's full lips tightened into a thin, angry line. "Damn whoever it is!" she said vehemently.

Ames nodded, fully understanding her anger and her frustration. "Don't you worry,

Jan," he said tightly. "I'll see to it you're not hurt any more'n you have been already."

She managed to smile weakly at him. "If anyone can keep such a promise, I think it'd be you, Arizona Ames." But then she quickly sobered, seeing the intense look on Ames' face as he peered along the barrel of his Winchester into gathering darkness. "Do you suppose he's still waiting for us up there somewhere?"

"Hard to say," he told her. "Be full dark in a few minutes, and he might figure to wait around until then and make another try at us. Then again, he might have gone on his way long ago."

"What are we going to do?"

"Reckon the only thing we *can* do," Ames said. "If he's up there, we've got to know it. And the only way to find out is to give him a target." He smiled wryly. "But not much of one, if I can help it."

"You're not going out into the open?"

"I don't see as how there's any other choice," Ames said quietly. He slipped the leather thong from the hammer and butt of his .44, took the Colt from its holster and pressed it into Jan's hand. "You might need this—in case he's still waitin' up in those pines, and in case I'm not as quick as I aim to be."

"Be careful, Arizona."

Ames inclined his head curtly, took a firm grip on the stock of the Winchester .70, and eased himself away from the pine log. He got his boots under him, keeping his head down, looking upward along the slope and some forty yards to his right. At that point was a small, jagged cluster of rocks and boulders which seemed oddly out of place on the grassy hillside.

He counted softly to five, and then burst from his crouched position into a low, zig-zagging run; the muscles along his spine were as taut as piano wire as he ran, and he expected any moment to feel a slug tear into his flesh from high in the ponderosas.

But there was no sound save for the wind and his own labored breathing, and he reached the safety of the rock cluster moments later. He crouched there, holding the Winchester at ready. Was the ambusher gone? It appeared so; there was just enough light left for a man to have a clear shot, and if the attacker had still been concealed in the pines he would surely have seized this last opportunity to fire upon the exposed Ames.

Still, caution was the watchword. Tensing again, Ames leaped back into the open and retraced his broken path to where Jan Holmes lay behind the scrub pine log, watching him with held breath and widened eyes.

There was only the sound of the night wind.

The ambusher was gone, all right.

After a few comforting words to Jan, Ames began to work his way up the slope toward the path; his eyes were sharp and watchful, and he held the Winchester with his index finger caressing the trigger. But he reached the path without incident. He glanced with saddened eyes at the now unconscious form of the chestnut gelding, and then went in search of Cappy.

He found the sorrel grazing peacefully in a small glen nearby and led him back to the path, rebooting his Winchester. Then he climbed down to the scrub pine logs, lifted Jan Holmes gently in his arms despite her protests that she could manage under her own power, and carried her up to where Cappy stood waiting. He sat her aback the sorrel, and then walked slowly to where the gelding lay. He disliked the chore he had to do next, but it could not be shirked.

Moments later, he mounted Cappy in front of the girl—with a single bullet gone from the .44's chambers, and the echo of one shot dying slowly in the now almost complete darkness.

7

WHEN Ames and Jan Holmes rode into the flickering firelight of the camped circle of wagons, they found Matt Harlen and Jake Ellison about to organize a search party for them. The Arizonan took Cappy past the gathered knot of men in the center of the encampment.

"Miss Holmes has been wounded!" he called out. "Somebody fetch the train doctor, and pronto!"

There was a shocked murmur from the men. Ames rode to the Holmes wagon and reined up—Ellison, Harlen, and the others following. Ames disengaged Jan's clinging arms from about his waist, swung down from Cappy's back, and reached up to help the grimacing but plucky girl dismount, careful of the wound around which he had tied his bandana earlier. He caught her up in his arms, carried her to the wagon, and laid her gently on the mattress inside.

As he came out of the wagon, Jake Ellison said anxiously, "Is she all right? Is she hurt bad?"

"Reckon it's no more'n a flesh wound," Ames told him.

Matt Harlen said, "What happened, Ames? We figured you'd fetched up some kind of trouble when you didn't come back by nightfall."

"Some varmint tried to bushwack us," Ames said, studying the faces of the other settlers who made a half-circle around him. "Winged Miss Holmes and shot her horse out from under her. Missed me with three shots at less'n two hundred yards. I'd say both of us were danged lucky to be alive."

"Damn!" Ellison exploded. "You get a look at the polecat, Ames?"

The Arizonan shook his head solemnly. "He was well hid-out, in a line of ponderosa above the path we were riding."

"Make way, here!" a voice said excitedly. "Make way!"

Ebenezer Benton, the train's short, nervous-appearing doctor pushed his way through the cluster of men. He was carrying his little black medical satchel in his left hand. Ames stepped out of the way and

187

Benton climbed into the wagon to attend the girl.

Ames moved away from Jan's wagon finally, took out his makings and began to roll a cigarette with tight-lipped concentration. Matt Harlen followed him, and said quietly, "Who do you think it was, Ames?"

"Can't rightly say," the Arizonan replied laconically.

"Connected with what happened to Tom Holmes, you think?"

"Seems like."

The wagon master took a plug of tobacco from the pocket of his Levis, bit off a chew; he worked his jaws rapidly for a moment, and then spat a thin brown stream toward a nearby campfire.

"Things appear to be gettin' out of hand hereabouts," Harlen observed with anger.

Ames struck a kitchen match on the seat of his trousers and put the flame to his smoke. He said nothing.

"Looks more and more like Wade Lamont," Harlen said. "I never did trust a cattleman, and coincidence only goes so far. Too many things have happened in the past couple of days, and I don't like none of 'em."

Ames did not want to commit himself.

"Maybe Lamont, and maybe not," he said. "One thing's sure, though—whatever's going on in Gallows Valley, it's near to poppin' a head."

"A fact," the wagon master said. "It—"

"Ames!" Jake Ellison's voice called out abruptly, and the younger man came up to them. The Arizonan turned to face him.

"Maybe I was wrong about you hangin' round Jan," Ellison said. "You saved her life tonight—she told me all about it just now while old Benton was patching up her shoulder. That bein' the case, I figured you'd want to be in on the showdown."

Ames frowned, and Harlen asked sharply, "What showdown, Jake?"

" 'Tween me and Wade Lamont," Ellison said, and the Arizonan saw in the light from the circle of campfires that the younger man's eyes were blazing with rage. "I'm fixin' to ride over to that ranch of his and have it out with him. I'm not going to stand still for a snake of a cattleman having my best friend killed, and then tryin' to bushwack his sister, the girl I aim to marry!"

"Hold on, now," Ames said placatingly. "We're none of us sure it's Lamont behind any of this."

"Who else could it be? There's just nobody else."

"Jake, Ames is right," Harlen said, coming to the Arizonan's defense quickly. "I reckon I figure it for Lamont, too, but there's nothing to be gained in walking into a cougar's lair. You go begging trouble at the Bar L, you'll find a passel more'n you can handle, I'll wager."

"You got any better ideas?" Ellison asked.

Ames said meaningfully, "None except staying alive. And seeing that nobody else in this train is killed or hurt."

"I'm damn tempted to go it alone, then!"

"I'll have you hogtied to your wagon, Jake," Harlen told him coldly, "if'n you make me do it. I won't have you getting your danged fool head shot off."

"Lamont's a no-good murderin' sidewinder!" Ellison snapped, his face livid with emotion. "We can't just let him get away with all he's done!"

"If he's guilty," Ames told him, "he won't get away with anything. There's sure to be a sheriff in Paradise—"

"Do you suppose he's going to arrest a big cattleman like Wade Lamont?" Ellison said contemptuously. "Fat chance! There's only one law to settle with a man like Lamont, and that's sixgun law!"

Before either Ames or Harlen could say anything further, Ellison turned and stalked off. The two men watched his retreating back for a moment, and then Ames said, "Do you figure he'll do anything foolish tonight?"

"I doubt it," the wagon master said. "Jake talks a big fight, and he's a hot head, but it don't fit him going off half-cocked by himself."

Ames nodded. "Reckon I'd like to spend another night with you folks, if there's no objection."

Harlen spat another thin stream of tobacco juice. "Glad to have you, Ames. Fact is, I was hopin' you'd stay on another day or two to kind of keep an eye on things."

"That can be arranged," the Arizonan said. "It'll be two-three days before my business is settled in Gallows Valley, and I can be on my way."

He didn't add that if Wade Lamont *was* behind the double-dealing thereabouts, and it could be so proved, his business would likely never be settled at all.

The wagon master clapped him on the

back. "Come on," he said, "Let's see if we can rustle up some vittles."

Arizona Ames snapped awake instantly at the vague, surreptitious sounds which came from the direction of the horses—sounds which a less trained man might have never heard. He cocked one eye open from his bedroll near a fire in the center of the wagon's circle, looking toward the tethered animals.

A shadowed, unrecognizable figure was moving swiftly, silently, there—untying one of the horses and leading the mount away from the train.

Ames did not move for a long minute, letting the shadowy figure think he was getting away unobserved. Then, with swift, silent movements, the Arizonan snapped into a sitting position and pulled on his boots. He noted as he did so, from the position of the moon overhead, that it was past midnight.

He made his way quietly across to the horses, and located his saddle in the neat row to one side of the makeshift corral. He stepped to where Cappy was tied, stroked the sorrel's muzzle lightly to keep him quiet as he threw on the saddle and cinched it down. Then he untied Cappy and led him away from the train, in the same direction the lone figure had gone.

Peering intently ahead of him, Ames could see the pale, almost indistinct silhouette of horse and rider against the backdrop of the moonlit sky; the figure sat his mount now. An instant later there came to the Arizonan's sensitive ears the soft echo of retreating hoofbeats; the silhouette seemed to grow smaller as he watched.

Ames swung astride the sorrel and urged him forward, cantering, his sharp eyes staring straight ahead of him. He was able, with his strong night vision, to keep his quarry in sight as they rode.

They picked up the wagon road minutes later, and followed it south. Ames remained a good five hundred yards behind the other man, staying just off the road so as to muffle the sound of Cappy's hoofbeats lest the other became aware he was being trailed.

When they reached the private road which led to Wade Lamont's Bar L ranch, the rider turned in to the gate, unlatched it and rode through, relatching it behind him. Ames, pausing in the shadows to watch this, waited for several moments and then followed, repeating the man's actions with the gate.

The Arizonan was not a man to make rash assumptions, but he was relatively certain that the rider ahead of him was Jake Ellison. The young man had spoken foolishly of carrying out a sixgun vendetta against Wade Lamont that night, and it appeared that Matt Harlen had been wrong about Ellison not being one to go off half-cocked by himself.

Ames frowned in the darkness as another thought suddenly struck him. Suppose Ellison was not going to Lamont to kill him at all, but to engage in some kind of rendezvous? Suppose Ellison had something to do with the murder of Tom Holmes, and the attempt on Jan's life that afternoon?

Ellison's friendship with the dead man might not have been as strong as everyone was led to believe—nor might his supposed affection for the girl. Perhaps Ellison had sold out to Lamont, and the two were somehow working together to drive the settlers from Gallows Valley.

Ames tried to put the tumbling questions from his mind; this was no time for conjecture. In either case—vendetta or partnership—Ames planned to be in a position to step in at the right moment. And in either case, he expected it was time to turn up a few logical answers.

As the rider neared the darkened buildings of the ranch proper—eerie black shadows in the silvery hollow below—Ames brought Cappy up into a walk. Now that he knew the man's destination, there was no purpose to be served in staying close and risking discovery. As it was, if Ellison looked back for any reason, he was almost sure to see Ames silhouetted against the moonlit sky.

In a narrow stand of trees, located just off the side of the road some three hundred yards from the first of the Bar L buildings, Ames saw Ellison stop and dismount. The Arizonan watched him lead his horse into the trees, blending completely with the grotesque black shapes. Ames brought Cappy to a standstill, swung down, and led the animal into some brush off on the other side of the road. He dropped the reins there, again stroking the sorrel's muzzle to assure silence. He waited.

Moments later, the form of a man afoot detached itself from the trees and began to move toward the buildings.

Ames could see the figure's progress clearly in the moonshine. It skirted the cinder path

195

which led to the ranch house and passed by the corral and stable at which Ames had watched the bronc-busting show that morning. It appeared to be heading for a large, two-storied hay barn whose whitewashed exterior shone spectrally in the moonlight.

As soon as the Arizonan was certain that the barn was the figure's ultimate destination, he left the brush and made his way carefully downhill, paralleling the road to where it widened into the ranchyard. He took the same course as the man he had been tagging, past the cinder path and the stable. The hay barn lay far to the left of, and somewhat behind, that building.

Moving with the sure-footed stealth of an Indian, Ames crossed the brightly illuminated ground fronting the barn and slipped into the shadows cast by the structure's walls. He remained motionless there for a time, ears straining for the slightest sound; he heard nothing.

He flipped off the leather thong over the hammer of his Colt, rested his palm lightly on the .44's textured grip, and began to inch his way slowly, cautiously, along the white-painted side wall of the barn. He had seen the figure move toward the wide double doors at the front of the building; but the Arizonan did not want to use that entrance if he could avoid it.

There had to be another way into the barn—a side or rear door, a window or ventilating opening of some kind—and if he could slip inside by such means, undetected, he would not only have a tactical advantage over those already in the barn but would be in a position to overhear anything that was being said.

The wall along which he was moving was void of an opening of any kind, he soon found, and he slipped around to the rear of the barn. He could see the outline of a door set into the planking there, and he went to it silently and tried the latch; it was locked securely. Ames cursed under his breath, and moved on. He edged around to the other side wall and began to make his way frontwards again.

He saw the small, rectangular, uncovered window at the same time he heard the indistinguishable murmur of voices coming from beyond it, inside the structure.

With cat-like quickness, Ames braced himself flat against the wall next to the opening, right hand still touching the butt of his Colt.

He leaned his head to the side, listening intently. The murmuring became two voices, low and muffled in the absolute darkness within the barn's hay- and dung-odored interior.

". . . have to do something about Ames, that's for sure."

"I had him dead to rights this afternoon, but the sight's off on my damned carbine. I winged the girl instead."

"We been plannin' this thing too long to let some saddle bum mess it up."

Familiar voices, but muffled enough so that the Arizonan could not be absolutely sure who their owners were. He chanced a quick look through the opening. Darkness, full and complete. And then—

One of the men inside struck a match to light a thin black cheroot in the corner of his mouth, cupping the flames in his hands. But that brief flash illuminated the two plotters for an instant, long enough for Ames to see their faces clearly.

The man who had struck the match was Roy Stringer, Wade Lamont's foreman.

But that did not surprise Ames nearly as much as the identity of the second man, the man he had trailed from the wagon encampment.

That man was not Jake Ellison at all..

It was Matt Harlen!

8

AMES pulled his head back quickly, his jaw set into tight, angry lines; he had been wrong on all counts. Instead of a prearranged meeting between Ellison and Lamont, this was one between Stringer and Harlen. But why? What was it they had been planning for so long? The Arizonan stood immobile, listening to the continued conversation from inside the barn.

"First it was that damned Tom Holmes, challenging my leadership of the train," Harlen was saying. "Then that young snip Ellison went and took up the call, especially now that Holmes is dead. And now this Ames jasper has stuck his nose in; hell, we were danged lucky he didn't come upon the wagon sooner'n he did or he might have saved Holmes' hide."

"Yeah," Stringer said. "Well, we got to take care of him afore he can do us any damage."

200

"Too bad he stumbled out of my line of fire in the Great Western today. I'd of put my lead in him 'stead of Guthrie. Maybe I should have plugged him anyway, then and there."

"The rest of 'em wouldn't have stood still for that," Stringer told him. "It'd of been murder, plain and simple. You done the right thing, Matt. 'Sides, with Guthrie out of the way, there's nobody can tie us to Holmes' killing."

"Reckon that's so," Harlen admitted.

"We'll get Ames afore long, no worry about that."

"And young Ellison, too. He's gettin' out of hand. He wanted to come up here tonight and have it out with Lamont. I sided with Ames and we talked him out of it. But there's no tellin' what he's liable to do."

The wagon master paused, and then continued, "Reckon I can doctor up the wheel on his wagon the way I fixed the one on Holmes', and see to it Ames is ridin' along with him when I send him into Gallows for more supplies tomorrow. Shouldn't take more'n a mile from camp for the wheel to work itself off then, and you could have some of your men waiting for 'em thereabouts."

"I don't know," the ranch foreman said

skeptically. "That Ames is a powerful tough hombre in a gunfight."

"Not if he doesn't get the chance to use that iron of his," Harlen told him. "Suppose you was to have your men mosey by the crippled wagon, like they were just passing, and offer to lend a hand fixin' the wheel. Then, have 'em open fire sudden-like; Ames and Ellison would never know what hit 'em."

"Might work at that," Stringer agreed. "How would you explain the ambush to the train?"

"Lamont and his boys." Harlen's reply was quick and triumphant. "I've planted the seed in most of the settlers' minds that Lamont's back of the trouble we been having, and when Ames and Ellison turn up dead, I'll lay it on thick. They'll believe me, all right."

"Sure! And then we got it accordin' to the way we planned. I put a bullet in Lamont, and say later that me and a few of the boys found out what he was up to, how he was tryin' to drive the settlers off'n their rightful land, and decided to rebel agin him in self-defense and the name of justice."

"I'll use my influence with the train to persuade settlers to stay on in Gallows Valley, since you'll be taking over the Bar L,"

Harlen continued. "They'll figure you to be on their side, especially after you give 'em your story, and they'll settle. Once that happens, once they put down roots and start farming this valley, we'll have 'em right where we want 'em on shipping and credit stores. They'll end up working for us afore long, and owing us their souls to boot. We'll be rich, Stringer!"

"More'n rich," the foreman said gloatingly. "Powerful, too; mighty powerful, what with all of Lamont's cattle and his holdings."

"You're sure, now, there ain't going to be any problem gettin' control of those holdings once Lamont's dead?"

"How many times do I have to tell you, Matt? He doesn't have any kin, and he's never bothered to make out a will—he figures to live to be a hundred. I had this lawyer over to Lovelock draw up a document all nice and legal-appearin' which leaves the whole shebang to me when Lamont dies. He copied the old man's signature so careful Lamont hisself wouldn't know it was a forgery."

"When do you figure to take care of Lamont?"

"Soon's Ames and Ellison are out of the

way," Stringer answered. "Reckon tomorrow night."

"No trouble from the hands loyal to him?"

"Nope. I picked out those jaspers to round up the two thousand head Ames bought for Reno delivery; they're scattered to hell and gone over Gallows Valley and around. Ain't nobody left but Lamont and maybe one or two of his men. The rest are workin' for me. We'll have complete control in no time, and when the others come back they either work for me or drift on."

Stringer laughed, a low unpleasant sound which seemed to come from deep in his throat. "And this way, we save that two thousand head to sell at top market dollar 'stead of the give-away figure old Lamont set out to Ames."

"Okay, Roy," Harlen said. "Then it's all settled?"

"Settled."

"I'd best be getting back to the train, then," the wagon master said. "No use chancin' being missed any more'n necessary."

"Right."

Ames, still pressed tightly against the barn wall outside the window opening, felt controlled rage stretch taut the leathery skin of his face and cord the muscles of his lean frame into the need for action. The conversation he had just overheard had brought forth consuming hatred for the two cold-blooded killers, an emotion the easy-going cowboy seldom felt toward any man.

He cursed himself for not having seen sooner that he—not Jan Holmes—had been the real target of the ambusher's bullet that afternoon; that Matt Harlen had purposely murdered the wounded bandit at the Holmes' wagon two days earlier to keep the man from implicating the wagon master and telling all he knew; that Harlen had fired too quickly, with Ames between him and Guthrie in the Great Western saloon, to have been aiming his bullet for the marauder; that the crooked trainsman had been more than ordinarily curious about the Arizonan's business in Gallows Valley, and more than ordinarily eager to have Ames around where he could keep an eye on him.

Ames' fingers clenched around the cross-hatched grip of his .44 as he heard the two schemers heading toward the front doors of the barn. He slid past the window, silently lifting the Colt from its holster, moving frontally toward the corner. When Harlen and Stringer came out into the open, he would get the drop on them and take them up to the main ranchhouse. Wade Lamont would be mighty interested in learning the gist of their recent conversation.

So intent was the Arizonan on his objective that he did not realize someone had slipped up behind him until the man fanned back the hammer on a Single Action .45.

The long years of drifting, of battling his way out of one scrape after another, had honed Ames' instincts and reflexes to the finest possible edge. The sound of the thumbed hammer acted as an instantaneous signal in his brain for those reactions to take command of his body.

He threw himself to the left, away from the barn, turning his body in mid-air and bringing the .44 around and under him at his belt. He squeezed off two quick, sure shots which shattered the moonlit stillness of the night, saw the shadowy blur of the man behind him jerk, drop the .45 he had held extended in his right hand, and fall over into the dust. The Arizonan landed on his right shoulder, rolled, came up into a squatting position. He was clearly outlined in the moonshine that flooded the night.

At that moment, another black shape appeared at the corner of the barn—Harlen or Stringer—and Ames snapped a quick shot there, driving the figure around to the front again. But the Arizonan knew he had been seen and recognized. He gained his feet, backing away and sweeping the area with the bore of his Colt.

All hell was breaking loose now, and all because of a guard he had not seen earlier or even expected to be present, who had somehow spotted him there in the shadows by the barn. There were loud, confused shouts from a long building some distance away on Ames' right, that he guessed to be the bunkhouse. Lanterns were lighted inside.

From the front of the barn came Stringer's bellowing voice: "It's Ames! He's killed Jigger! Spread out of your bunks, boys, and don't spare the lead!"

Ames knew that as soon as Stringer's men had strapped on their sixguns and came pouring out of the bunkhouse, he would be trapped. They would surround him, cut him off from the road and from Cappy waiting in the brush along it, and pick him off in their own sweet time. He still had a chance, though a slim one; but he had to move, and move now.

He turned to run sideways, facing over his right shoulder with his .44 at the ready to cover his back. He cut diagonally past the rear of the stable to intercept the cinder path which led to the main ranchhouse. Stringer and Harlen, moving boldly out from their protective positions at the front of the hay barn, sent a volley of bullets at him.

Ames saw the bright orange flashes from their sixguns, heard one of the slugs whine overhead, but their aim was hurried and none of the lead came closer than that. He gave them a pair of answering shots from his Colt, and then he was onto the cinder path and running toward the ranchhouse and Wade Lamont.

As he neared the sprawling structure, a light appeared through the partially draped front window, casting an oblong of yellowish brilliance over the railed veranda. Ames jumped onto the porch without bothering with the stairs, landing solidly in a crouch just as the front door and the flyscreen burst open. Wade Lamont's burly form appeared, dressed in a long nightshirt. The rancher held a Sharps rifle, the muzzle pointing at Ames' midsection.

"What in tarnation is goin' on out here?" he demanded loudly, angrily.

Ames had a quick look in the direction from which he had just come, saw Stringer and Harlen running directly toward the house. Behind them several of Stringer's men were beginning to empty out of the outhouse. Ames turned his attention back to Lamont and said urgently, "It's Roy Stringer, Mr. Lamont! He's aiming to kill you and take over the Bar L!"

"*What?*" Lamont shouted in disbelief. He had recognised Ames in the moonlight, and the rifle had dipped low to the floor of the porch; he both liked and trusted the Arizonan from their earlier meeting. But now the Sharps leveled once more on Ames' belly.

"I reckon you'd best put up that iron you're holdin', Ames, and explain yourself."

"There's no time!" the lean cowboy snapped. "Stringer and the others—"

Before the Arizonan could finish his plea, the Bar L foreman shouted something to his men—and a dozen guns were spitting fire and lead at the two men on the ranchhouse porch.

9

AMES dove forward reflexively at the sound of Stringer's shout, slamming into Lamont and sending both of them crashing to the veranda floor. The hail of bullets sent showers of wood splinters from the railing and the white-painted wall onto their backs, and broke one of the windows with a shattering crash.

The Arizonan sighted along his right arm from his prone position, squeezed off the final two rounds in his .44. He heard one of the running men cry out, stumble and fall—but he did not think it was either Stringer or Harlen. Then he scrambled onto his knees, relieved to see that a cursing, redfaced Wade Lamont was doing the same thing. The rancher hauled the Sharps up, began to fit the stock to his shoulder.

"Inside!" Ames yelled at him.

Lamont understood immediately, and he and the Arizonan scuttled through the doorway and inside the ranchhouse. Ames reached up and threw the door closed, gained his feet, and found the heavy wooden crossbar for it sitting to one side; he dropped the bar into its iron brackets.

"The windows!" Lamont snapped.

Ames nodded and jumped to the one at the door's left while the ranch owner stepped to the one on the right. Ames hurriedly dug cartridges from his belt and began to load the empty Colt, thinking that Lamont—in spite of the fact that the old man had no real idea what was going on—was reacting to the situation with the coolness and courage which had been attributed to him.

Ames finished loading the .44, and snapped the chamber closed. He used the barrel to break out the glass in his window, peering into the moonlit night. Stringer and Harlen and the foreman's crew were fanned out now, having taken every inch of available cover facing the ranchhouse. Ames knew that some of them could soon be coming around back, to try to get in that way, and that in a matter of minutes he and Lamont would be completely encircled.

He called across to the grim-faced rancher,

"Watch our flank. They'll try to back-shoot us if they can."

"Right," Lamont said.

They were in a comfortably furnished parlor, lighted by a single kerosene lantern on the dining table. The old man turned from the window and moved across the room to the one inner doorway, which opened onto a hallway leading to the rear of the house. When he reached it, he swung the door closed and pulled an ornate parlor cabinet with twin bevel-plate French mirrors over from the wall to barricade it. He went back to his window, pausing on the way to douse the lantern and plunge the room into darkness.

He said as he resumed his position, "What in hell is this all about, Ames?"

The Arizonan told him, outlining in terse sentences what he now knew. He finished with, "When Stringer saw the two of us together on the porch just now, he must have figured that there wasn't any use in waiting to kill you. He could get two birds with one stone, this way. That's why he had his men open up on us."

Lamont rattled off a string of vehement profanity. "I never would have thought it of Roy Stringer! I knew he could be a hardcase at times, but I never pegged him for this kind of low-down, back-stabbin' coyote!"

Ames grunted, staring through the broken panes of glass in his window. One of the men had left cover, was up and running toward the ranchhouse. He brought the Colt up and fired with lightning speed. The man yelled in sudden pain, fell sideways, and lay still.

Lamont said with respect, "You handle that iron like you was born with it in your hand."

Ames did not reply, his eyes searching the front yard for some other sign of movement; there was none. He looked over at Lamont finally. "How much ammunition do you have in the house?"

"There's rifle cabinet on your side of the room, on the front wall," the cattleman told him. "Couple of boxes of cartridges for this here Sharps, and maybe half a dozen boxes that'll fit that Colt sixgun of your'n. You figure us to be here for a spell, that it?"

"I came in alone," Ames said, as if berating himself for not having thought to bring assistance. "And they can wait us out, if they've a mind." His voice was grim.

"Hell, if'n all you told me is pure fact, then I don't put it past 'em to fire the house."

213

"We'd best hope they don't think of that," Ames said, but he had had the same thought as Lamont. He knew that chances were it would not be long before Stringer or Harlen came up with that idea as well. And if they managed to put a torch somewhere and Lamont were unable to get to it to snuff out the flames . . .

The Arizonan shook his head, dispelling those depressing thoughts. There was no use in climbing into your grave while you were still breathing. As long as they had their wits and plenty of ammunition, there was still hope.

Lamont said to him, "Reckon we can try to make it down to the stable and pick up a couple of horses. Might take 'em by surprise if we rushed out sudden-like, throwin' lead."

Ames shook his head in the darkness. "Moonlight's too bright, and the stable's too far away," he said. "We'd be dead men before we got a hundred feet."

"Yeah," Lamont said with sardonic irony. "I know that, Ames. But at least we'd die on the move, 'stead of sittin' in here like a couple of fatted calves in a slaughterhouse pen."

The Arizonan said nothing, but he was prone to agree with the rancher. They would move out into the open, all right, but only as a last resort; only when all the other possibilities had been considered and discarded. Until that time they would remain where they were.

A sudden volley of shots came from the concealed marauders in the yard, peppering the outside wall, shattering more panes of glass in both windows above where Ames and Lamont were crouched. The barrage had come too abruptly, in too full a force, to suit Ames, and he wondered if it was a cover for some kind of assault on the ranchhouse. Had they already thought of setting the building on fire? Had Stringer sent one of his men around to the rear with a torch?

A chill moved along Ames' back, and he left the window, starting across the darkened floor toward the blockaded doorway. He could see well enough in the darkness to skirt the room's furniture.

Lamont called out above the fusillade, "Ames? Where in hell're you goin'?"

"To check the rear of the house," the Arizonan replied.

"Go easy, then. I'll hold down things at this end."

Ames moved the parlor cabinet as quietly

as possible from the door. He pulled the door open a crack, peering into the hallway. There was no sign of anyone. Ames slid through and made his way stealthily along, his eyes sharply watchful. He passed the entrance to Lamont's den, and a few steps further on the doorway which opened into a bedroom with a rumpled four-poster.

The hallway emptied into a wide, narrow kitchen, its furnishings ink-colored shadows against the lighter black of the night. He saw that the kitchen led onto a porch at the far left, and he took two steps into the oblong room, starting for the porch.

A looming black figure seemed suddenly to fill the entranceway.

Ames threw up his .44 and fired, his hand a blur of motion. The Colt spat flame, and the figure flew backward, crashing into a galvanized iron washtub on a low wooden table and sending it clattering to the floor. In that instant, Ames sensed a flickering, dancing light coming from a section of the porch that he could not see. He ran to the entranceway, and a second man was on a stairway leading up to the utility porch outside, holding open the flyscreen with one hand.

He held a burning pine-pitch torch in the other.

The Arizonan brought the .44 to bear again, but the man hurled the flaming firebrand at Ames before he could fire, jumping back and letting the flyscreen bang shut. Ames dodged to the right, felt the heat singe past his face. He fired three quick shots, and three round scorched holes appeared in the screening, belt-high and less than five inches apart. The man on the stairs screamed and toppled backward, rolling into a heap at their bottom.

Ames pivoted, looking at tongues of flames which lanced upward from a thick stack of cordwood against the far wall, crackling as the fire spread from the torch and gained intensity. The Arizonan looked frantically about him, saw a well pump on a wooden platform next to the body of the first man he had shot. He reached down, caught the grip on the iron washtub, and dragged it over to the platform. He grasped the pump handle, began to work it up and down until water splashed into the bottom of the tub with a metallic raining sound.

He worked feverishly. When he judged that there was enough water, he released the pump handle, and hefted the washtub. He carried his burden to the fire—now threatening to engulf the whole side wall of the porch—and then overturned the water onto the flames. There was an angry hissing noise, and acrid smoke bit into Ames' nostrils, but most of the fire was extinguished. He beat at the remaining flames with the washtub, confining them, stomping them into cinders with his boots.

When the fire was completely out, Ames dropped the tub and went back inside the house to confer with Lamont. His face was scorched and blackened by the flames, and he knew that some of the skin on his hands had been blistered. But he could still grip his .44 and that was all that really mattered now.

He was halfway along the hallway when he heard Lamont shouting, "Ames! Ames!"

He ran into the parlor. "What is it?"

Lamont was standing by the window, holding the Sharps rifle crooked in his right arm. He was grinning widely. "Lookit there, will you? Just lookit there!"

Ames stumbled across to the window beside him, staring out. He blinked, and blinked again at the scene unfolding before his eyes in the bright moonlight.

Harlen and Stringer and the foreman's men were out from their cover, flushed like jackrabbits and running every which direction. Some were firing, others just running for their lives. And chasing them across the silvery ranch yard, shooting and yelling and raising clouds of dust, were some twenty mounted riders.

All were members of the settler's wagon train.

And leading them was Jake Ellison.

"They come ridin' down my road hell-bent," Lamont said joyously to Ames, clapping him on the back. "They came up here with a vengeance and opened up on Stringer and the other varmints like the Seventh Cavalry. I don't know who they are, but they're sure a mighty welcome sight!"

"They're your new neighbors," Ames said, feeling some of Lamont's elation rub off on him. "Come on! Let's see if we can give 'em a hand!"

Ames and Lamont rushed to the door, threw off the crossbar, and stepped out onto the veranda. Just as they did so, Roy Stringer rose up on the far side of the porch, sixgun leveled in his hand, lips pulled back from his teeth in a snarl. His eyes blazed with hatred, and they were resting on the broad and unprotected back of Arizona Ames, who was watching the settlers ride herd in the ranch yard.

Suddenly, Lamont shouted, "Grab some dust, Ames!"

The Arizonan dove off the porch in a head-first lunge just as Stringer's sixgun belched fire. The bullet passed harmlessly over the spot where Ames had stood, and then the Sharps rifle cracked from Lamont's belt line. Stringer threw up his arms, staggering backwards, and crumpled onto his side. He did not move.

Ames, who had hit the dust rolling and came up braced on his knees with his Colt at the ready, slowly relaxed. He got to his feet, climbed up onto the porch again. His eyes held respect and admiration and warmth for Wade Lamont.

"Reckon I owe you my life, Mr. Lamont," he said softly.

"Hell!" the rancher said, grinning. "It was my pleasure, Ames. After what you told me Roy Stringer was plannin' for me, it wouldn't of been fitting for anyone else to give him his just due."

The commotion was dying down in the

ranch yard now. The settlers had captured, or wounded, or chased into the hills all of Stringer's men. There was no more fight left in any of them. And as Ames and Lamont watched from the veranda, Jake Ellison came riding up from behind the house dragging a man who had a rope cinched tight about his middle. The man was Matt Harlen.

Ellison dismounted, leveled his old Harrington and Richardson at the wagon master. Harlen just lay there in the dust, his face sullen and blank, not moving. He was a beaten man, and he knew it.

Ames and Lamont walked slowly over to the headstrong young settler, and the Arizonan felt as if he were looking at Jake Ellison in a new light. He had thought of him previously as nothing more than a brash, acid-tongued trouble-maker—even as a conspirator in a plot against Jan Holmes that never existed—but by riding in here with the trainsmen tonight, he had no doubt saved both Ames' and Lamont's lives, and proved himself a capable man in the bargain.

Ames said quietly, "Looks like you made yourself a right nice catch there, Jake."

Ellison turned. "Well, howdy, Ames," he said with a twisted smile. "Reckon I did at that, sure more than I bargained for. I persuaded Harlen here to straighten out a few things for me about what's been goin' on roundabouts of late when I threw a loop on him a few minutes ago." Ellison paused, looking at Lamont. "This'd be Mr. Wade Lamont, wouldn't it?"

The old man measured him with his penetrating eyes. "Sure would be, sonny. And you?"

"Jake Ellison."

"The new wagon master of the train that brought Gallows Valley its new settlers," Ames put in. "Not that they'll be needing one now."

Ellison and Lamont stood looking at one another, and after a moment the younger man said, "Reckon we got a mite to talk over, don't we, Mr. Lamont?"

" 'Pears that we do, at that," Lamont said, his face splitting into his wide, infectious grin. The two men shook hands.

Arizona Ames thought, as he watched them, that there would be no more trouble in Gallows Valley.

10

THE barbecue which Wade Lamont threw two days after the showdown was proving to be a great success. The Bar L corrals were filled with horses and wagons of the settlers, and the children were playing tag around them, trying to see who could yell the loudest. Women bustled about the long, groaningly full tables, setting out great loaves of home made bread and bowls of preserves, and the men were moving about, laughing and talking to the ranch hands. Liquor was available, but a fight could not be had if wanted, not with the succulent smell of barbecuing beef in the air.

Mouths watered, and as noon approached appetites were kindling to famished proportions. The air was just crisp enough to add further incentive, and somehow almost everybody gathered around the huge roasting steer which revolved on a steel spit over the glowing pit midway between house and barn.

Lamont, taking the host's prerogative, had been in charge of the basting, and was using a new broom to swab the crisping sides with his own special sauce, which was in a wash-tub beside him. Then he stepped back and instructed one of his men to throw green sagebrush in the fire, and thick billows of fragrant smoke enveloped the barbecue, adding the last touch of perfection. The Bar L owner grinned, and walked over to where Ames was hard at work whetting the carving knives.

"Just about ready, Arizona," he said. "It'll be done in just a few more minutes."

"Well, I reckon!" Ames replied, his weathered features breaking into a deep smile. "That's a pit-roaster beef if I ever smelled one!"

"No steer of mine ever died a more glorious death," Lamont laughed, his eyes sparkling. He turned to look at the crowd now milling around the pit expectantly while the sage smoke rolled away in a down-valley breeze. "This sure makes me feel good, Arizona. Folks living in peace, happy and friendly. I can't say I'm sorry the government went and sold Gallows Valley, not when I can throw a shindig like this! Goin' to be fun havin' some neighbors."

Just then Jan Holmes approached, her dark eyes sparkling in spite of the sling her arm was in. Even though it was just a shoulder graze, Ebenezer Benton had thought it best, knowing it would heal better if her arm was steady. Right behind her was Jake Ellison, all spruced up in his one suit, his unruly red hair slicked back, and an infatuated smile on his freshly shaved, pink-scrubbed face.

"Hello, Arizona, Mr. Lamont," Jan said.

"Why howdy, Jan," Ames replied. "Don't you just look as pretty as a picture in that dress. I can't say when I've seen a nicer sight!"

Jan laughed. "Thank you, Arizona." Ellison came up to stand beside her. He shook hands with Ames and then with Lamont.

"I wanted to say how much we all appreciate this," he said to the rancher. "Mighty fine of you, especially after what I thought about you."

Lamont chuckled. "Don't give it another thought, son. If you hadn't figured I was the polecat behind all the trouble, you would have never come riding in when you did. And that," he added with a nod, "I'm glad of."

"Jake!" Jan said, turning to him, "You mean you thought Mr. Lamont was in cahoots with Matt Harlen?"

"Well," Ellison said sheepishly. He scuffed a toe in the dirt. "It had to be somebody, and Tom and I didn't know that Harlen and Stringer were in the Army together years ago. But dagnab it, at least we weren't fooled by Harlen, like the others. Like a certain young lady I can name."

Jan blushed slightly. "It was Tom who thought something was wrong about Harlen from the first. I recall a powerful lot of talking before he convinced you, Jake Ellison, and—"

Both Ames and Lamont had to laugh. "Easy there, Miss Holmes," Lamont said, chortling. "The important thing is that Jake did think Harlen was crooked. If he hadn't, he probably wouldn't have been sleeping lightly and see Arizona here leave the camp. Then, when he found out that Harlen was gone as well, he properly put two and two together, and figured Harlen was on his way here and Arizona was followin'. He rounded up the men and came ridin'."

"I just had the feeling Ames could use some help," Ellison said.

"I sure enough did," the Arizonan said. "We couldn't have held off Stringer's men for long."

"But where were your men, Mr. Lamont?" Jan asked. "Some of your hands were loyal to you and would have stopped Stringer."

"Most of them would have, I'm glad to say," the rancher answered. "Only Stringer had sent my men after Ames' cattle, leaving only his crew of varmints at the ranch."

"When we came riding in, Jan," Ellison explained, "they started shooting at us, so naturally we opened up on them. I caught Harlen trying to sneak away, and it didn't take long for him to confess to everything." He shook his head in wonderment. "I still can't get over how long Stringer had been waiting for the chance to take over your ranch, Mr. Lamont."

"He saw his chance when the government sold my land," the ranch owner said. "He got hold of his old crony, Harlen, and Harlen signed on as master of your train."

"He said he knew the area, and none of us did," Ellison explained. "He sure did, having lived in Nevada since his army discharge."

227

"I thought it mite peculiar when he told me he had never been in these parts before," Ames put in. "Familiarity with the territory is one of the reasons a wagon master is picked."

"Well, it's all over," Lamont said, "and there won't be any more trouble now."

"This is your last night with us, isn't it, Arizona?" Jan asked. "You're leaving tomorrow with your cattle, I hear."

"That's right," Lamont answered for Ames. "And I'm riding with him as far as Reno. Sam Playford is supposed to meet us there, and I've heard too much about this brother-in-law of Arizona's to miss the chance."

"In that case, I'll save a dance tonight for each of you!" the girl said brightly. "That is, if you'll make an announcement at lunch for us, Mr. Lamont."

"Be glad to, Jan."

Ellison cleared his throat and a spot of red tinged his cheeks. "We . . . that is . . . I . . ." he faltered. "I mean, Jan and me . . ."

Jan giggled lightly. "He's trying to tell you that we're engaged."

"No!" Lamont cried.

"My congratulations," Ames said.

228

"Well, ain't that great!" The rancher slapped Ellison on the back warmly. "This makes it a double celebration. A going-away for Ames, and an engagement party for you young 'uns."

He turned to the Arizonan. "Aren't those knives sharp enough by now? I'm just itchin' to spread the good word!"

"Sharp enough to cut stone," Ames replied, handing Lamont the glistening utensils.

Lamont rolled up his sleeves, said, "Let's go!" and then the four of them walked toward the pit. Ames glanced at the surrounding happy faces, at the rich valleys beyond, and then across to the snow-whitened peaks of the Santa Rosas. This was a good land, he thought, and it had not seen the last of him, even if his name was Arizona.

Danger Rides
the Dollar Wagon

1

ARIZONA AMES, brooding over a beer in the Lucky Buck, the only saloon the town of Phileaux River boasted, became alert at the sound of a commotion in the street. Two men came through the doors of the saloon, their boots hard on the wooden floor. They were yelling at one another angrily, and Ames could hear them clearly over the rest of the noise.

"You're a danged fool!" one of them said. He was the larger and the older of the pair. "My own brother!"

"Mebbe so. But I tell you it was a sure thing! I don't know what went wrong!"

They sidled up to the bar and ordered rye. The older brother said, "You let them take us proper! What will Martha say when we tell her? And Sue? Less than six months married, boy, and with a child on the way!"

"But I could've been rich! We all could've been!"

"Could've don't pay the mortgage, Danny, or put bread on the table!" The older brother downed his drink and ordered another.

"It was a sure thing, I tell you. The dealer would never have known!" He sank his head, though, the realization of what he had done overwhelming his pride. "I'm sorry, Norm, powerful sorry," he said contritely.

"Bein' sorry don't help none."

"Beggin' your pardon," Ames interrupted, "I couldn't help over-hearing what you were saying."

"Yeah?" Norm demanded. "Who said you could butt in?"

"A good friend of mine got taken in a monte deal like the one next to Doc Modora's Dollar Wagon," Ames said, as pleasantly as he could. "It sounded like you were taken just the same way."

"I wasn't taken," Danny snapped. "It was just my bad luck, that's all. This other fellow and me asked to see the cards. You know, inspect 'em, and when we did, the fellow bent one edge of the queen so we'd be sure to know it."

"Uh-huh." Ames nodded in agreement. "And then when you put your big bet down and turned over the dog-eared card, it wasn't the queen after all."

"How—how did you know?"

"I told you. The same trick was played on a friend. Reckon this fellow suddenly disappeared, too, didn't he?"

"Couldn't find him nowheres around, mister, and I looked."

"You check inside the wagon, boy?"

"The wagon? Doc Modora's wagon?"

"That friend of yours was a shill, put in the crowd to stir up business. The dealer was in on it, too; when he got the cards back, he took the bend out of the queen and put it on another card."

"Gol-darn, I knew it!" Norm roared. "We've been hornswoggled!" Norm grabbed his brother's collar and shook him. "A cheap tinhorn trick! And you fell fer it!" He flung Danny against the railing, almost upsetting the drink in Ames' hand. "Well, I'm goin' back there and get our money back!"

"Reckon you can't," Ames said.

"What do you mean?"

"You can't prove you were cheated," Ames explained. "You try that and it'll look as if you were just plain robbing 'em."

"What can we do?" Danny asked the tall stranger.

"I owe that group something for a long time," Arizona Ames said, his teeth clenched tightly together. "And I don't have a wife or babies to think about. Besides," he added slowly, as he remembered years past, "I don't have anything much to lose any more. You better be grateful for what you have."

2

IT had been mid-afternoon when Arizona stopped his old horse Cappy under the shadow of a ledge on the small hill overlooking Phileaux River. He had taken off his wide-brimmed, deep-crowned sombrero and wiped his brow with his bandanna. They were almost finished with a long slow trek from the west, and the town below looked cool and inviting.

Ames had just left a stint at the Cornwall spread in Wyoming. The place had had a bad reputation, and after working it, Ames knew that it was not undeserved. Old man Cornwall was a cantankerous buzzard, the land having made him sour and bitter. He paid but half the going wage, and worked the hands mercilessly. His cowpunchers themselves were rejects and castoffs.

But Ames had not been in any position to be particular, not with his past, though he tried to do his job well and keep out of trouble. The foreman, however, had taken a liking to Cappy and tried to steal the animal, leaving Ames for dead in the grasslands. Ames had revived and returned to the ranch. The foreman would never try to steal any other man's horse.

Ames had half a month's wages in his pockets, and as he looked at the town, he hoped there would be work for him there. Cappy smelled water and whinnied; and, after a pat on his lean neck, Ames let the sorrel trot down the trail at his own tired pace.

Phileaux River was small, little more than a group of stores bordering a single, dusty street. It had been one of the first towns to be built after Custer's expedition confirmed gold in 1874. The gold had not made Phileaux River's fortune, nor the fortunes of Yankton, Bon Homme, and other Dakota settlements. Large companies had brought cattle into the area to help feed the miners, and soon afterwards the prairie sod was broken by the plow.

After a number of disastrous winters, the ranchers learned to keep smaller herds and shelter them, and there were many spreads dotting the area which might need an extra hand. They did not often find one as willing to work as Arizona Ames.

With the heat of day pressing on him, Ames passed along the street with its narrow, planked sidewalks and low curbs to the livery stable on the other side, not bothering much to look around. There was not a great deal to see in any case. Schirmer's General Store was the biggest single dwelling, a two-story wooden frame building with a galvanized iron roof. Ames had the feeling it would be like an oven in there. A dog slept under the porch roof, its ears scratched occasionally by an old man resting in a chair beside it.

There was a sheriff's office next to the one saloon, a branch of a Dakota Territory bank with its window shades pulled down, a funeral parlor, a ladies' boutique with a frilly sign in French, and the hotel which was nothing more than a sprawling, one-story house. It looked clean enough to Ames.

The livery stable was cool. Its owner was wise enough to have covered the roof with sod, which not only helped keep out the heat, but insulated the stable as well during the winter blizzards.

Ames rode up and dismounted before the barn-like doors. The owner, a fat old man with a heavy beard and a plug of tobacco bulging one cheek, came out, squinting from the sunlight. Ames haggled over prices, but the man would not compromise. Ames boarded Cappy for fifty cents, and strode back to the hotel.

Ames had passed one rider while in town, a farmer in his wagon. When he walked into the Lucky Buck Saloon and ordered a beer, there were only two other patrons in the place. The beer was luke warm and almost flat. Ames switched to rye. He had two shots and felt sleepy. He drowsed in the saloon the whole afternoon, waking up in the cool of the evening. He had dinner in the crowded hotel dining room, full of laughing and shouting townspeople. The streets had blossomed with cowboys and farmers and a few bonneted housewives and bareheaded ladies.

Ames went back to the Lucky Buck. The piano was playing raucously, and the bartender was having difficulty waiting on the noisy crowd. Ames felt his spirits pick up.

A young ranch hand burst through the swinging doors, yelling that a peddler had arrived. The crowded saloon emptied almost at once. In such desolation, an outside man, especially one as colorful as a peddler, was highly welcome. People bought his wares to keep him around, to have him tell and retell the news from other parts of the country, as well as because they needed the products he was selling.

Ames strode outside and watched the brilliantly-painted wagon come slowly up the street, being pulled by a handsome dappled gray. The man who drove it wore a big smile and an outrageous brocaded vest. He waved to everybody, and by the time he stopped in the center of Phileaux River a large crowd had gathered around the wagon. The peddler had a round, open face, as though he were an angel, but Ames knew him for what he was: a charlatan, a thief, and a swindler.

He was Jersey Jack Kelson, not the Doctor Modora printed on the wagon, and, though Ames had not seen the medicine pitch, he was sure it was a false one. Jersey Jack had run a different game in Oklahoma City, and had taken a number of Ames' friends. Ames wondered what the swindle would be this time.

He did not have long to wait. Jersey Jack pitched the ladies first, showing gowns and glass jewels and shiny pots and pans, everything selling for one dollar. The most favored of all feminine items was, of course, needles;

they broke or disappeared rapidly in the Dakotas, and without them, the women could not mend otherwise good clothing.

Next he talked to the men, hustling a patent medicine called Doctor Modora's Tapeworm Remedy. For some reason, the major ill that year was tapeworms. Lack of correct diet, overwork and fatigue, any imagined ailment was the fault of worms. Ames had a good idea there was just enough laxative in the medicine to make the buyers think it was doing some good; chiefly, Doctor Modora's Tapeworm Remedy consisted of alcohol and rain water.

Then Jersey Jack brought out his real pitch. Or rather, one of his men did. Behind the dollar wagon Ames could see another group of men, and investigating, he found a three-card monte game in progress. It was a simple little con, in which the operator put three cards face down on a board and defied anyone to pick out the queen. There was a deft amusing spiel that went with it, and at first none of the players lost. Then the bets became higher, and luck changed to the operator's favor. Only Ames knew it had nothing to do with luck, but to the manipulations of the dealer.

Disgusted, he had returned to the Lucky Buck—and now he was leaving the saloon ready to see justice done—or at the least, some interesting action. . . .

3

ARIZONA AMES strolled at a measured pace along the dusty street to where the gaudy Dollar Wagon stood. The crowd had thinned out somewhat now, but there were still several men grouped around the three-card monte game. One of them was Jersey Jack Kelson; he had apparently discontinued his pitching due to the late hour.

Arizona approached Jersey Jack, who was standing near a tall, angular man wearing dun-colored chaps and playing monte with much laughter and merriment. Unless Ames was badly mistaken, the angular man was one of Kelson's shills; he turned up the queen three out of four times, "winning" sizeable sums each time.

Ames stood next to Jersey Jack and gawked at the angular man, and when the shill turned yet another queen he said, "Hell! That don't figure to be too danged hard." He did his best to sound ignorant and arrogant—an easy mark.

Jersey Jack looked at him with interest. Even though Ames had seen Kelson work his swindle in Oklahoma City, he was reasonably certain that he was not known to the crooked gambler.

Jersey Jack smiled and touched Ames' arm. "Well, you're sure right about that, friend. It ain't hard at all. If you've got a little cash, and some sporting blood, you ought to take a whirl."

"I will, at that," Ames said.

"Make room, gents," Jersey Jack said to the monte players. "Here's a cowpoke with a hankerin' for some sport."

They made room. Ames took a handful of silver dollars from the pocket of his trousers and stepped forward, swaggering just a little, reinforcing the gamblers' impression that he was for all the world an easy mark.

As he expected, they let him win the first few hands. He began doubling his bets. The dealer let him win twice more, and then his eyes flickered past Ames' shoulder to the spot where Jersey Jack was standing. From the corner of his eye, Ames saw Kelson nod almost imperceptibly.

The dealer laid the three cards face up on the barrel top they were using for a table. Ames looked at them briefly, and then fastened his eyes on the dealer's hands as the man turned the cards over and began shuffling them about on the barrel top.

If Ames had not been looking for it, he would have missed the deft way the dealer palmed the queen, substituting another card for it from the long sleeve of his silk shirt.

Ames reacted instantly, his hand shooting out to clutch the dealer's wrist, twisting it over, shaking it. The queen fell out onto the barrel top, and the gathered men could see clearly that there were four cards there now. Angry murmurs began to fill the night air.

Ames pulled the dealer forward, upsetting the barrel, and then releasing the man's wrist; the dealer sprawled into the street. The shill in the dun-colored chaps stood up, starting toward Ames, and Ames hit him once in the face with a quick right hand. The shill reeled backward.

Ames turned then and threw two short, sharp jabs into Jersey Jack's stomach; the con man's breath whooshed out in surprise and pain and he doubled over, clutching at his stomach.

It turned into a free-for-all then. The locals had realized that they were being swindled, and if there was one thing the men of the small Dakota Territory towns did not cotton to, it was slick grifters.

They moved in on Jersey Jack and the shill and the dealer, and two others who were roused from the wagon by the commotion. Ames joined in with grim determination; he, too, hated the grifter and the con artist— perhaps even more than they did. The man who had ruined his sister, Lee Tate, had been of the same stripe.

The sheriff—a big, powerful man with silvering hair and an authoritative manner—and two of his deputies finally broke up the melee. Jersey Jack and his men were badly beaten by that time; two of them lay in the street unconscious.

The sheriff demanded to know what all of this was about. One of the angry locals said, "They're a bunch of cheatin' sidewinders, Boone. This here fellow caught one of 'em palmin' cards and gave him what fer."

"What's your name, stranger?" the sheriff asked, turning to Ames.

Ames told him. There were murmurs from the crowd.

"So these here Dollar Wagon boys were pullin' a swindle, eh?" the sheriff said.

Ames nodded. He indicated Kelson, who was kneeling near the wagon, dabbing at the bloodied lip with a red kerchief. "That one's called Jersey Jack. I saw him work the same trick on some friends of mine out in Oklahoma country a couple of years back, and I figured he had a lesson coming to him. That's why I played the game."

"Reckon mebbe he did at that," the sheriff said. "Well, we sure don't want his kind in Phileaux River. The boys and I'll see they don't stay long."

"They took more than a few of the townspeople," Ames said. "Including a couple of brothers named Norm and Danny. Reckon they'd like to have their money back."

"They'll have it," the sheriff assured him. "Sure do appreciate what you done here Ames."

"My pleasure," Ames said. He moved off, rubbing his bruised knuckles, and returned to the Lucky Buck Saloon.

A couple of the locals followed Arizona Ames inside and insisted on buying him a drink, and he drank with the men for a short while.

248

Then he decided to walk down to the livery stable to check on Cappy before turning in for the night. He was in the habit of making certain the faithful animal received proper treatment wherever the two of them went.

It was very dark when Ames reached the sod-roofed building, and the area seemed to be quiet and deserted; most of those men still up and about were congregated at the saloons. He did not think the fat man would still be there, but he had noticed a single window on one side. A quick look through there would satisfy him as to Cappy's comfort.

Ames started around the building, stepping into the shadows there. Just as he reached the window, the low, muffled sound of voices came to him. At first, he could not make out what they were saying; but then, one of the voices raised in anger and Ames recognized it as belonging to the brash young Danny he had spoken to in the Lucky Buck earlier.

"You dirty skunk!" Danny said, and Ames caught the unmistakable slur in the voice that could only be caused by too much rye. The boy was drunk, or close to it. "I ain't goin' to let you get away with what you done!"

The second voice spoke, but the words were low and indistinguishable.

"Sure I got my money back!" Danny shouted. "But that don't even the score. Only one thing's goin' to even the score."

"Simmer down, boy," the second voice said, and Ames stiffened. It belonged to Jersey Jack Kelson.

"Hell I will!"

"Go on home, boy, if'n you know what's good for you."

"I know what's good for me, right enough! This here's what's good for me!"

Ames knew what those words meant, recognized the inflection in Danny's liquored tone; he had heard it in the voices of dozens of men throughout the west. He leaped forward, his right hand flipping off the leather thong across the butt of his .44.

Just as he reached the rear corner of the livery stable, two shots rang out.

Ames turned the corner, the .44 held in his hand now, just in time to see a shadowy group of figures standing near the huge bulk of Kelson's Dollar Wagon. The sheriff must have given them time to get out of Phileaux River instead of escorting them out personally. Across from the wagon, at the rear wall of the livery stable, Ames saw another shadowy figure lying prone on the ground, one arm outflung. That lone figure was Danny.

"Hold it right there!" Ames shouted, feeling anger and revulsion rising inside him. "You murdering coyotes won't get away with this!"

Jersey Jack's voice yelled, "Luke!"

In that instant, Ames heard movement behind him, coming from the deep shadows of a shed-like structure parallel to the livery stable. He started to turn, bringing the .44 around, and then pain exploded against the back of his neck.

Ames went down, pinwheels of light that were at first brilliant and then grew gradually dimmer, erupting behind his eyes. He heard, as if from a great distance, the sounds of scurrying boots and the excited voices of men. He felt a hand remove the .44 from his fingers, and, a moment later, return it.

The pinwheels of light vanished, and blackness swept over him.

It was only a bare few moments before Arizona Ames regained consciousness. He staggered to his feet, leaning against the rough boards of the livery stable. He felt the back of his neck, dimly noticing his sombrero was gone. He raised the .44 and it was then he saw that the gun in his hand was not his.

The finely balanced weapon the old trapper, Cappy Tanner—for whom he had named the sorrel—had given him was gone. The one he held was a far cry from that one. The Dollar Wagon was also gone, now, and Ames knew what had happened: they were trying to put the blame for Danny's death on him.

"Hold on here," came a loud voice from the street. Turning, Ames saw the sheriff running toward him. There were a group of locals behind him. "What's all the—hey!"

The sheriff strode to the boy on the ground. Ames noticed then that his own sombrero was clutched in Danny's hand. The sheriff stood after a moment and said coldly, "He's dead. Shot in the back."

"In the back?" Ames cursed softly, realizing that one of Jersey Jack's men had ambushed the boy, probably the same one who had hit him from behind.

"That's right. And you're standin' here with a smokin' gun." He walked slowly toward Ames, his eyes hard and his jaw set rigidly.

"It is not my gun, sheriff," Ames said. "I

came to help the boy and one of them hit me on the head. Then they switched guns with me. And put my sombrero in the boy's hand."

"One of who, Ames?"

"The Dollar Wagon boys. They're the ones you want."

"Ain't nobody here but you," the sheriff said. "Looks as though you tried to rob the boy of his money. Don't figure, what with your name and what you done this evenin', but facts is facts, right enough."

Ames knew what this talk was leading to. A man's reputation, no matter how good, was soon forgotten when one of the locals was killed and all the evidence pointed to him. Few criminals were lower than a bushwhacker, especially one that preyed on a mere boy. Those same men who had bought him drinks in the Lucky Buck Saloon and thanked him so profusely for exposing the con game Jersey Jack Kelson was working would now clamor just as profusely for his hide. There was only one decision for Ames to make.

"Don't try for your gun, sheriff, not while I have this one. Reckon I don't want to shoot anybody, but if it comes to that—" Ames let the sentence hang meaningfully in the night air.

The sheriff did not try to draw, for he was a prudent man, but Ames knew he would not hesitate if there was a chance he could drop the cowboy.

"Get him!" somebody shouted wildly from the crowd.

"If any man makes a move, the sheriff dies," Ames warned.

"Danny! Danny!" Norm's voice came through, and the crowd was pushed aside as the boy's older brother shouldered his way to the front. "What's happened to Danny?" he asked, almost hysterically.

"Ames here shot him," the sheriff said laconically, watching the .44 in Ames' steady hand.

"Why you—" Norm reached for his gun without thinking.

Ames had no choice. He fired once, close to the brother, but not intending to hit him.

"Hold it," he snapped. "I'm telling all of you, I'm not the killer. I know it looks bad, but it wasn't me. It was Jersey Jack and his crew."

"They left town," the sheriff said. "I seen

to that. Reckon I wish it was them, but I don't know how it coulda been."

Arizona Ames was in a bad position. He had the silver-haired sheriff on one side of him and the vengeful brother facing him from the other. It was useless trying to talk sense to them, and he had to move fast before they closed in. Without warning, he jumped toward the sheriff, knocking the lawman to the ground.

Before anybody could stop him, Ames raced through the unlocked side door of the livery stable and bolted it behind him. Four volleys of shots peppered the planks immediately, sending Ames back into the stable.

The great barnlike structure smelled of horses and sweat and dung. In the dim light, Ames could see halters and hackamores and bridles hanging from wall pegs, and the mounds of hay and array of equipment used for animal care. There was a wagon near him with one wheel off, the axle being repaired.

Ames was trapped. He heard the townspeople collecting around the stable, the sheriff directing them loudly. "Now I don't want anybody hurt," he yelled. "Don't take any fool chances."

Ames walked as quietly as he could through

the stable, so as not to give away his exact location. Unless he acted quickly, the townsmen would become restless and finally rush the stable. Ames did not want to have to fight his way out, not only for his own sake, but for the sake of the innocent people who might be harmed.

The Arizonan found his horse, and untethering him, backed Cappy out of the stall. "Easy there," he soothed the sorrel, who seemed to have caught the scent of death which pervaded the air. Cappy was tossing his head nervously.

Ames figured that it would be no more than another half hour before the sheriff would be unable to contain the angered populace; and with each passing minute, more men came, heard the story and vowed to help catch the killer of the well-liked boy, Danny.

After saddling Cappy, Ames led the animal as close to the front doors as he could without risking a bullet, and then hurried to the rear of the stable. He did not waste any shots, but instead upset a large shelf of saddles; they made a tremendous clatter as they tumbled to the floor. Then Ames swatted a couple of horses smartly, and they began whinnying and kicking in their stalls.

The sheriff yelled from outside, "He's tryin' to get out the back!"

Ames heard the sound of many boots running around to join the others at the rear. He ran for Cappy, vaulted into the saddle and spurred the animal. Cappy surged forward. There was a split second in which Ames kicked loose the brace across the doors, and then Cappy galloped full speed out into the night.

As he had hoped, the noise had distracted the bulk of the men to the rear, and the few who remained around front were caught off guard by the charging rider. They shot wildly, and Ames felt a sharp pain in this left shoulder, as if a wrangler had burned him with a branding iron. There was a momentary blur of shock, and then the arm became leaden, but Ames held on and rode for the town's limits.

He knew it would be close. The men were near their mounts, which for the most part were fresh, and a posse would be on his heels in no time. He leaned into the wind, urging Cappy to put as much distance between them and Phileaux River as possible.

He saw that the only direction he could go was north, since that was the side of the town the livery stable had been located, and the road followed a steep slope and paralleled the river to Sawyer.

Ames realized he did not have a chance if he stayed on the road, as already the telegraph wires would be singing his description and word of his escape to the sheriff of Sawyer, and more men and more guns would be waiting for him there. He rode for about half a mile, until the lights of Phileaux River were no longer to be seen. Then he cut into the surrounding country.

The dust gave him away. Every twist and turn, every back track and switch was observed and followed as he attempted to shake off the pursuing hunters. Ames thought about the river, but in the height of summer it was low and surrounded by adobe mud flats which would bog Cappy down. His only chance lay toward the west and the buttes.

As midnight neared, Cappy began to tire noticeably. Wearied from the long run and the previous day's ride, even the sorrel had to slow down. Ames, disappointed though he was at the realization, had to admit Cappy had done a yeoman job. He patted the horse gently, as if telling him it was not his fault.

They slowed to a canter, and then to a trot, and finally to a slow walk. Ames was thankful for the fact that there was less dust this way, and with luck, the night would conceal their direction.

They continued west, circling occasionally and zigzagging at other times to throw off the posse. Yet at daybreak, in the first faint rays of the new sun, Ames was able to see that the riders were still close on his trail.

4

THE vast, open Dakota prairie, just west of the Black Hills, lay beneath the blazing summer sun like kindling under a firebrand. The hot July wind blew flame breath across the barren expanse of buffalo grass and sagebrush and three-foot turfs of bluegrass, and Cappy's coat glistened with flecks of lather as the sorrel fled toward a line of limestone buttes in the distance.

Ames' tall, lean, sun-bronzed figure rose slightly in the saddle, turning to look briefly at the billowing dust cloud rising lazily into the brilliant cobalt sky behind him. The movement made the bullet wound in his left shoulder spasm with pain. He was still unable to make out the individual riders in the posse, but he knew that they were gaining steadily.

Cappy, blowing heavily through vented nostrils, had not had much rest the previous night; he was beginning to flag beneath Ames now. The posse had comparatively fresh mounts, and the men knew the land far better than he. His trail was as obvious to them as theirs was to him, and he was fully aware that he had no better than an even chance to reach the bare, trackless sanctity of the buttes before they overtook him.

The sun had already begun its slow descent into the shadows of late afternoon, and Ames felt its blaze across his right cheek. The light played tricks on his eyes, making the myriad domes and spires of the buttes seem closer than they actually were, outlining them against the fiery sky like black fangs of a rattler.

Again he twisted in the saddle, and this time the dust cloud seemed larger, looming in drifting brown waves. The dots of the pressing riders suddenly became visible. Just as sudden were the tiny flashes from their unholstered sixguns, and Ames realized that they had finally gotten to within shooting distance, and were wasting no time taking advantage of this.

The shots seemed popgun-loud in his ears, faint echoes swallowed by the vastness of the plain; but then they became louder, closer, and he dropped low over Cappy's flowing mane, making himself as small a target as possible for lead which was by no means popgun-harmless.

The sudden forward hunching caused pain more devilish than before to lance through him, and the wound in his shoulder began to bleed again. He felt warm liquid soaking the faded yellow material of his shirt, flowing freely down along his side.

Weakness began to overtake him. He felt strength rapidly ebbing; it would not be long before he blacked out from the steady loss of blood. His vision, already blurred by sweat streaming down from his wide forehead and by dust raised from Cappy's pounding hooves, clouded even more—and there were slowly gathering shadows at the edges of his vision.

Ames lifted his head to gaze quickly into the distance. The buttes were closer now, much closer—were his eyes still playing tricks? No, he was coming into higher ground, beginning to climb. The autumnal colors of the limestone cliffs were discernible now: pale yellows, reds, burnt umbers and golden bronzes, shining radiantly in the distance. The sight of them brought renewed hope rising within him—even though the posse was almost at his heels now, and their bullets were coming dangerously close.

Arizona Ames had taken this route because, though the most arduous, it was the closest to the protective buttes. He had not wanted to try for the town of Iron Flats, which was to the south. The buttes were his only chance.

The terrain became rougher, still climbing, and Cappy's hooves clattered for the first time against solid rock. Ames heard the buzzing of the pursuing gunshots grow faint again as he climbed still higher, searching for a trail which would lead him to any semblance of safety. He had gained a precious few seconds as the posse was forced to slow their mounts and regroup into single file.

He saw, then, what appeared to be an old Indian trail. Wiping sweat from his eyes with the back of one hand, he urged Cappy onto the winding, barely discernible track. They passed through an expanse of boulders, entering a deeply eroded canyon. He turned, looking to the rear again; he was hidden momentarily from the posse's sight. He let his eyes roam the canyon walls feverishly, seeing that it was a box, with the only entrance seeming to be the one through which he had just passed.

Ames walked Cappy quickly along the base of one of the sheer walls, his eyes probing the huge crags for a spot from which to make a stand. Finally he located the possibility of one, buried in a deep pocket of shadow, and dismounted.

The large, irregular boulders had a deep recess between them, with the rocks overlapped in such a way as to offer plenty of cover, as well as a vee notch for the Winchester rifle nestled in a scabbard on Cappy's flank. He led the sorrel behind the largest of them. He was about to drop the reins when he saw that the recess seemed to continue deeper into the canyon wall.

Another quick look satisfied him that the posse had still not discovered his entrance to the canyon, and he decided that he had enough time to determine how deep the recess ran. Entering the gap, he saw that it was not altogether unlike a cave. The faintest of drafts from the blackness within told him that there might be another entrance, that the recess might lead through the wall to emerge somewhere behind it.

Gathering strength, Ames led Cappy inside. They inched their way along, the jagged sides of the rock scraping their bodies in the darkness of the narrow, hidden tunnel. Rocks slipped beneath his boots, and the bright light of the entrance shrank until it was little more than the glow of a kerosene lamp hung waist-high. The passage seemed to grow narrower, until he thought the walls would press them into an impossible cul-de-sac, trapping them there.

But then the path shifted sharply to the right, rising upward, and Ames saw another thin shaft of light fifty feet along. He took Cappy toward it, watching the light grow to reveal an entrance, nearly as wide as that in the canyon, in the ceiling of the tunnel, with the erosion-gravel of centuries having sifted down to make a steep but navigable path up to it.

They went up the path, through the opening into sunlight which burned Ames' eyes with its glare. When his vision grew accustomed to the brilliance again, he saw that they stood on a small ledge on the opposite side of the canyon wall.

The tall, lean rider turned to look back the way they had come. The tunnel was a kind of culvert nature had dug to drain the sudden squalls and pounding winter rains from the butte, perhaps only one of dozens of similar run-offs burrowed through the limestone, emptying into the canyon on the other side, or others like it. There was a good chance that the men in the posse would not know of this particular one, or be able to find it unless they were as blind lucky as he had been.

Laboriously, Arizona Ames climbed upward, leading Cappy, until he reached the canyon's rim. There he let the sorrel's bridle fall in a protective overhang of shale, and made his way to a flat table rock, sinking onto it slowly. From there he could look down into the gorge below. Heat waves shimmered, and he shaded his eyes against the brilliant glare, licking parched lips.

The posse had just come into the canyon. He counted ten men, eleven. Sunlight reflected from a tarnished star on the chest of the lead rider, and even at this distance he knew that the man was the sheriff of Phileaux River.

The sheriff rode deeper into the canyon, the other men at his heels; just before they reached the wall upon which Ames rested, the sheriff raised his hand to halt the posse. They turned their horses in all directions, studying the shale and limestone cliffs, but none seemed to see the hidden passage. The sound of the animals' shod hooves on the bare rock floor drifted and echoed faintly throughout the confines of the canyon.

Finally, the sheriff and two of the other men dismounted and stood in a tight circle. Ames could hear nothing of what was being said, of course, but he knew that it was an argument as to whether to continue the search for him. After a time, having reached a decision, the three men remounted their horses and the sheriff motioned the posse around. They made their way quickly out of the canyon.

Ames released a soft sigh; they had apparently decided that he had not entered that particular box after all, that he had bypassed it for another gorge, another place of concealment. They would give it up soon, he thought, and ride back to Phileaux River.

Painfully, he gained his feet again. On weakened legs, he returned to where Cappy stood in the shale overhang, caught up the reins, and led the sorrel along the rim of the canyon.

His brain was fatigued and sluggish now, with the release of tension, and planned dimly what he would do next. Plain Creek was nearby, or he thought it was, and he had to have water soon. The leather of his boots burned maddeningly and he felt blisters rising on the soles of his feet; but he did not mount the sorrel. If Cappy died in this desolation, Ames' remaining vestige of hope would die with him.

It seemed like an eternity before he saw the thin juniper-green line marking the beginnings of Plain Creek. But there was no gleam of water ahead. He reached the thick clump of juniper which grew over the stream and pushed his way through the branches. One look at the cracked earth told him all he needed to know. Plain Creek was dry until the autumn rains.

Exhausted, Ames slumped to the ground. His shoulder ached with increasing fervor, and he felt he was nearing the end of his endurance. He followed the green line with his eyes back the way he had come until it disappeared and the blue basalt rocks began, and he had a difficult time keeping the line in focus. Heat waves danced in front of him, and fire spilled down from the brilliant blue of the sky. A slight breeze from the south blew dust unceasingly.

Mechanically, Ames led Cappy toward a

dimly-remembered water hole which lay some three miles ahead. His body ached terribly as he moved, the trail almost an unseen blur before his eyes. The sun had just begun to drop behind the rim of the horizon when he trod through a thick strain of sallow brown grass and a sparse stand of cottonwoods, and saw the water hole.

It was dry.

Ames sank to his knees, his brain whirling. Thirst was a terrible, agonizing way to die. If only he had a few drops of water. Suddenly, the memory of another dried water hole made its way into Ames' heat-fogged mind. He still had one slim chance. With some special reserve of energy he crawled to the middle of the sun-baked area and began scooping at the sand with cupped hands.

There was always water buried somewhere beneath the surface of a dry hole such as this.

The meager shade of the cottonwoods blotted out some of the rays of the setting sun, but still Ames had to rest many times in his labor. At long last, the sand became slightly damp, and with renewed hope he worked more rapidly. Some two feet down, the first sweet-smelling wetness began to seep through.

Cappy nosed nearer, the scent of water overwhelming in the animal's nostrils. Ames pushed him away gently and continued to scoop until there was a small, dark puddle collected at the bottom.

Ames sank back, then, letting the sorrel drink first. Then he widened the hole and leaned forward, his parched lips touching the cool, sustaining liquid.

But before he could drink more than a few scant drops, the fatigue and the throbbing pain in his shoulder combined to send waves of empty blackness through him, and he lapsed into a deep yet somehow welcome unconsciousness.

5

AMES became aware of a swaying, jouncing motion which amplified the pain in his wounded shoulder, but in his numbed state of shock he was unable to fully orient himself. Instead, he had the oddly detached feeling of being in a dream, and the people and places of his troubled past washed over his fevered brain like disembodied fragments.

For an instant the problem of Crow Grieve flashed vividly before him only to be replaced by the searing portrait of Esther Halstead. The picture of the beautiful girl lingered longer than the others and was joined by the outline of her father and brother, for that portion of Ames' life was an important one. He had saved Fred Halstead's ranch in Troublesome, and in return was made part owner and later became engaged to Esther.

Shortly before their marriage, however, an ambusher's bullet meant for Ames had cut

271

Esther down in the streets of Yampa, and she had died in his arms. It had been a sharp, agonizing climax in Ames' search for happiness, and now, involuntarily, a moan escaped from the cowboy's lips.

His mind continued to drift, all the way back to his beginnings into Tonto Basin, where as Rich Ames he had avenged his twin sister Nesta's seduction. He had killed the man responsible, the town's crooked sheriff, and had maimed the man's nephew. From then on, he had been a hunted man, an outcast from his family and friends. Only fourteen years later, when Nesta wrote of misfortune and he returned to his birthplace to help, did Ames succeed in clearing his name.

As an Arizona Ranger, he ended the gun trouble in Tonto Basin, saved his brother-in-law Sam Playford from the clutches of the amoral Slade Gorton, and met and briefly loved the daughter of the man he had originally maimed.

But the years of nomadic wandering were too strong within him; he soon felt restless and uncomfortable, and was forced, heavy-hearted, to admit that he was not cut out for settled life. He had left the star of the ranger, and Miss Anna Belle Tate, and with the money of his share of the Halstead ranch, once again rode alone.

Truly, Ames personified the West, for he was a product of its wild and untamed spirit, a man who could not fit a tamer role and would be hard put to survive in one, loving lustily the land which sustained him. The traits which were embodied in other cowboys were distilled to the purest essence in this man, for not only could he ride, shoot, and lasso remarkably; he had as well a largeness of spirit which made him unique.

But trouble followed him relentlessly, everywhere he went, and Phileaux River had been no exception.

Suddenly, the swaying motion sent a sharp jolt of pain stabbing through Ames. He managed to open his eyes, and after a moment the dream-like images faded and his vision was clear. He lay looking up at the dark night sky. The moon was rich and golden, drifting higher and giving off a soft, pale light. His ears caught the familiar clatter of a wagon or buckboard, traveling an uneven trail; his head was pillowed by a bedroll and his lower body was draped in a heavy woolen blanket. He blinked several times, turning his

273

head. The short wooden sides of a well-used buckboard were visible then.

He put the palms of his work-roughened hands flat on the gapped boarding of the buckboard's floor and raised himself slowly and painfully into a sitting position. He saw Cappy then, tethered to the rear of the wagon, trotting along behind. The animal's head seemed to jerk with relief to see Ames sitting up.

Ames twisted his tall body to peer upward at the raised seat of the buckboard. A solitary figure sat there, dressed in a plaid shirt and denim trousers, wearing a large hat cinched tightly by a rawhide drawstring under the chin. The individual was leaning tensely forward, holding the reins easily in one gloved hand, urging a roan mare silently forward. On the wooden seat by the figure sat a Spencer seven-shot carbine.

Ames ran a thick, cottony tongue over the roof of his mouth. He had no idea who the man driving the buckboard was. Could he be the law? No, if that were the case, the others in the posse would have been along—at least the sheriff and one other to act as deputy. Then who? And where was the man taking him? He could not recognize the surrounding terrain in the darkness.

If the man were a neighborly citizen who had happened by the water hole, discovered Ames unconscious there, and, seeing the bullet wound, decided to take him into Phileaux River or Sawyer for medical attention, then Ames had to get away before it was too late. He knew what would happen if he allowed himself to be taken back to Phileaux River, and word of the murder of Danny would have long since reached Sawyer.

Ames let his good right hand slide down to touch the black carved leather of his cartridge belt, across the silver buckle, and come to rest on the holster ornamented with a large silver "A." His fingers closed over the unfamiliar butt of a .44 which was not his.

He smiled humorlessly in the blackness; the fellow was in for a surprise, and although Ames disliked treating in this way a man who was apparently attempting to help him, he knew that it was the only thing he could do under the circumstances.

Arizona Ames lifted himself into a kneeling position, at the same time silently drawing the .44 from his holster. He eased the hammer back slowly, and then leaned over the back of the seat and pressed the muzzle gently but firmly into the man's back.

"Slow that mare down, mister," he called over the rattling of the rig. "Nice and easy-like."

The man stiffened and began to turn. Ames applied a slight pressure with the .44. "Just keep your eyes held frontways," he said.

The man pulled back on the reins, bringing the mare up sharply. When they were standing silent on the trail, Ames said, "Reckon I'm sorry for doing this, mister, but there just isn't any other way. Now suppose—"

Ames stopped abruptly, his eyes widening, for in that moment the driver of the buckboard turned, lifting one hand slowly to sweep back the hat.

It was not a man at all.

It was a woman, a pretty, light-haired woman with a pale face and dark eyes who stared at Arizona Ames levelly, showing no sign of fear at the gun which was being held against her spine. She appeared strong and capable, and Ames did not wonder at her being able to lift him into the buckboard, as she apparently had done.

"You won't need that gun, mister," she said coldly.

Ames lowered the .44.

"You need attention," the woman said. She turned around, ignoring Ames, and clucked the roan into a walk. "Lie back down. Put the blanket over you, or you'll get a chill to the bones."

Ames had never had a woman speak to him that way. As amazed at himself as he was at her, he did as she told him to, sinking weakly against the buckboard's side. Neither of them spoke.

They rode along for more than half an hour. Ames finally asked, "Begging your pardon, ma'am, but this isn't exactly country for a lady. What might you be doing up in these hills?"

She did not reply at once. Then she answered in a bitter voice, "Lookin'. Just lookin'."

"For what?"

"Doesn't matter, mister."

Ames did not try to pursue the matter. As curious as he was, he had been around women enough to know better than to press them. He said only, "I want to thank you, ma'am."

"Least I can do, considering it was my own son who shot you."

That statement caught Ames completely off guard. "I don't understand, ma'am," he said.

"I—I never thought I'd see the day when my own flesh blood would bushwhack anybody. Please try to—" She ended in a short, tearful sob.

Ames understood the woman's terseness now; her cold approach had been only a cover for the distress she must have bottled within her. Yes, she was a strong woman, but one driven to despair.

"Ma'am," he said quietly, "Your son didn't shoot me."

"No? He vowed vengeance, young as he is, and I've been trying to find him ever since he ran off. And I know he came this way. Oh, my God, I don't want both my men to die!"

Ames could not reply. The woman had not been too clear, and she was fighting with herself to keep from breaking down. It was an internal battle, one he was unable to assist with. At last the women straightened up and cleared her throat.

"I'm sorry," she said haltingly.

"It's all right, ma'am," Ames said. "I understand."

"But you don't. You see, my husband died two weeks ago in Sawyer. He—He was shot down in the street. Robbie, my son, swore to get the man responsible. I tried to turn him away from the idea, but he wouldn't listen. He took my husband's holster and gun and strapped it on the afternoon they brought Tom's body home. He practiced every chance he got. I could hear him, but there was nothing I could do. Every shot tore me apart inside."

"Easy there," Ames comforted. "I'm sure your son thought he was doing right. He must have loved his father a lot."

"Yes, he did. He left early this evening. Just packed up his saddlebags and rode his pinto off before sunset. I—I've been searching for him ever since. That's how I chanced on you at the water hole."

They rode on in silence for a while. The country evened out, turned once again into the plains, only on a somewhat higher elevation, and sparse grass appeared, waving gently in the night wind.

Ames knew there were many small ranchers and cattlemen who lived out here, in between the towns of Phileaux River and Sawyer. Their crops and herds were watered by the many streams coming out of the buttes and out of the Doubleday range farther north. Life was day-to-day, and one was thankful just to see sunset with a full stomach.

Arizona Ames studied the woman for a third time. It took strong women to stand next to their men, and the Spartan life eroded and dissipated their looks and charm almost before they had fully bloomed. He pictured the pretty features of the woman when he had faced her. She was one of the few who had withstood the erosion, and that made her special somehow.

"I really thought Robbie had shot you," the woman said suddenly. "For a minute I was sure you were dead."

"If it hadn't been for you, I reckon I would be." Ames settled against the side of the buckboard, moving so as to ease the pain of his shoulder. He noticed she had put a crude bandage around his wound. He fingered the material.

"You needn't have used your petticoat," he said.

"I never wear it anyway," she said ruefully. "Not out here. It was under the seat; Lord knows how it got there. I'll clean the wound when we reach the ranch. It's not too serious, but you lost a lot of blood."

Again the silence set in. A stiff breeze rose on the heels of the south wind, and Ames draped the blanket over him. The woman rested her elbows on her knees and urged the roan on.

They arrived at the ranch. It was pitch-black as they rode through a split-rail fence gate and along a dusty path of a weatherbeaten wood-and-adobe ranch house. It was too dark for Ames to observe much, save for a spreading cottonwood in the front yard, but he could determine that the ranch was small and poor. The woman stopped the buckboard in front of the door and offered to help him out of the wagon, but Ames refused.

"It's all right, ma'am," he said. "I can manage just fine."

"Just like a man," she said, smiling thinly. She had a very pretty smile, Ames thought. "Obstinate as the dickens." She helped him anyway, putting a hand to his good arm. "By the way, my name is Virginia. Virginia Sands."

"I'm Ames," he said to her.

"Ames? Just Ames?"

"Some call me Arizona, because that's where I'm from."

"Arizona it'll be," Virginia said.

They went into the dwelling. Ames could hear the wind whistle through the chinks in the wood siding, even before he was able to see anything in the darkness. Virginia struck a match and raised the glass of a kerosene lantern which was hanging by a nail next to the door. She lit the wick and snuffed on the match, turning as she did to smile charmingly at him.

He was struck by her beauty. She had seemed a pretty creature when he glimpsed her face in the buckboard, but now, illuminated by the soft, rosy glow of the lantern, Ames was drawn to her. Virginia was not too tall, but she was slim with a well-curved shape. Her clothes did not hide her womanliness, even though she wore a loose man's outfit. Her face was haloed by rich, gold hair that hung in ringlets about her shoulders. The naturally wavy blondness accentuated her large brown eyes, which looked at Ames brightly. They were wonderfully bold, Ames thought to himself; this woman was not afraid to look any man square in the eyes.

Ames glanced about the room then. It was sparsely furnished, though neat and well-scrubbed; chintz curtains over the single window by the heavy door added a small hint of color to the somewhat cheerless interior, and there were stitched quotations from the Bible on the walls. A stone-and-mortar fireplace was at one end; the hearth was scorched from countless fires built and carefully tended throughout the night to ward off the freezing cold of the Dakota winters.

Virginia carried the kerosene lantern into the center of the room and placed it on a thick, oblong table ringed on three sides by homemade, square-backed chairs. She scraped one of the chairs back.

"Set here, Arizona," she said. "I'll fetch some water and bandages."

Ames obeyed. He watched her walk through a doorway into the cabin's only other room. She was a mighty fine-looking woman, he thought, and a mighty proud and durable one, too. With her man dead only three weeks, and her boy run off swearing vengeance, she was still able to show concern for the needs of a stranger. In spite of his own problems, Ames felt compassion for her and found himself hoping there were some way he could repay Virginia Sands.

She emerged from the other room after a time, carrying an earthenware bowl and several lengths of cloth stripping. She laid the bandages on the table and favored him with a small smile.

"I'll just bring some water in from the pump," she said.

She went outside, and Ames suddenly felt the need for a smoke. With his good hand, he lifted the sack of tobacco and the wheatstraw papers from his shirt pocket. Holding the sack in his teeth by its drawstring, he spread the paper into a V with his thumb and forefinger.

But he had difficulty with his left hand—it had almost no feeling now—and he could not seem to get the sack open. He was fumbling with it when Virginia returned, the earthenware bowl filled with cool spring water.

"Here, now," the brown-eyed woman said sternly, putting the bowl on the table next to the bandages, "let me do that for you."

Arizona Ames smiled wanly. "Thanks ma'am."

She opened the pouch and tapped tobacco

from it evenly into the V'd wheatstraw. Ames rolled it deftly into a cylinder, licked the edge, and placed it between his lips. Virginia struck a wooden match and applied flame to it.

Ames pulled smoke into his lungs, closing his eyes. With a gentle sureness, as if she had been tending to bullet wounds all her life, Virginia opened his shirt, removed the petticoat bandage, and began to clean the caked blood around the wound with one of the strips of cloth daubed in water. Ames' blue eyes did not flicker, and if he felt any pain or discomfort from the probing, gentle though it was, he showed no visible signs of it.

As she worked, Virginia seemed to find the need to unburden herself to Ames. She began talking about her husband, Tom Sands. He was, she said, a kind and tender-hearted man who had worked from daybreak to sunset to provide a good home and a comfortable exist-ence for his family. They had started with a dozen white-faced Herefords he had bought with a loan from the Cattleman's Bank in Deadwood, and had built them into a modest-sized, well-paying herd over the years.

Then, five winters ago, all but twenty head

had perished in a prolonged blizzard. Since that time, they had had a run of unbroken hard luck which resulted, finally, in their being left nearly penniless. The cattle were all but gone, and they were forced to depend on the two dollars a week their son, Robbie—a strapping, headstrong lad of fifteen—was bringing home from his job in Taggert's General Store in Sawyer.

Tom Sands had been inordinately proud, however, and he had not been able to accept for long what he called "charity from flesh and blood," even though Robbie insisted upon helping out until his father was able to make the ranch pay off again. Sands decided to ride into Sawyer for supplies and to attempt to promote a loan towards the purchase of more Herefords.

He had never come back.

"Sheriff Dodds told me what happened when he rode out that night," Virginia said. Her lower lip trembled, and Ames felt his heart go out to her. "Mr. Proctor, at the Sawyer Bank, refused to give Tom the loan. He—he must have been desperate then. I suppose that's why he took up with the gamblin' men."

"Gambling men?" Ames asked sharply.

"Yes." Virginia finished applying the fresh bandage and rose wearily. She went to the hearth, where she built a small fire from a stack of kindling wood there. She laid a blackened coffee pot over the embers. "Sheriff Dodds said they were part of a travelin' wagon that came through, full of things to buy. Tom and some other men got into a game with them."

"What sort of game?"

"Sheriff Dodds didn't say."

Ames thought for a moment. "Three-card monte, I reckon. Your husband caught them cheating, likely."

"That's what Sheriff Dodds suspected," Virginia said. "But he had no proof. Everything happened so fast he said, that nobody was able to tell exactly what it was all about. All he knew was that a man named Jersey Jack had shot Tom. The man claimed self-defense, and Sheriff Dodds had to accept his word."

Ames' lips drew into a thin, bloodless line. The sinewy features of his face set into a granite hardness, and his eyes blazed with an inner fury. Virgnia stared at him.

"What is it, Arizona?" she asked.

"That same bunch was in Phileaux River,"

Ames said softly, as if talking to himself. "This fellow Jersey Jack is their leader. They were taking the lifeblood of other honest men the same way they did to your husband and plenty of men before him. I stepped in to put a stop to it."

Virginia moistened her lips. "Is—is that how you were shot?"

"In a way," Ames said laconically. He had already said too much.

Virginia leaned toward him. "Please," she said. "Please tell me what happened."

Arizona Ames was a strong and silent man, as reticent as the country through which he drifted. He looked into Virginia's soft brown eyes. He felt he could trust her, was sure she would not think any less of him, but nonetheless he hesitated. She might not take the account well, and he would not want her any more upset than she was.

"Please," she said again, touching his arm timidly.

"Can I have some of that coffee?" Ames asked, looking toward the hearth. He was still debating the advisability of confiding in her.

She hastened to the hearth and removed the coffee pot. She poured some of the steaming black liquid into a tin mug and brought it to him, saying in a low voice, "This was Tom's cup. I hope you don't mind."

"It's an honor, ma'am," Ames said. He wrapped his large hand around the mug and lifted it, tasting the coffee gratefully. He had reached his decision. "Reckon you have a right to know what went on, seeing that your husband died because of those sidewinders."

He began to tell her what had happened in Phileaux River.

6

AMES leaned back in the hard, straight-backed chair and closed his eyes wearily. The recounting of what had happened left him feeling drained, and a welcome lethargy began to flow through his body; he needed rest, needed it desperately.

Virginia realizing this, did not press him with questions. She said only, "Come along now, Arizona. You'll sleep in my bed tonight."

"Mighty nice of you, ma'am, but I reckon just a blanket and the floor'll do fine."

"Nonsense. I'll take Robbie's cot out here."

Ames was too exhausted to protest further, and he allowed himself to be led into the other room. He sat on the soft mattress of an iron-framed bed, while Virginia removed his cowhide boots and shirt.

Gently she eased him back until his head lay cradled in the cool softness of a feather pillow. Then she covered him with a patchwork quilt and stood looking down at him for a long moment before moving silently out of the room. Ames was asleep almost instantly.

He awoke to the smell of coffee and food cooking, and raised himself into a sitting position on the bed, rubbing sleep from his eyes with one huge hand. The pain in his shoulder was almost gone, he noticed, though the area around the wound was still numb; his left arm, he knew, would be useless for some time.

He swung his feet down and managed to pull on his boots with his right hand. He stood and found that a fresh shirt—probably one belonging to Tom Sands—had been laid out for him. He put it on and then walked into the other room, feeling a little weak but otherwise able enough.

Sunlight slanted in past the chintz curtains, and Ames saw that the sun was starting a slow descent toward the west. It was mid-afternoon now; he had slept for more than twelve hours.

Virginia was at the hearth, stirring a large kettle suspended on an iron bar over a low fire. He saw with some surprise that she was wearing an old but clean calico dress and that

291

her golden hair was pulled to the back of her neck and fastened with a bright blue ribbon. She looked up at the sound of his boots on the wooden floor and smiled warmly.

"How do you feel, Arizona?" she asked with no little concern.

"Considerably better than last night, ma'am," he answered wanly. He seated himself at the oblong table.

"Hungry?"

"Reckon I could use some food, right enough. Smells mighty good."

The brown-eyed woman blushed prettily at the compliment. "Nothing but some rabbit stew," she said. "Robbie shot a couple of jackrabbits before he—" She broke off, the smile disappearing; a frightened look took its place.

Virginia filled a hammered tin dish with thick, steaming stew from the kettle and set it before him. He ate slowly, so as not to make himself ill; it had been over thirty-six hours since Ames had last eaten, and his stomach ached from the lack of food.

Virginia watched him, her pretty face grave now. When he had finished eating, she poured him coffee. She waited until he had rolled a cigarette and lighted it before she

292

said, "What will you do when you're well enough to ride, Arizona?"

He exhaled a thin cloud of smoke. "Reckon I'm well enough to ride right now," he said.

"Oh, no!" Virginia put a hand on his arm, and then blushed again and removed it quickly. "You're still too weak!"

"Can't afford to stay here, ma'am," Ames said, sipping some of the coffee. "The sheriff isn't going to give up searching for me. He'll have men combing this entire area, and it sure wouldn't do if he found me here with you."

"But if you try to ride out, you might be seen."

"I'll have to take that chance, ma'am. Jersey Jack and his boys are getting farther away by the minute, and I can't find them if I'm in jail."

"You're going after the Dollar Wagon, then?"

Ames nodded. "I have to," he said. "I have plenty to settle with them. It's the only way I can clear myself. Besides, there's what they did to that boy Danny." He met her soft brown eyes. "And what they did to your husband Tom."

"Then if you're determined to leave, I

want to go with you. I can help you."

Ames was startled. "Running down side-winders isn't a fit chore for a woman," he said quietly.

Her jaw firmed resolutely. "Arizona, my boy Robbie has gone after the Dollar Wagon. I told you that. I don't want anything to—to happen to him. He's all I have left now."

Ames patted her hand. "Don't you worry about your boy, ma'am. Nothing's going to happen to him."

But Ames was remembering what had happened to another young boy behind the Phileaux River Livery Stable when he tried to go up against Jersey Jack Kelson. If Robbie Sands had already found the Dollar Wagon . . . Ames did not put voice to his fears; there was no need in frightening her even more than she was.

"Arizona, please take me with you," Virginia said plaintively. "It—it might be days before you find them. You won't be able to go into any town for supplies for fear of being recognized. I can. And I can ask about the Dollar Wagon, maybe find out where it is."

Ames shook his head. "I don't think it'll take long, ma'am," he said. "They were in

Sawyer before they came to Phileaux River, which means they're moving south toward Iron Flats. That's no more than a two-day ride, and if I push a little I catch up to them before they get there. They can't travel too fast in that wagon."

Virginia moistened her full lips. "What will you do then? Will you kill Jersey Jack?"

"I don't rightly know," Ames said. "Reckon I'll have to take him alive, if I want to clear my name in Phileaux River."

"Then you'll need help. You'll need *me*."

"There isn't anything I could let you do, ma'am," Ames said. "I can handle what has to be done."

Virginia stood up and went to the single window. She stood there with her arms folded, staring out at the vastness beyond. "I'm going with you, Arizona," she said slowly, flatly. "I'm going, and that's all there is to it. You can't stop me short of tying me to a chair."

"I wouldn't want to do that, ma'am," Ames said. "But if I have to, then I will."

She turned, her eyes meeting his levelly. "Will you? Suppose no one comes by for a week or more? We seldom get visitors out here, you know. Would you want me to starve to death, Arizona?"

"No, ma'am, but somehow I think you'd manage."

"I'll manage just as well with you, Arizona. I won't be in the way."

"The ranch—"

"I left once to look for Robbie, and I will again, even if you won't let me come with you. I'll just follow you."

Ames studied her, knowing it was useless to argue further. "All right," he said slowly. "Pack what you'll need."

She seemed to find it necessary to reassure him. "I'm a good rider, Arizona. Don't worry about that. I grew up in this country."

Ames only nodded.

Within twenty minutes the young widow was ready. She had changed into the man's outfit of the previous night and had packed two bedrolls and some food. Ames helped her take everything outside and tie it on the roan's flank. The buckboard, Ames noted, had been placed alongside the small lean-to where Cappy had been bedded.

Ames walked over to the sorrel after the saddlebags were in place and Virginia had gone back for her Spencer carbine. Cappy was rested and, much to Ames' surprise, curried and rubbed down. The animal's coat glistened in the sun, and he looked as though he had never traversed the miles of plains the day before.

"Thanks, ma'am, for seeing to Cappy last night," he said to Virginia when she returned.

She fastened the long scabbard onto the saddle and swung up onto the roan. "He's a fine animal, Arizona. It was a pleasure."

Ames, impressed, could do nothing more than nod as he mounted Cappy. Together, they rode out of the ranch yard and down the dusty road.

7

AMES and the widow Sands did not head back toward Phileaux River. Figuring that Jersey Jack Kelson and his men would have headed south to Iron Flats, they cut diagonally across the Dakota hills, hoping to make up lost time that way.

To an outlander, the hills were cold and foreboding; but to Ames who had ridden the area before, they were full of rough but negotiable trails. Virginia proved to be helpful, for having lived there, she had a keen and experienced eye which picked out the quickest routes. And, just as importantly, she knew what lay on the other side of the rugged and towering hills. Ames decided that he would have wasted much time if she had not come.

The barren buttes dotted the landscape, contrasting with the level plains which the two of them rode during the afternoon. Occasionally they would dip into a sheltering valley or through tall, screening trees, and the change was refreshing. From the scorched earth they would enter lush, brilliantly green grass jeweled with little clusters of wild flowers that ran a rainbow of colors.

In spite of the urgency of their mission, of their single-mindedness of purpose, Ames and the woman stopped along about four in the afternoon and let the horses graze and drink at a small spring in just such a copse.

Virginia removed her hat and tossed her hair. Again Ames was caught by its brilliance. She flashed a smile at him, and he could not help but be thankful she had insisted on accompanying him. They walked down to the spring, which was in the shadow of a large cottonwood. Ames saw little tracks of small plains animals around the water hole, as well as the larger prints of coyotes and occasional bison.

Kneeling, Ames filled a battered tin cup with the sparkling liquid and handed it to Virginia. Virginia thanked him and took the cup. She sat on a flat rock near him and, bringing her legs up almost to her chin, watched the lean, weathered man as he stooped and drank the water directly.

"You've barely been sipping the water,

ma'am," he said to her as he joined her on the rock. "By the looks of things, this spring is the only one around these parts. I'd not be dainty about drinking all I could."

"We have the canteens."

Ames nodded but said, "For some reason folks think you should save water, only wet your lips with it or take a few swallows. The Sioux know better. Saturate yourself with it, and you'll keep your strength up."

Virginia's mouth perked into a smile. "If you say so," she said and finished the cup. Ames took it and refilled it for her from the pool."

"There you are, ma'am."

"The name is Virginia. If I can call you Arizona, the least you can do is return the favor."

"Thanks, ma'am," Ames said. "I mean Virginia."

She laughed, stretching her arms over her head. Then she sobered. "Don't you think we'd better be going, Arizona?"

"Reckon so."

They walked back to the horses, the woman stopping quickly to pick some goldenrod and a small cluster of iris and violets. She handed them to Ames and said simply, "Haven't they the sweetest smell?"

"Perfume," he replied.

The next hours of riding proved how wise they had been to rest. From the comfortable coolness of the cottonwoods, the terrain began to slope upward, and stone and shale were strewn around as if thrown indiscriminately by some giant hand. The trail wound between huge, sun-bleached boulders and sun-hardened parched earth and patches of grama grass. Hawks circled lazily in the late afternoon sky, and black and white magpies chattered occasionally. Now and then a sharp-tailed grouse or a prairie chicken scurried across their path.

They were plodding up a short, stony pass when Virginia's roan suddenly came to a halt. No coaxing by the woman could persuade the animal to move, and he attempted to wheel around twice.

"What's the matter, Arizona?" Virginia asked.

"Snakes, I reckon," Ames said. "Cappy here is a little skittish, too, and that's usually a sign he's caught wind of a nest of them."

Ames dismounted, and taking the reins

from Virginia, he walked the roan through the area. The roan pranced, tossing his head, but followed. After approximately five minutes afoot, Ames handed the reins back to Virginia and remounted Cappy, and they continued.

Ames did not like to travel after dark. Once the sun set, the plains were shrouded in absolute black, and the horses were forced to test almost each step for fear of falling into unseen prairie dog holes or slipping on the rough ground. Luckily, there was a full moon again tonight, and the last few miles were traversed slowly but safely by the pale, reflected light.

They were nearing the Phileaux River now, about halfway between the town of the river's name and Iron Flats. Chances were that Jersey Jack Kelson and the Dollar Wagon were still ahead of them, but not by far.

They reached the wheel-rutted main road and turned south. Inside of half an hour, they came upon the Phileaux River. It was wide and flat, but since this was summer the expanse of water was considerably narrower than it would be when the rains came and melting snow flowed down to feed it from the mountains. The pale moonlight reflected thin silver images along its muddy surface.

On both banks were swamp-like areas of thick mud, which made an attempted crossing extremely dangerous, if not altogether impossible. A grove of willows grew on the far bank, and where Ames and Virginia reined in their horses after leaving the main road, clumps of juniper and an occasional black raspberry bush dotted the landscape. The sound of crickets and buzzing mosquitoes filled the night air.

Ames surveyed the river for a moment, and then said to Virginia, "We'll bed down here for the night. The way I see it, Jersey Jack and the Dollar Wagon can't be more than an hour's ride ahead of us, and it's likely they'd have put up until morning somewhere along the river. I'll scout along a way and see if I can locate them."

"And if you do?"

Ames smiled grimly. "Jersey Jack and I might have a little set-to."

Virginia bit her lip. "You—you be careful. Please, Arizona."

"Don't you worry."

"Can't I come with you? I don't want to stay here alone."

"You'll be safe enough," Ames said.

"We'll build a little fire; that'll keep the coyotes at a distance."

Ames thought for a moment that she was going to argue with him, as she had back at the ranch. But she only sighed very softly and swung down from the roan and began to untie the bedrolls and saddlebags from the animal's flanks. Ames dismounted and went in search of wood. He collected an armload of dry branches, and in the shelter of a lone cottonwood nearby, built a small fire.

Virginia spread out both bedrolls, side by side, on the soft ground, and then sat cross-legged on one and began to remove a skillet and tin dishes and food from the saddlebags.

Ames said, "I don't reckon I'll have time to eat anything now. But you go on."

"You have to take something," Virginia told him. She produced hardtack and a slab of peppered deer jerky from the saddlebags. "You can eat this while you ride."

He accepted the food, studying her by the flickering orange-yellow light of the fire. She appeared no more than a young girl, fresh and beautiful, her sweet lips curved into a small, weary smile. Ames felt a catch in his throat; seldom had a woman affected him this way; seldom had he allowed his mind to give rise to the tender thoughts which now flooded his brain.

He wanted nothing more than to sit beside her there in front of the fire, to put his strong arm about her slim shoulders, to comfort her and listen to the sound of her soft voice like the whisper of the gentle summer breeze.

But he knew that he could not. Jersey Jack Kelson was somewhere ahead of them, and the business Ames had with the murderous con man was festering like a raw wound inside him. And there was no time, no room, for other things while that wound still existed there.

He stood abruptly. "I'll be back shortly, Virginia," he said and was surprised at how easily he had used her given name. "No more than a couple hours, probably."

Quickly he went to where Cappy waited. He climbed into the saddle, and without looking back urged the sorrel forward, across the short expanse of grassland and once again onto the main road.

Arizona Ames rode for more than half an hour, nibbling at the hardtack and jerky, his eyes following the twisting line of the Phileaux River. He saw nothing in that time—no sign of the Dollar Wagon, no other riders along the rutted road.

When the road rose sharply upward to wind along the crests of a series of low bluffs paralleling the river, Ames had just about decided that he had misjudged Jersey Jack's nearness. He would ride only a short way farther, he thought, and then he would return to where Virginia waited at the camp. It would not do to leave her alone too long.

It was then that he saw the wisps of smoke creeping skyward from a section of the river hidden by the bluffs.

He jerked back on the reins, bringing Cappy up short. Lifting his lean body in the saddle, he stared in that direction; he had not been mistaken. He guided the sorrel off the road and across rough, bare ground toward the edge of the bluffs. When he had neared it, he dismounted, dropping Cappy's reins, and stroked the sorrel's forehead to keep him quiet. Then he crept forward to the edge of the bluff, dropping prone, and peered down a somewhat steep slope to the river.

The Dollar Wagon was there, pulled off a secondary trail that would have, he thought, its beginnings somewhere farther along the main road. A large, blazing campfire had been built before the wagon, and four men lay sleeping around it. The river, with its bordering mud flats, was beyond the wagon and the men's unsaddled horses grouped near it.

Ames moistened his lips, shifting his position on the rough ground. Four men. If he recollected correctly, there had been five altogether at the Dollar Wagon in the town of Phileaux River. That meant that one of them was either sleeping inside the wagon or was standing guard, hidden from his view.

Ames debated. He did not think they would have posted a sentry; what reason would have had for doing that? They were not expecting any trouble, any night visitors, and Jersey Jack would have figured the killing in Phileaux River to have landed Ames in the lock-up. No, he decided, one of them was inside the wagon, all right. And that one could only be Jersey Jack.

Ames knew he was going down there, despite the danger, despite the odds. If he could get Jersey Jack back to Phileaux River, he could clear himself of the charge of murder. It was a risk he had to take. If he died, then, it would not be unjustly at the end of a hangman's noose.

The slope, Ames saw, was grown heavily with sagebrush and wild blackberry and gooseberry bushes. It would afford him all the cover he would need to make it down to the secondary road, as long as he moved stealthily. Once he made it there, he would be vulnerable if any of the sleeping men roused—there was no cover between the road and the wagon, some thirty yards—but if he were again stealthy he would be able to reach the wagon undetected.

His hand went to the still unfamiliar .44 in his holster, loosening the thong. Then Arizona Ames rose up and slipped over the edge of the bluff and began to make his way down the slope.

Thorns from the gooseberry bushes scratched his hands and face, but Ames took no notice of the stinging pain. His eyes were watchful, and he made sure each step was silent. It took him a long time to reach the bottom of the slope, but when he did, none of the sleeping men had wakened. Ames was about to try crossing the road when a few small rocks came clattering down a nearby slope.

A coyote or possibly a mule deer come to

nibble the berries had dislodged some shale likely. Instinctively Ames pressed into the niche of rock, letting the shadows hide him. There was the chance that one of the men would hear the sound.

There came a rustling of brush high atop the neighboring cliff as the animal which had started the noise moved away. Then the crackling fire and an occasional groan as one of the men stirred were the only sounds. Ames waited longer. A screech owl made its peculiar call in the distance. A horse neighed.

Still Ames waited; he had the feeling all was not right. Too many years, too many close experiences had taught him the lessons of caution. The trapper reflex made him freeze in the dark niche in which he stood, and the hunter instinct warned him he would not make the thirty yards of space alive.

Ten, fifteen minutes passed. Then Ames heard the first slight sound. He recognized it as the shuffle of boots. He eased the .44 out of the holster and held it up beside his face, still making not the slightest movement which would give away his place of concealment. The walking came closer, and Ames heard the heavy breathing of the man long before he saw him.

Jersey Jack was more cautious than Ames had first surmised. Even though he had no reason to post a guard, nonetheless he had.

Ames decided that the guard had heard the rocks and had come slowly from his hiding place to investigate. If those rocks had not tumbled when they had, or if Ames had disregarded his instinct, he would have been lying dead in the trail by now.

The guard was never aware of the cowboy. The large, hulking man passed by the niche without a glance. Ames waited until the man had stepped past him, and then he brought the barrel of the .44 crashing down on the man's skull. The guard made no sound, falling to the ground like a discarded sack of corn meal, his rifle thrown to one side. Ames picked up the rifle, a new Winchester '70 and then crept across the trail.

Ames made his way closer to the fire, keeping in shadows. He reached the wagon. The four men were on its other side. He eased himself up onto the tailgate; the back was a canvas curtain, tied at either bottom corner and made to roll up like a window shade. He laid the rifle silently on the tailgate and went to work loosening the knot holding the canvas. After he had gotten one end

310

untied, he lifted the flap. Now he was sure that his recollection of five men was correct.

The Arizonan slid off the wagon and crept between its wheels. He studied the four prone figures, but the blankets effectively hid their face. He had no other choice than to go amongst them. Even more slowly than he had descended the slope, he edged closer to the men, every move exact.

As careful as he was, there was always the possibility one of them might awaken accidently. It was truc that he had the rifle and the .44 but there were four of them, and those were not good odds in any circumstances. And then there was the added responsibility of Virginia Sands.

No, Ames realized that his only chance was to take Kelson a prisoner without disturbing the other men and then ride out at full speed for Phileaux River. Then, in the morning when the men found Jersey Jack gone, there would be enough distance between them to make their flight successful.

Ames eased the hammer back as he approached the first sleeper. It was the monte dealer, snoring lustily. Ames stepped to the next, only to find that this was the shill who

311

had been wearing dun-colored chaps. The third man was Kelson. Ames smiled grimly and put the sixgun into his holster. Then he unwound his bandanna. He crawled up to the con man with it balled in his right hand.

Jersey Jack lay on his side, his head turned and his mouth open. He had a nasal sound as he breathed. Ames moved around so that Kelson's mouth was directly below him, and then he acted.

With swift, sure movements, he stuffed the dirty bandanna into the con man's mouth, at the same time unsheathing his hunting knife and holding it at Kelson's throat. Jersey Jack woke up, his eyes bulging, but he could not cry out with the cloth in his mouth. He felt the cold steel blade then, and realizing instantly what it was, lay back. His eyes narrowed like a snake's and glared at the man crouched over him.

Ames ran the blade lightly across Kelson's throat, not hard enough to draw blood, but hard enough to make the message clear. Ames wanted no sound.

He got Jersey Jack onto his feet and moved him away from the other three sleepers. Just outside the illuminating circle of fire Ames took Kelson's gun and realized it was his own, as he felt its familiar coolness. He put the other sixgun in his waistband and holstered his own weapon. He then prodded Kelson forward with the muzzle of the Winchester. Ames skirted the horses, not wanting to alarm them, and the two men started up the secondary trail.

The con man made a low, gurgling sound in his throat when they passed the unconscious guard. After they had gone another hundred yards, Ames took the handkerchief out of Jersey Jack Kelson's mouth.

"Make a noise, and it'll be your last, hombre," he warned.

"You're a fool," Kelson said in a low voice.

"You shouldn't of tried to frame me for the boy's murder in Phileaux River," Ames said.

"What are you planning to do?"

"Take you back and turn you over to the sheriff."

The con man snorted. "My men will get you before that. You're as good as dead, cowboy."

"We'll see who ends with his boots up first," Ames snapped back. "If you're smart, you won't cause me any trouble. There's nothing I'd like better than settling a few matters privately with you. Like murdering

Tom Sands in Sawyer a couple of weeks back."

"That was self-defense."

"It wasn't an equal fight, and you know it. Not between your gunslingers and a mild farmer like Sands. His widow is broken up over what you did, and I mean to see her happy again. Her and her son, Robbie." Ames felt his anger growing, and he jabbed the con man in the ribs again, starting him up the trail before he lost control of himself.

The trail joined the main road about two hundred yards ahead, up toward the bluff from where the rocks had tumbled earlier. Ames figured that in another hour he would have collected Cappy and returned to the camp for Virginia. Their horses would have to take turns carrying Kelson, but that should not slow them down too badly.

Just as they neared the top of the bluff, the bushes rustled and parted. A young boy jumped down to the trail, feet planted wide apart, eyes blazing. He held a long-barrelled Colt in one hand.

"Murderer!" he yelled at Jersey Jack. "Lowdown murderin' polecat!"

The sixgun spat flame.

8

THE night erupted in shattering echoes of sound. Reflexively Arizona Ames sent Jersey Jack sprawling to one side with a thrust of the Winchester, at the same time hurtling his own body forward, head low, legs driving on the irregular surface of the trail. One of the wild shots sang past his left ear; another kicked up a spray of dust near one boot.

It took Ames only a single second to cover the short distance between the boy and himself, and then his shoulder rammed into the youngster's legs just above the knees. The force of his rush knocked the boy down, and Ames landed on top of him, dropping the Winchester as he did. His right hand groped frantically, found the hot muzzle of the Colt, and wrenched it loose from the boy's grip. Ames rolled off him then, flinging the weapon into the surrounding brush. He came up onto his knees turning.

Jersey Jack Kelson had recovered and was hightailing it down the trail toward the safety of the wagon. Ames could still see the flickering light of the campfire from where he was; the remaining three men there were on their feet now, clustered together uncertainly. But they would not be uncertain for long. Ames could hear Jersey Jack yelling, shouting for them to fetch their rifles.

Cursing violently, Ames gained his feet. The boy was just struggling up, breathing heavily. Ames felt for the second .44; it had fallen from his waistband in the struggle. He picked up the Winchester and let the boy look into the yawning black bore. There was no time for talking now, no time for questions or explanations. It would only be a matter of moments before Kelson and his men came up the trail after them.

He said quickly, "Move, boy!"

The boy's face was sullen.

"I said, move fast, unless you want to get shot!" Ames grabbed the boy by the shirt collar and threw him up the trail.

The boy stumbled, then ran. He was a thin lad, and although not very tall, his legs were long. Ames had difficulty keeping stride with him.

The boy ran for a black mound of rocks near the entrance to the main road in whose shadow stood a small Indian pinto. Almost without hesitation, he mounted. Ames leaped behind him.

"Head up the road, boy," Ames directed. "And this pinto had best be fast."

"Fast enough," the boy replied. He dug his heels into the horse's ribs and swung the pony north.

Ames cast a quick look over his shoulder. He could see commotion around the campfire now, and the four men began to run up the trail. There was no time to spare, and Ames shouted that to the boy. The lad leaned into the pinto's mane and the animal stretched into a full gallop.

They reached the bluff where Cappy was, and Ames jumped off and ran to the sorrel. "Get going!" he yelled to the boy "I'll catch up!"

The boy nodded and spun the pinto around. Within minutes Ames had pulled Cappy astride the running horse. They rode hard for almost half an hour. Finally the two of them neared the spot along the river where Ames had left Virginia. Slowly, Ames eased

317

Cappy to a canter, watching to make sure the boy did the same with the pinto.

"You're Robbie Sands?" he asked then.

"How did you know?" came the astonished reply.

"Your ma told me what you were figuring to do," Ames said. "But damned if I had the notion you'd pull a fool stunt like you did back there."

"My ma?"

"That's right."

"How do you know my ma?"

"I reckon we'll talk about that, too."

"Who are you, mister?"

Ames told him, and then said, "Why'd you come out throwing lead like that?"

"Kelson murdered my pa," Robbie said. His jaw trembled. "He deserves to die."

"Maybe so," Ames answered laconically. "But it's not your place to do the killing."

"Whose place is it, then?"

"I figure it's the hangman's," Ames said.

Robbie did not say anything for a moment. They reached the point in the road where they would turn off, and Ames led them into the grasslands heading toward the river. Then Robbie said, "What were you doing with Kelson back there? I saw you sneakin'

318

down into their camp from where I was hidin' on that bluff."

"Kelson and I have business together," Ames said. "It might have been finished business if you hadn't come out with that sixgun."

"That was my pa's gun. You shouldn't of thrown it away."

"Your pa doesn't have any more use for it," Ames said harshly. "And I don't think you're going to be needing a shooting iron for a while, anyway."

The boy fell silent. After a time, they came in sight of the small fire Ames had built in the shelter of the cottonwood. At first there was no sign of the widow Sands, but as they brought their horses up and dismounted she came out from behind a clump of juniper cautiously, her slim hands competently levelling the Spencer carbine.

She recognized the small figure beside Ames immediately, and letting the rifle fall forgotten, she rushed toward them. "Robbie!" she cried. "Oh, Robbie!"

"Ma!"

Virginia gathered her son into her arms, hugging him. He pulled away finally, as if

319

being embraced by his mother was not befitting to his manliness. She stepped forward and put her arm about his shoulders, her eyes brimming with tears.

"Thank you, Arizona," she said haltingly. "Thank you for bringing Robbie back to me safely."

Ames felt embarrassment color his cheeks. "You can thank me when this business is over," he replied gruffly. "We're not out of trouble yet."

"What happened?" Virginia asked. "You didn't find Kelson, did you?"

"I found him, right enough," Ames answered. "I had him safe out of his camp when this boy of yours jumped out and began throwing lead."

"Robbie!" Virginia cried, her eyes growing wide.

"Lucky thing it was dark," Ames went on. "He didn't hit either one of us, but Kelson hightailed it back to the Dollar Wagon. You can wager he and his henchmen'll be out hunting us before long, and I don't want any of us to be here when he shows up."

"Ma, who is this man?" Robbie demanded of his mother. "Why is he here with you?"

"There's no time for explaining now,"

Ames said. "Your ma'll tell you about it when you get to your ranch." To Virginia he said, "You take Robbie and ride home, pronto. Cut cross-country."

"But what about you?"

"Don't you fret about me," Ames said. "I'll be along later."

"Arizona, you're not going after them alone!"

"No, he ain't," Robbie said stolidly. "I'm goin' with him."

"You're going with your ma, boy," Ames told him. "She's a brave woman, but she needs a man along riding in this country at night."

Robbie seemed to consider that statement for a moment, and then nodded quickly. Ames smiled grimly, and then helped the widow up into the roan's saddle.

She said, "I—I don't want you hurt, Arizona. Please be careful. Please."

Ames nodded curtly.

Her large brown eyes began to grow moist again, and Ames looked away to where the boy sat astride his pinto now. "You take care of your ma, Robbie, hear?"

"I will."

Ames nodded again, and then reached out

and slapped the roan's rump sharply. The animal snorted and leapt forward, Virginia's slim figure sitting proud and capable in the saddle. Robbie spurred the pinto after her, and Ames watched them galloping off across the grasslands toward the road.

Then, quickly, he gathered the bedrolls and saddlebags together and tied them on Cappy's flank. He paused for a moment to say a grim and silent prayer for the safe passage of Virginia and Robbie, and then he mounted the sorrel and took him into the heavy growth of juniper along the bank of the river.

Ames decided to forsake the main road, lest he meet up with Jersey Jack or his men on the way back to where the Dollar Wagon was camped. He reasoned that the con man's men would not search this far north and that they would likely stick to the main road in the darkness. He also reasoned that only one, or perhaps two, men would have been left to guard the Dollar Wagon. The last thing Kelson would expect would be that Ames would come back there, and he thought he would have the element of surprise in his favor once again. Maybe some lead would fly, but he would have to take that chance; there was too much at stake.

Depending on the amount of vegetation along the river bank, he cantered or walked Cappy for the better part of an hour. Once he frightened a large pronghorn antelope that had come down to drink at the river, and the animal made a good deal of noise escaping through the juniper. Another time, a small animal darted across Cappy's path, startling the sorrel and causing him to rear momentarily. But aside from these, Ames encountered no difficulty.

Finally, he rounded a sharp bend in the river and ahead of him saw the short bluffs which hid the Dollar Wagon encampment from the main road. The moon had retreated behind a low, rolling bank of clouds, and although he could not yet see the campfire, he knew it was not far ahead now.

He dismounted and led Cappy as quietly as he could through the underbrush. After five minutes of walking, he saw the glowing coals of the fire and the shadowed bulk of the wagon ahead of him. He wound the sorrel's reins around the decayed, moss-covered trunk of a felled cedar, and eased forward in a low, cautious crouch until he was within a hundred feet of the wagon. He stopped there, his body concealed behind a bush.

Peering through the thorny leaves, he could see a lone man seated before the fire, his profile visible in the thin light from the dying coals. The man was drinking from a tin cup. The dappled gray, still out of harness, was the only horse within sight; it was tethered to the front of the wagon.

Ames lifted his .44 from his holster. The others were still out searching, apparently. Although he was not sure, Ames thought the man was the guard he had knocked unconscious earlier.

He crept out from behind the gooseberry bush, circling around behind the man, carefully, quietly. He closed the gap between them to fifty feet, to twenty-five, to twenty. He reversed the .44 in his hand, but extended, and took another step.

His boot came down on a dry, brittle twig.

There was a sharp snapping sound, and the man whirled away from the fire at the sudden noise, coming up into a crouch, his hand instinctively drawing the sixgun at his side. Ames threw himself flat, rolling, trying to get the .44 reversed back again.

At almost point-blank range, the man by the fire squeezed off three shots in rapid succession.

9

AMES landed flat in the thin brush just as a bullet ripped along his shirt, opening the fabric across his back but not breaking the skin. He rolled again, onto soft ground. A second bullet came so close that it sprayed bits of dirt into Ames' face. blinding him momentarily. He got his finger on the trigger of the .44 finally and shot back automatically, fully aware that the next shot from the other man might tear through him like a hot arrow.

Ames could not see, his eyes watering violently from the kicked-up dirt. He heard a strange mixture of sounds, combining the ricocheting chink of metal against metal, another whistling shot, a clatter which made him think the man had dropped his gun, and finally a savage, high pitched yell. He tried to clear his eyes, to see if he had winged the man, but when he did he only had time to see a black looming figure leap at him from the wagon.

Ames' shot had hit the man's .44 probably rendering the gun useless, but had not wounded him. Ames rolled again, just as the man landed where he had been. Through his still blurred vision, he saw the glint of a Bowie knife.

It was one of the most deadly of hand weapons—horn-handled, with a curved, single-edged, foot-long blade—and Ames, a veteran of many fights with many weapons, had great respect for it. Compared to the knife, his gun was useless, for he wouldn't have time to bring it around and aim it before the man stabbed at him.

That was the evil beauty of the Bowie knife. Legend has it that the knife was named after James Bowie or his brother, invented by one of them shortly before Jim Bowie died at the Alamo in 1836. Whether true or not, the knife soon earned a reputation for itself in the West as a perfect combination of size and weight. It could slice, stab, skin, or be thrown with equal exactness. Long after guns were outlawed in the small cow towns, men carried the Bowie knife as a constant companion.

Ames' hunting knife was not much of a

weapon in comparison. He thought of it nonetheless. But he did not have enough time to unhook the leather thong holding it—the man lunged at him with a curse. Instantly, Ames kicked out with his hard leather heels and caught the man in the knees. The man staggered back. Ames brought his legs under him and sprang into a standing position just as the man attacked again.

Ames knocked the knife-wielding wrist away with his .44, but before he could bring the gun into play, the man fell against him. They both toppled to the ground, Ames on the bottom. He lost his breath as he struck the earth, and his hand inadvertently relaxed, the gun tumbling from his open fingers. The man shoved a forearm against Ames' throat to keep him down, then raised the knife high.

Ames, in one desperate attempt, twisted downward and brought his legs up in a somersault, locking his boots around the man's head. Then he jerked backwards, and the man fell off him. Ames scrambled to his feet, choking, his throat on fire from the arm which had held it.

The man scuttled away and kicked Ames' gun out of reach. Then he began circling Ames, waving the Bowie, waiting for a safe opening. Ames darted his hand for his hunting knife; the man thrust suddenly, narrowly missing Ames' fingers. But the slash had left him exposed for a second too long, and Ames threw himself on the man. They tumbled to the dirt again.

The man became limp beneath Ames and let out a small sigh much like a balloon losing air. Ames stood up. The man did not stir, staring wide-eyed at the stars overhead. A dark patch of liquid began to seep from beneath his body at the spot where his right hand was pinned. Ames could not see the knife. There was no need for him to—he knew where it was.

Ames looked down at the dead man for a moment, catching his breath. He had figured Jersey Jack correctly, but he did not get much satisfaction from the knowledge. It was not worth a man's life.

Kelson had a bigger ego than a brain. If he had been smarter, he would have remained at the Dollar Wagon after Ames' first, futile attack. Ames would have had to follow the wagon, then, hoping to catch the wary con man alone.

As it was, Ames had the opportunity he needed. There was no safer place to be than near the wagon while Kelson and his men were out scouring the hills. Even if he had been discovered, Virginia and her son would be a bit safer as they rode in the opposite direction. Most importantly, if the wagon was not guarded, or lightly guarded as it had turned out to be, Ames would be able to get inside it.

And Ames wanted to get inside the Dollar Wagon badly. He hoped he would find stolen money in there, money that belonged to many luckless victims, money that could possibly be returned. Also, Ames wanted to uncover evidence of other crimes, so that when he brought Kelson to the Sheriff of Phileaux River, the con man could not squirm his way loose. Lastly, Ames wanted to stop the crooked games once and for all. Five minutes inside the Dollar Wagon would be enough, he vowed, to destroy every piece of equipment.

Ames left the man where he lay, collected his gun nearby, and slowly walked to the wagon. He jumped up on the tailgate again, and for a second time untied the canvas back and rolled it up. By the waning light of the fire, he started to search.

The search was extensive and brutal. Ames cleared the few pots and pans away from wall hooks to get to the narrow cabinets behind. He found eighteen packs of cards, which he took outside and dumped in the fire. The added fuel caused the fire to blaze, helping the cowboy see more clearly. The monte board and a roll of felt which had a craps layout printed on it went into the fire next, and the dice were thrown into the bushes.

There were some grub-sacks of flour and rice, bacon, some dried fruit, and a box of salt which Ames left alone. He found no money, and he cursed Kelson silently, for the con man must have carried it with him. Jersey Jack had also been careful enough not to leave any incriminating evidence lying about, for Ames was only able to find a yellowed newspaper clipping about another Kelson (Jack's brother?) being hanged for horse thievery ten years before.

He found two breech-loading rifles and a couple of boxes of ammunition for them and the handguns. He took the boxes outside and scattered the bullets. He was in the wagon continuing his search, when he heard a horse galloping down the secondary trail.

Ames froze. He was in the shadows and

silently then he took his .44 from his holster and waited for the rider to halt.

The rider came up to the wagon, but stopped near the front, out of Ames' sight. "Jason?" a man called out. "Hey, Jason, where are you?"

Ames grunted as though in answer.

"What're you doin' in the wagon, Jason?" the man asked. Ames heard him urge the horse closer to the rear. "We got to move out. Jersey Jack's waitin' for us."

Ames grunted again. He trained the gun on the side of the wagon where he thought the man would be on the other side. The barrel swung in an arc as the horse moved slowly along the side, and then Ames saw the horse's nodding head and the man's loose grip on the reins as the rider came into his view.

Ames tensed as the man leaned forward in the saddle, peering into the darkness. It was the monte dealer. "Jason, damn you, come on out o' there. We got—"

The dealer broke off abruptly, for he apparently recognized the shadowed figure of Ames. His right hand dove for leather, his left jerking the reins to bring the horse—a big blood bay—around.

Ames had no choice; it was shoot or be

shot. He squeezed the .44's trigger, felt the recoil of the big Colt. The horse reared, tossing its head wildly, and the dealer flew out of the saddle. He hit the ground and pitched over on his side, shouting with pain.

Ames could not be sure if his bullet had driven the man off the animal, or if he had simply been thrown when the horse reared. He jumped down out of the wagon and approached the now writhing figure cautiously, his weapon extended in front of him. The dealer rolled over on his back, staring up at Ames with pain-clouded eyes. He was clutching his chest, high on the left side.

"You busted my shoulder," he said, grimacing.

"If you make a move toward that iron of yours," Ames told him, "I'll put a bullet in the other one."

"I ain't movin'."

"Where's Kelson?" Ames asked. "I heard you say something about him waiting for you."

"I ain't got nothin' to say."

"You've got plenty to say." Ames clicked the hammer back on the .44. "And not much time to say it in."

"You—you wouldn't kill me," the dealer

said, but there was fear mixed with the pain in his eyes now.

"Try me, hombre."

The dealer saw the expression on Ames' grim face. He rubbed the back of his uninjured forearm across his mouth. "All right," he said. "All right, I'll tell you."

"Where's Kelson?"

"In Crescent."

"Crescent?"

"It's an old ghost town up in the hills to the west. 'Bout a forty-minute ride."

Ames frowned. He remembered the place now, a gold boom town that had been financed by a large Eastern bank until the bedrock vein had been worked dry. Then the bank had pulled out, forcing the miners to abandon the almost vacant settlement.

"What would he be doing there?"

"That's where we chased the woman and the kid," the dealer said. "We come on 'em in the grasslands and took out after 'em. They tried to hole up in one of the shacks, and we—"

Ames' heart began to pound furiously in his chest. He dropped to one knee beside the dealer and gathered the man's shirt front in his big hand, pulling the white face close to his. The dealer howled in pain at the sudden wrenching.

Ames snapped, "You what? Killed them? By God, if I find one hair harmed on that woman or that boy's head—"

"No, no," the dealer protested. "We didn't kill 'em! Jersey Jack had 'em hogtied when I left."

Ames cursed himself for a fool. He should not have let Virginia and Robbie ride out alone; he should have gone with them, seen them safely back to their ranch, before riding after the con man again. But how could he have known Kelson would leave the main road and ride off to the west in his search? How could he have known?

He said to the dealer, "So Kelson sent you back here to fetch the Dollar Wagon up to Crescent."

"That's right."

"And then what?"

"I—I don't know."

Ames knew. If he was any judge of a snake like Jersey Jack Kelson, the con man would want no one alive who might present a threat to him. And Virginia and Robbie presented just such a threat. He would not hesitate,

Ames felt certain, to kill a woman or a boy.

"Which building has Kelson got the woman and the boy in?" he snapped.

"The old general store."

He released the dealer's shirt; the man sank back on the hard ground, moaning softly, his fingers kneading the blood-soaked area where Ames' lead had taken him.

The Arizonan stood then, trying to think. He had to get up to Crescent before Kelson decided to put a couple of bullets in Virginia and Robbie. But how? If he remembered correctly there was only a single road leading into the ghost town—it was walled by steep shale bluffs on two sides, and a deep, sheer-sided canyon on a third—and Jersey Jack would be sure to have that road watched as a precautionary measure. He could not just ride in—.

Or could he?

An idea came to Ames. He knelt once again beside the dealer. The man had passed out now, from shock and pain. Quickly, Ames began to strip his clothes from him. When he had dungarees, hat, and blood-stained shirt, he shed his own clothes and put on the dealer's. They fitted him snugly, but he could move freely enough.

Ames went quickly to the man's horse, then, and found a sheepskin jacket rolled up in the bedroll. He put that on; it covered the dark stain on the shirt. He took the bedroll over to the unconscious dealer and covered him with it as a protection against the cool night air and then dragged the limp form over near the fire.

That accomplished, he set about harnessing the dappled gray to the Dollar Wagon. When he had completed the chore, he ran into the undergrowth along the river bank and located Cappy. He led the sorrel back to the camp, where he tied him to the wagon's tailgate.

Ames climbed up onto the seat of the Dollar Wagon and took the reins in his hand. In the darkness, it was just possible he could pass for the dealer. And if he could, he had a chance of getting into Crescent alive.

Grimly, he brought the gray around and up onto the secondary trail. When he reached the main road, he urged the animal forward at full speed. But before long, the lurching, bone-jarring jolt of the wagon on the rough roadbed forced him to slow down. He kept the gray at a steady, even pace, though every fiber of his being cried out for speed, and his

337

muscles and nerves were stretched into an almost painful tautness.

He could not risk a broken axle, or a possible weakening of the undercarriage—especially since the road leading up to Crescent, which would veer off to the west several miles farther on, was bound to be in a state of disrepair. If he did not get the Dollar Wagon safely into the abandoned town, then it would be all over.

Not for him, but for Virginia and Robbie Sands.

10

AMES headed north again, past the spot where Virginia and he had camped. He gave the turning point a quick glance as he drove the wagon by, the terrible anguish he felt inside deepened by the familiar terrain. After another few minutes he arrived at the small road which veered to his left, to the northwest.

At one time, probably at the height of Crescent's boom, somebody had nailed a large sign to a tall spruce at the apex of the fork, welcoming visitors to the thriving metropolis, the "*City of Golden Opportunity.*" It hung in two rotting pieces now, swaying slightly in the cool night breeze, its paint long since faded.

Ames urged the gray onto the narrow road, which was barely more than two ruts side by side, and the wagon teetered and bucked as it passed over the rough, pocked ground. The horse wheezed slightly as he labored up the steeply sloping path. It wound through the boulders and clearings, the treacherous surface often overgrown to the point where the trail was indecipherable.

Ames looked back once, but the looming trees and thick brush had already sealed off any view of the river or the main road. They passed over a rise and headed into a small, level meadow, and the gray's speed picked up to the point where Ames had to ease him back with the reins for fear of the wagon flying apart. The gray took that as a sign for rest, and he stopped to nibble on a tuft of grass.

Ames did not urge him on, satisfied with the unexpected progress they had made. The fragrance of the surrounding flower clusters made Ames' head swim, and for an instant, he too let himself relax slightly, releasing tension. Then the horse stirred himself and plodded on to the end of the meadow and again they started their weary climb through the black and barren valleys.

The Dakota gold country had been a wild sector, where extremes were the ordinary way of life. Indians had been pushed there, Custer had died there, and settlers who had lived for the gold ended up with the plow there. In a few short months the hills were latticed with tunnels, flumes and hydraulic monitors; miners paid a dollar for a beefsteak and another dollar for the plate to eat it from. And towns like Crescent blossomed and wilted like quick-blooming desert cactus.

Ames was without a concrete plan of attack as he neared the ghost town, although he knew he was going to have to be silent about whatever he did. One shot, one outcry, and Kelson would kill Virginia and Robbie. His one hope lay in his masquerade, and he was going to have to bluff the same way he would do if he was running a busted flush in a high-pot poker game.

The trail ran along the cliffs of shale which bordered the town, and for a while, Ames had trouble holding the wagon on the land-slid road. He looked down the sheer sides of the canyon on his left, unable to see the bottom in the dense shadows of night.

There was one final curve before the trail entered the wide box clearing which held Crescent, but already he could see the silhouette of the headframe of Consolidated Mining Union's shaft towers against the moonlit sky. He stopped the gray and dropped off the wagon. He stood for a moment, ears straining. Jersey Jack would have posted a guard, Ames was sure. He only hoped he had not gone too close before halting.

The desolate country of poor dry grass and drought-resistant spruce was alive with the sound of scurrying squirrels and crafty coyotes which were never seen, and with the constant buzz of insects. Ames did not hear anything out of the ordinary.

The Arizonan stepped to the back of the wagon and untied Cappy. He brushed the horse's nose and led him to an outcropping of grass and tied the reins to a spruce there. Then he returned to the wagon and continued into Crescent. He kept his head low and his back bent into a slouch until the guard showed himself.

He had been hidden in the darkness, high on the shale bluff behind several boulders, and if Ames had tried to hunt him without knowing his exact location, he would never have found him. As it was, the man stood up and waved to Ames, Ames raised his hand and waved back. Not a word was spoken between them.

The road wound around an especially tall and sharp spire of rock. Ames stopped the gray there. For the first time, he could see the outline of the whole deserted town. It was as he remembered: completely silent. Crescent had had more than its share of violence, and legend had it that there had been a stretch of five months when there was at least one murder every weekend. Yet as a ghost town, nothing stirred, nothing made sound in the wind, nothing rustled in the tall grass.

Ames could almost believe that when something crumbled or fell, it did so noiselessly. It was as if Crescent drew in sound now that it was dead, to atone for all the vitality it had poured out when alive.

Crescent had been a rich boom town, and many of the buildings had been built to last. It had produced over $15,000,000 in gold in its short life span, and at the beginning, before the surface placers ran out, it had not been uncommon for miners to take out $1,000 a day. Then the eastern bank put in the shafts, and beyond the town Ames could see the black forest of Consolidated Mining Union's holdings.

The tallest of Crescent's buildings was the Odd Fellows-Masonic Hall. It stood at a tilt at the intersection of an alley and the main street, its pointed roof collapsed into the third story. Next to it was the Adams Express

Building, constructed of rhyolite tuff, a material common to the area; sandwiched between the butcher shop and it was the jail, a small iron-and-wood structure. The butcher shop had a floor of marble, and visitors had been known to stop in there as though it was a part of a guided tour just to see the sleek, polished surface.

Across the street was the infamous hotel known as Mitch's, made of brick and limestone. Mitch's had been run by a woman named Mitch, who had been caught by her husband in a compromising situation and then shot. The husband had not been too popular before the incident, and the townspeople had taken the killing as an opportunity to string him up on one of the hotel rafters.

Crescent did not lack saloons, either. There had been a half dozen of them ready to accomodate the thirsty miners, and the ground floor of Mitch's actually held two separately operated bars. Eastward was the Old French Bakery, the remaining four walls of Jon's Apothecary, and another brick-front building with the legend, *"Moran Bros. Cheap Cash Store"* painted across its side.

A flickering light came from Morans, shining through the cracks in the boards and out from the glassless windows. There were five horses tied at the crumbling hitching post in front of the store. Ames recognized Virginia's roan and Robbie's pinto. The other three belonged to Kelson and his two remaining men.

Having oriented himself fully with the town, Ames jumped down from the wagon and walked rapidly to the rear. Before he could go in after Kelson and the other man, he had to eliminate the threat of the guard—escape would be impossible otherwise—and he had to do it quickly and quietly. Gunshots or any warning yell would immediately alert Kelson that something was wrong.

Ames jumped up on the tailgate and climbed into the wagon; after a few seconds he found what he was looking for—a small coil of rope. He attached the rope to his belt, dropped to the roadbed again, and began to run. He rounded the tall spire of rock, keeping his head bent forward so as to prevent recognition in the wash of moonlight. When he reached the vicinity of the guard's hiding place behind the boulders high on the bluff's side, he pulled up and began waving his arms wildly.

There was no sign of movement from the irregular black shapes of the boulders at first, but finally the shadowed figure of the guard rose up. He stood motionless for an instant, and then began to make his way down the steep slope to the road, his rifle held up at his chest. When he reached the road, he shambled toward Ames, the moonlight showing a puzzled expression on his thin face.

Ames continued to motion, turning his body away from the approaching guard and taking a single step back along the road. "What's the matter, Luke?" the guard called, coming up beside Ames. "What's all the—"

The sentence was never finished. Ames pivoted suddenly and swung his balled right hand in a sweeping upward arc. The hard, muscled fist exploded on the point of the guard's chin, almost lifting him off his feet as it sent him sprawling backward. Ames was upon him immediately, but there was no need for further action; the guard was unconscious in a thick patch of sagebrush beside the road.

Ames lifted the coil of rope from his belt and tied the guard's arms and legs securely, using the comatose man's own bandanna for a gag. Then he picked up the rifle, emptied the magazine into the surrounding brush, and carried the weapon with him back to the wagon. He put it under the seat.

He paused for a moment, then, pondered his next move. He had two basic alternatives: he could drive the wagon directly into the town, bring it up in front of Moran's General Store, and hope the arrival brought Jersey Jack and the third man outside where he could get the drop on them; or he could go in on foot, under the cover of darkness, and hope to surprise them that way. He discarded the latter immediately; he would run too many risks if he went in without the wagon.

For one thing, Kelson would likely have heard the Dollar Wagon approach earlier and would wonder why it had not continued into town; for another, Ames felt sure his only chance of rescuing Virginia and Robbie lay in getting Kelson out of the General Store, away from the hostages, and he had no assurance of being able to do that if he proceeded on foot.

No, he would have to take the wagon in. He still had no guarantee that its arrival would bring the con man out of the building. But an idea was forming in Ames' mind and if it worked, both Kelson and the third man would come out, all right—come out in a hurry.

Ames climbed up into the seat again, took hold of the reins, and clucked the gray into a walk. The road passed the rim of the canyon, widening somewhat as it became the main street of Crescent. Tall grass grew in random patches on its surface, and there were tangles of brush and debris which had been pushed by the wind against the high curbs of the board sidewalks.

Ames felt a chill course through him as he neared the first decaying structures lining both sides of the street: two saloons, all of their windows either removed by the departing residents or broken by wind and rain and sleet, a small dry-goods store, a mercantile shop with its front door hanging oddly by a single hinge. There was no sound, save for the clatter of the wagon's wooden wheels on the rough street; and the low mournful song of the north wind as it blew down from the high cliffs beyond the town.

When Ames came parallel with Mitch's Hotel—and across the street, the Odd Fellows-Masonic Hall—he lifted his .44 onto his lap with his right hand, holding the reins

348

with his still partially-numbed left. His heart hammered with increasing rhythm in his chest, and the inside of his mouth was dry with the taste of impending conflict. The corded muscles in his neck were wiredrawn.

He let the gray walk slowly for another fifteen feet, and then he took his hand from the .44 and grasped a long quirt from a slot on one side of the wagon, near the brake. He snapped it sharply over the gray's head, once, twice; the horse balked momentarily and then lowered its head and began to run.

Ames cracked the whip another time, urging the gray to an even greater speed. He then let the quirt fall on the seat beside him, taking hold of his gun again.

They raced past the Old French Bakery, the apothecary shop, bearing down on Moran's General Store. Ames leaned his body forward, pretending to jerk back on the reins; at the top of his voice he yelled, "Runaway! Look out! Runaway horse!"

Just as they passed by the entrance to Moran's, the front door flew open, letting an amber elongation of light illuminate the cracked boarding of the sidewalk in front, and two men rushed out.

Ames hauled back on the reins then, bringing the gray up just a little—they were past the far corner of the General Store now, in front of the assayer's office—and then he stood up on top of the swaying floorboards and leapt out to the side.

Ames landed on his feet, stumbled, went down. He hit the rough surface of the street on his left shoulder, causing a searing fire to explode in the healing bullet wound, and then he rolled and came up on his knees. He had kept a solid grip on the .44, and he raised it in his hand, finger whitening on the trigger.

The two men were into the street now. They had pulled up at the sight of Ames jumping from the wagon, uncertain, thinking he was the dealer because of his clothing. But in the moonshine as Ames came up onto his knees, they recognized him.

One of them—Ames saw it was the shill in the dun-colored chaps from Phileaux River—had his gun already drawn. He brought it around and fired at Ames, missing; the Arizonan squeezed off a single shot. The bullet took the shill squarely in the chest, and he toppled over, sprawling face down in the street.

Kelson had hesitated for a fraction of a

second, as if undecided whether to make—suicidally—for the General Store's bright light, draw on Ames, or head for protective cover. He chose the latter, and before Ames could fire at him, he dove headlong behind a rough-hewn wooden horse trough in front of the assayer's office.

Ames snapped a quick shot to keep the con man pinned down; then, realizing what a perfect target he made himself, he ran for the opposite side of the street and the dark shadow at the side of another of Crescent's saloons.

He made it there safely and stood peering across the shadowed street. A standoff, he thought grimly. Both Kelson and he needed to reach the General Store—and Virginia and Robbie—to win the battle. Kelson must regain his hostages. Then he could force Ames to throw down his gun and surrender by threatening to kill the woman and her son. And Ames knew that once Virginia and the boy were released and safely on their way out of Crescent he would be free to wait the con man out; and on his terms he knew he would be victorious.

Yet as it stood now, to attempt to reach the store, with its flood of lantern light through

351

the open door, was to meet certain death at the hands of the other.

The dark and deadly game of cat-and-mouse was going to be played in the ruins of the buildings, in the black niches and gloomy corners of Crescent. Both men knew it, accepted it; the waiting began.

Neither made a move for almost five minutes. Then Kelson fired three shots which splintered the siding to the left of Ames. Ames pulled back slightly. But he saw Kelson scurry into the narrow space between the General Store and the assayer's office; the con man fired again from there, coming no nearer to hitting Ames.

There was little chance that Jersey Jack, or Ames for that matter, could score a hit while they were concealed in darkness, but Ames was not a man who cared to be pinned down. He preferred the quick and open course, and he knew, knew with a grim certainty, that he was about to make his own violent move.

11

AMES waited impatiently. Then he suddenly left his cover and ran along the wooden sidewalk in front of the saloon, trying to keep in the shadows of the building's front wall. Two quick shots followed him, missing, and then Ames reached an alleyway between the saloon and another mercantile store and ducked into its protective darkness. Listening there, he could hear frantic scratching sounds from across the wide street. Kelson had emptied his gun and was reloading.

Seizing the scant few seconds while the con man's weapon was useless, Ames made a dash across the street.

He was far enough away from the open doorway to be out of the lantern's glare, but the moonlight made him nonetheless vulnerable. The expanse of the street seemed endless, and Ames braced himself for the bullet which would surely slam into him if Kelson managed to reload in time.

But none came. He reached safety along the opposite side wall of the General Store just as Kelson stepped slightly into view, gun held high. Ames tumbled and rolled into a squatting position, dropped forward only long enough to fire one quick wild shot, and then ducked back. He waited; silence. Time seemed to have stopped. Ames held his breath, trying to catch the slightest movement which would tell him what Kelson was up to. No sound reached his ears.

Ames wondered if he had been lucky enough to have hit Kelson with his shot, but dismissed the thought immediately. Even if he had, he could not walk out into the open to find out. He mulled over Kelson's possible course of action. The con man could continue to play a waiting game, or possibly—

Ames heard a slight scraping sound from the rear of the store. Was Jersey Jack sneaking around the building in an effort to get the drop on Ames from behind? If so, now was his chance to break for the doorway. But Ames did not move. It was just possible that the con man had made the sound purposely and then doubled back to his original position so as to catch Ames in the light if he broke for Moran's entrance.

Ames let his eyes circuit quickly, knowing he could not stay where he was. The General Store was next to the apothecary shop on this side, and the one-story building looked as sturdy as any in Crescent. A low false balcony ran along its front, shadowing the sidewalk beneath. It had fancy gingerbread trim and came around to the side, concealing the sloping roof above. The trim had for the most part been torn away, and the supporting timbers looked decayed. Ames decided to take the chance that the rotting beams would still have the strength to hold his weight.

He holstered his .44, and wiping his hands on his dungarees, he judged the leap. Then he took a deep breath, crouched and jumped. His fingers curled around the gutter, and he could almost feel the locust pegs which held it together break apart under his hands. He swayed slightly, catching the heel of his boot on the window ledge in front of him, and using it as support, he hauled himself up until he could roll onto the balcony. Quickly, he twisted around there, digging for his Colt as he went. He had a complete view of the

355

doorway and this side of the General Store now.

Kelson was coming around the back of Moran's. The first thing Ames saw was the con man's gun, then his arm, and finally one side of his face as Jersey Jack drew a bead on the spot Ames had been. Ames fired then, but missed high—although he had the satisfaction of hearing Kelson give a startled yell as he disappeared around the corner again. But then, almost immediately, came the crash of a boot against wood, and the squeal of protesting hinges, and Ames suddenly realized he might have outsmarted himself.

As long as he had been on the ground, Kelson could not chance kicking in the back door of Moran's. Virginia and Robbie were obviously in the main part of the store, up front where the lantern was, and if Kelson came in through the back, he would never reach the hostages before Ames made it through the front entrance. But with Ames up on the balcony of the apothecary shop, Kelson must have figured he had enough time. He must have known where Ames was from the flash of the .44.

Cursing, Ames threw caution to the wind and tumbled off the balcony. He had learned the art of falling from many years of breaking wild stallions, and instead of leaping down feet first, he allowed his body to go slack as he fell. As a fortunate result, he landed in a cat-like stance, feet and hands down, and was up and running for the lighted doorway almost the instant he struck the dirt.

Ames went in crouching low, moving diagonally toward the left-hand wall of the almost barren interior. Kelson was caught off guard. He had not expected Ames to be able to get in there that quickly. He was just into the main part of the store, near where the defenseless woman and boy were tied and gagged in one corner. He pulled up as he saw Ames and threw himself to one side, sending an empty, dust-covered barrel toppling over. His boots slipped on the rotting floor, and he went down to his knees.

Ames, still crouching, snapped a quick shot at Kelson that chipped wood from an empty shelf just above the con man's head. Jersey Jack crawled behind a large crate and returned the fire. His shots were wide, but sent Ames diving for cover behind an over-turned display table. Kelson fired another shot then, and the store room went dark for a split second, only to explode into whooshing, flickering light again.

Ames realized instantly what had happened. Kelson's third shot had purposely shattered the kerosene lamp on the long counter paralleling the left-hand wall; flames spread across the counter from the ignited kerosene in the reservoir, consuming the dry, deteriorated wood with incredible speed.

The fire had almost reached Kelson's place of concealment when the con man suddenly jumped to his feet and rushed through the entranceway into the rear of the store. Ames sent a bullet after him, but then the fire covered the opening, licking at the walls, at the floor, sending billows of choking black smoke into the room.

Ames left the display table and ran to the corner where Virginia and Robbie lay bound. Swiftly, he tore at the gags in their mouths, pulling them free. His hunting knife was in his hand now and he cut the ropes around their wrists and ankles. Virginia was coughing violently from the smoke as Ames pulled her and the boy into the center of the room. Fire claimed the corner almost immediately; the whole rear section of the store was now a blazing sheet of flame.

Virginia gasped, "Arizona, how—how did you find us?"

"There's no time for talking now," Ames said. They had neared the open doorway, off to one side of it. Robbie started toward the door, but Ames caught his arm, restraining him.

"This whole place is going up any minute!" Robbie yelled over the roar of the fire. "We've got to get out of here!"

"Not yet," Ames told him.

He knew, instinctively, that if they simply walked out of that door there would be three bullets waiting for them. Jersey Jack was ruthless, and he would not leave Crescent without making sure that the three people who could send him to the gallows were dead.

Ames was positive that Jersey Jack had doubled around the side of Moran's and was waiting now with a readied gun for them to emerge from the burning store. Kelson knew that they could not leave by the rear entrance, which was blocked by the wall of fire across that half of the building, and that the only other way out was through the front door.

Ames only had a few seconds in which to make a decision. He would have to go out first, alone; that much he realized. But what he could not know in advance was which side of the building Kelson had come around, which side he lay in waiting. If he made the wrong choice of sides, then he was a dead man.

And if he died, so would Virginia and Robbie.

Ames turned to the boy and pressed the hunting knife into his hand; he had to have the .44 himself. The smothering cloud of smoke was thicker now and the fire had crossed the floor with searing heat that threatened their clothing. Quickly, Ames bit off instructions, telling them to wait until he was outside, wait until the shooting had stopped before they exited.

A protest from Virginia died in a spasm of coughing. Robbie held grimly onto the hunting knife, but Ames knew that it would be of little use against the conman's sixgun if—

He forced his mind away from that possibility. He had to act, and act now. He bent his body forward, took a half-step toward the center of the room, and then ran for the open doorway.

As soon as his boot hit the threshold, he left his feet to twist his body sideways, facing south toward that side of Moran's where the

apothecary shop was. He hit the rough planking of the board sidewalk on his right
shoulder, rolling off the high curb onto the
street.

Two flashes of orange light erupted from
the direction in which he was looking; Ames
had guessed correctly. One bullet tore the
heel off his right boot, a second splintered
wood from the planking. He rolled again,
under the hitching rail where the horses had
been tied—they had reared and bolted at the
first sign of fire—and brought his .44 up just
as Kelson fired again.

Ames felt the bullet pass close along his
right cheek. Through eyes watered badly
from the smoke, he saw that Kelson was
standing spread-legged at the corner of the
building, lips skinned back, gun held straight
out in front of him. Ames squeezed off twice,
feeling the buck of the .44 the length of his
arm.

The con man jerked upright, firing a fifth
shot wildly into the air, and then he spun in a
half circle and fell into a pile of debris at the
end of the sidewalk.

Ames got painfully to his knees. Virginia
and Robbie rushed out of the burning
General Store at once, running to Ames in

the street. Virginia knelt beside him, flinging her arm across his shoulders, hugging his face close to her breast. "Arizona," she wailed, "Arizona, are you all right?"

He looked at her out of half-closed eyes. Then he smiled, "Virginia, I reckon I'll live, right enough." He saw her pretty face was heat-reddened and tear-streaked. "How about you and the boy?"

"We're fine," she told him, weeping openly now with relief. "But we couldn't have stayed in there another second. If you—" She broke off, holding him, crying.

Ames felt the strength and the warmth of her body, and fatigue made him want to stay within the enveloping circle of her arms, rest there. But there were things left to be done. Gently, he held her away from him and then stood, helping her to her feet. She seemed to understand. Together they walked to the place Kelson lay, Robbie behind them.

When he turned Jersey Jack over, Ames saw that his bullet had penetrated Kelson's chest, high on the right side. It was not a fatal wound, and for this Ames was thankful. There was still the matter of clearing his name in Phileaux River, and Ames would have been hard pressed to do that without Kelson alive.

He glanced up at the General Store. The fire had taken all of it now, and the flames from its blazing roof were licking at the assayer's office and the apothecary shop. The sidewalk was burning in front. Ames bent and grasped Kelson and dragged him into the middle of the street. Then he went back and picked up the con man's gun and gave it to the boy.

"You watch over him while I round up the horses, Robbie," he told him. "Virginia, you wait here, too."

When he had their nods, Ames hurried on bone-weary legs to the north end of town. Virginia's roan and Robbie's pinto were there, near one of the Consolidated Mining Union's hydraulic monitors. The Dollar Wagon, still in one piece after their flight through the town earlier, was nearby; the gray was peacefully chewing on a big clump of grass.

Ames led the roan and the pinto to the rear of the wagon, tied them there, and then picked up the reins and climbed into the seat. He brought the gray around and returned to the center of town.

363

The assayer's office and the apothecary shop were ablaze now, the flames racing through the dry, brittle timbers. It would not be long, Ames knew, before that entire half of the block went up—and perhaps the whole town.

Robbie helped him lift the unconscious Kelson into the rear of the wagon. Ames tied Jersey Jack's hands and feet as a precautionary measure, even though he did not think there would be much fight left in him when he roused. Then the three of them boarded the wagon, and Ames drove the gray south to the section where the street narrowed into the winding road.

They stopped on the other side of the tall spire of rock to lift the trussed guard—conscious now, eyes alive with hatred—into the rear of the Dollar Wagon. Then they continued to the spot where Ames had left Cappy tied on the side of the road. He gave the gray's reins to Virginia.

"Can you handle the wagon on this road, Virginia?"

She nodded gravely. "Yes," she said. "I can handle it, Arizona."

Ames jumped down and went to where the sorrel stood, swinging up into the saddle. He waved to Virginia to begin the long journey down the road and back to Phileaux River. If they made any kind of time at all, he thought, they would get there shortly past sun-up.

As he brought Cappy on to the road, Ames looked back in the direction of Crescent. The spires of rock hid the town from his view, but the sky beyond it was illuminated with a brilliant, orange glow. Unaccountably, he felt a touch of sadness at the final cremation of the once-thriving settlement; but perhaps it was better that way than if the town simply rotted away during the slow but inexorable passage of time.

Tiredly, Ames cantered Cappy after the wagon.

12

AMES finished the last bite of what had been a huge, thick elk steak, wiped his lips with the linen cloth from his lap, and emitted a long, slow sigh of contentment.

"Virginia," he said appreciatively, "I can't recall that I've had a better meal than this one."

The widow Sands beamed at him radiantly across the table. "Why thank you, Arizona Ames!" she answered, greatly pleased.

She wore a simple gingham dress that accentuated her firm, youthful body, and her hair was long over her shoulders on this night. She looked to Ames like a girl of eighteen, with freshly-scrubbed skin and just a hint of lip rouge.

She began to clear the table, humming very softly to herself. Ames leaned back in the chair and rolled a cigarette, gazing wistfully into the fire in the hearth, knowing that it was growing late in the day. He would have to leave soon—perhaps he would ride south into Texas, or southwest into New Mexico—and there was an odd confusion of emotions in him at the thought.

There was, first of all, the wanderlust, the need to drift with the prairie wind, to see new places and new things; and there was, as well, the fervent desire to establish roots, some kind of home, where he could settle peacefully at last.

The door burst open and Robbie ran in, out of breath. In one hand he held a long willow pole; in the other, triumphantly, a string of catfish. He had ridden off early that morning for a favorite fishing spot—a narrow stream that wound through the lush green meadows in the northeast.

"Lookit here!" he announced proudly. "Ain't these beauties, Arizona?"

Ames smiled quietly, nodding. "You did yourself proud there, son," he said.

"Give them to me, Robbie," Virginia said, extending her hand. "I'll clean them later."

Robbie handed over the string, and she took the cats over to a corrugated iron tub, laying them inside. She looked at Ames and sighed as if to emphasize the fact a woman's work is never done.

Watching her, Ames thought that there was love in this poor house; good and honest emotion which made up for the lack of worldly goods tenfold. He hated to admit it, but he was going to miss this fine woman and her boy.

Robbie suddenly blurted: "Well, maw? Is he stayin'?"

"Robbie!" Virginia said, startled. She blushed a bright red color that matched the crimson design on her dress. "You hush up!"

"But you promised to ask him! You said!"

"Ask me what, Robbie?" Ames inquired, turning to the boy.

"Why, about you stayin' on here with us," Robbie said plaintively. His eyes searched Ames' face, eagerly hoping for an affirmative answer. "You will, won't you?"

"It's mighty nice of you to ask me, son," Ames said. "I'm flattered. But, well—"

"You might consider it," Virginia said haltingly, rubbing her hands on her apron. "I mean, there's lots of work around here, and what with Tom gone an' everything, maybe we could hire you."

"As the foreman, Arizona," Robbie said. He turned solemn for a moment. "Course, there's nobody here 'cept me and ma."

Ames had to smile. "Sounds like that would be enough for any man to handle, Robbie."

Then he, too, became grave as the weight of the offer made him think carefully. He did not answer right away, but stared at the empty table before him. Finally he looked at Virginia and felt sadness in his heart.

"It wouldn't work out, I'm afraid. You heard what the sheriff told me about clearing out of Phileaux River."

"But you cleared yourself!" Virginia protested. "It's not fair! You brought Kelson in, and that other man, and put an end to their swindling and murdering."

"Lawmen are proud people, Virginia. No matter that I brought Kelson in; I held a gun on the sheriff and escaped from his town and led him a long chase across the prairie. He's not likely to forget that, not ever. If I stayed around here, more trouble would come some day, the way it always does to me." Ames shook his head sadly. "No, Virginia, I think my leaving is for the best."

The widow's eyes began to brim with tears and her chin trembled slightly with emotion. He wanted to stay—and yet he wanted to go;

but his choice was clear. Abruptly, Ames rose. He looked at Robbie and Virginia, at their crestfallen faces, and he felt a lump form in his throat. He could ride and shoot and rope with the best hands, but when it came to a situation such as this, he was absolutely helpless. Quickly, he spun on his heel and went out through the door and walked across to the barn; he began to saddle Cappy.

He pulled the cinch tight after a moment, tested the security of the tack, and then led the sorrel across the front yard. Virginia and Robbie stood in the shade of the spreading cottonwood, her arm about the boy's shoulders. As much as he hated goodbyes, Ames knew that they had to be said. He walked hesitantly up to Virginia.

"I reckon it's time now," he said.

She nodded. "You'll—you'll be back, won't you, Arizona?" she asked. "Some day?"

"Some day, Virginia."

"Do you promise?"

"I promise," Ames said, and he knew that he would keep that promise—some day.

Virginia, trembling with pent-up emotion, stepped as close as she could to Ames. "I have something for you, Arizona," she said. "For all—all the good you've done Robbie and me."

She suddenly reached up and grasped the cowboy by his lapels and kissed him. Her lips were cool, but her kiss was not. It was as much a plea for him to reconsider as it was in gratitude.

"Ma!" Robbie yelped.

"There!" Virginia said, blushing, letting go of Ames. "You should remember us after that!"

Ames, tremendously embarrassed, was speechless for a moment. Then, grinning, he mounted his sorrel with a single leap. "Lord!" he exclaimed. "You shouldn't have done that, Virginia." He leaned over and smiled shyly at her. "But I can't say I'm sorry you did." He turned to the boy. "Robbie, you take a real good care of your ma, you hear me?"

"I will, Arizona," Robbie vowed, sadness set in his face.

Ames brought Cappy around, snapped a farewell gesture, and heeled the horse into a gallop. He rode through the gate and onto the prairie road. The wind blew coolness across his face, gentling the turmoil inside him, and the stark, flat grasslands stretched out before him, shining with shaded golds and ambers and browns in the distance.

He rode until he reached a chalky knoll to the southwest; there he reined Cappy in, and after waiting for his trail dust to settle he gazed for sometime at the tiny speck that was the Sands' ranch against the hazy backdrop of the sky. He could not be sure, but he thought he discerned the vague motion of two slim hands upraised from the miniature figures by the spreading cottonwood.

Ames turned away then, looking to the southwest. The Crow Buttes, and the two peaks called Castle Rock and Square Top, rose to meet his eye. Looking at them, he felt very small and very insignificant, and somehow, just a little remorseful.

Arizona Ames spurred Cappy forward into the deeply purpling twilight of the Dakota plains.

THE END

GUIDE
TO THE COLOUR CODING
OF
ULVERSCROFT BOOKS

Many of our readers have written to us expressing their appreciation for the way in which our colour coding has assisted them in selecting the Ulverscroft books of their choice. To remind everyone of our colour coding— this is as follows:

BLACK COVERS
Mysteries

*

BLUE COVERS
Romances

*

RED COVERS
Adventure Suspense and General Fiction

*

ORANGE COVERS
Westerns

*

GREEN COVERS
Non-Fiction

WESTERN TITLES
in the
Ulverscroft Large Print Series

Gone To Texas	*Forrest Carter*
Dakota Boomtown	*Frank Castle*
Hard Texas Trail	*Matt Chisholm*
Bigger Than Texas	*William R. Cox*
From Hide and Horn	*J. T. Edson*
Gunsmoke Thunder	*J. T. Edson*
The Peacemakers	*J. T. Edson*
Wagons to Backsight	*J. T. Edson*
Arizona Ames	*Zane Grey*
The Lost Wagon Train	*Zane Grey*
Nevada	*Zane Grey*
Rim of the Desert	*Ernest Haycox*
Borden Chantry	*Louis L'Amour*
Conagher	*Louis L'Amour*
The First Fast Draw *and* The Key-Lock Man	*Louis L'Amour*
Kiowa Trail *and* Killoe	*Louis L'Amour*
The Mountain Valley War	*Louis L'Amour*
The Sackett Brand *and* The Lonely Men	*Louis L'Amour*
Taggart	*Louis L'Amour*
Tucker	*Louis L'Amour*
Destination Danger	*Wm. Colt MacDonald*

We hope this Large Print edition gives you the pleasure and enjoyment we ourselves experienced in its publication.

There are now more than 1,600 titles available in this ULVERSCROFT Large Print Series. Ask to see a Selection at your nearest library.

The Publisher will be delighted to send you, free of charge, upon request a complete and up-to-date list of all titles available.

Ulverscroft Large Print Books Ltd.
The Green, Bradgate Road
Anstey
Leicestershire
England